MURDER AT THE LUNATICS' BALL

MURDER AT THE LUNATICS' BALL

R S LEONARD

‘Revenge may be wicked, but it’s natural.’
Becky Sharp in William Thackeray’s *Vanity Fair.*

rsleonardbooks.com

Ebook: ISBN 978-1-7395889-2-2
Paperback: ISBN 978-1-7395889-3-9
Edited by Cat Cobain and Claire Baldwin
Cover art by Damonza
Layout by Damonza

For Mum, 10 January 1943 – 30 August 2023.
'Your hand is my glove.'

PART I

HAMPSHIRE, ENGLAND

CHAPTER 1

Mr Harris Mortimer

I AM IN A hackney carriage on the way to the lunatics' ball. I am not afraid to confess that I feel some trepidation at the prospect, for I am frightened that the sight of those unfortunate creatures inside the asylum will bring back painful memories. My poor mad mother died in a private lunatic asylum when I was a boy of ten years of age.

Of course, I am told that the bad old days of manacles, strait-waistcoats and flogging are gone, and I am assured that modern establishments for the care of the insane are exemplars of the cultivated and humane civilization that is ours under the reign of Her Majesty Queen Victoria, in the year 1875.

It is a dismal November afternoon in rural Hampshire. I cannot see much through the grubby carriage window nearest to me due to the poor light and rain-lashed wind, though I can feel that we are now on an upwards incline towards the great house. I jump as the driver shouts and cracks his whip at the poor beast struggling to pull the cab up the hill. It is prescribed that public lunatic asylums are built on high ground, where the air is pure, and the patients can aid their recovery with the bountiful and beautiful nature that surrounds them. I do not understand such notions myself. I never could abide the real countryside. 'Tis true, I live in a moderately peaceful place – Chelsea – just outside of London, renowned for its artistic heart, and so in sympathy with my own. But it has noise and life enough; and then I am close enough to the city itself to get my fill of din, hurry and smoke, and to let my soul surge along with the rush of the crowd. A few weeks in a place like this would certainly certify me as a proper resident; I would run mad from the never-ending skies, the deathly silence punctured only by the desolate cries of animals, and, above all, the scarcity of people.

I am jolted again and thrown hard to my right, banging my head on the sharp frame of the carriage window. I touch my face near to my right temple and notice a little blood on my ink-stained fingers. The driver shouts and the horse cries long and loud; it must be rearing up on its hind legs. I clutch my seat until the carriage stops and settles. I look out of the window nearest my head, which is a little clearer than the other one, and am shocked by the sight of a white face confronting me. I blink several times. Fear moves up from my stomach to my throat – is it a ghost? Surely not, I tell myself. I do not even believe in them. Really, my nerves are quite gone. But the face is still there. It is that of a young woman, oval-shaped, deathly pale, the eyes wide-set. I hear a faint tapping; she is trying to get in.

Ghost or woman, I grasp at the door handle, turn, then shake it desperately, to no avail. I grab the pull handle and bang on the roof of the coach to alert the driver, but he seems to hear nothing. The door gives suddenly, and I have to stop myself from falling out of the carriage. A wet, ice-cold hand grasps my right one and instinctively I pull it towards me, the body of the poor creature following her hand. She lands on the hard seat next to me and I reach over her to secure the door.

'Sir, sir,' she says. 'I cannot thank you enough. They are keeping me here against my will. I am sane; indeed, I assure you. But there is a terrible man here who, who…'

The carriage lunges forward, and the woman grabs onto my right arm with both of her hands. I turn to her and put my left arm onto her right shoulder to settle her. The carriage moves again and settles to a steady pace. We stare at each other. She is quite beautiful, no doubt about it; her eyes are an unusual pale brown colour, like creamy toffee. Her figure beneath the wet, coarse fabric of her gown seems slender but ample enough. Auburn hair falls in wet strands across her face and over her shoulders, a fallen white cap hanging at the back of her head. What a shame that such a woman is a lunatic, condemned to a life shut away from the world. Her beauty would grace any society drawing room. I shudder, not from the cold, but from the thought of all the women whom I encounter in social life, and what might lie beneath their calm, rational exteriors.

I let go of her, conscious that I am too close to this female stranger.

'Is there anything I can do to help you?' I ask. 'Are you hurt?'

'Oh no, sir, I am quite well. But you can help me. You must aid me to get out of here. I am now imprisoned against my will. I am certified sane, but they delay my release. It is that terrible man, that repulsive creature, who wants to keep me here. You are a gentleman, I see, and I am sure you are a good man. You can speak to dear Mr Rockingham, the Chief Superintendent, about me. Please, I beg you.'

The carriage is slowing down and now draws to a stop.

'I must go,' says the woman. She presses my hand, looks at me imploringly, and opens the door to the carriage.

'But your name, Miss?' I say.

'Rosetti. Miss Titania Rosetti.'

She is gone.

I remain sitting on the carriage seat, shaken physically and emotionally, the cold touch of the woman's fingertips still present on my hand. This has not been an auspicious start to a visit I have been already dreading.

I force myself to be calm; I practice a smile, and try to sharpen up my brain. I am here to do a job, after all, and intend to do a good one. I am a writer, a journalist, commissioned by the London *Times* to do a number of articles on life in a public lunatic asylum. The reputation of the latter has been deteriorating recently, what with one scandal or another, and arguments from a new breed of mad doctors – a frightening breed of men, I find them – that see the mad as a degenerate portion of a degenerating society. I am to visit here daily for a week, with no part of the asylum inaccessible to me and no question I cannot ask. I was offered a room in the visitors' accommodation here at the asylum, but declined firmly. Instead, I am staying in the city of Portsmouth, which is a little far from this corner of the Hampshire countryside, but a manageable enough distance. I must have my dose of noise and people if I am to get through the week with my sanity intact.

It was the Medical Superintendent – the man in overall charge of this place – Mr Roderick Rockingham, who suggested I commence my work by attending the lunatics' ball. I am still amazed at the very idea of balls taking place in lunatic asylums, but they are all part of the benevolent system of lunatic care known as moral management. Rockingham hopes that my beginning my work by attending a ball will confound my expectations, and open my mind to the varied wonders of the moral system that I will encounter during the week.

I force myself to get up and I step out of the carriage awkwardly; I will have a few bruises coming up in the morning.

'Did you not see that poor woman?' I ask the driver, who is clambering down from his seat. 'She could have caught her death out here in this abysmal weather.'

'Never mind that woman, sir,' says the driver, a morose man with a long, deeply wrinkled face and a strong Hampshire accent, 'she could have killed us all appearing like a ghost before us and spooking my poor, old horse.'

He strokes the horse's mane, then pulls an apple from the pocket of his great brown cape and feeds it to her. 'There, old girl, there; you're alright now.'

'Well, we three are alright, happily,' I say, 'but cannot yet say the same for that woman. I will seek help inside; we must do what we can.'

I barely have chance to take in the imposing, three-storey building spread out before me as I hurry across the gravel to the central portico, the driver still muttering behind me, something about lunatics being treated like royalty.

I flick my head round to him, suddenly angry. 'Why should they not be treated well? They are not criminals, I assume, deserving of punishment?'

'No, sir, but…'

I turn away again and approach the door; this is not the moment for a philosophical debate with a cab driver on our society's treatment of the insane. I take a deep breath and ring the doorbell. My heart is pounding. Once I am let in, what if I am never let out? I remind myself that I am a rational man, and must not let wild thoughts overtake me. It is not long before the solid oak door creaks open. A tall man with slightly angular features, a Roman nose and thick brown hair and beard stands in the doorway.

'Good afternoon,' he says. 'Mr Mortimer, I believe? I am Mr Friend, Matthew Friend, the Clerk here at Allingsford.'

'Good afternoon, Mr Friend. Yes, I am Mr Mortimer.'

He has a reassuring name, at least, but can anyone in such an institution be truly a friend?

'But come in, Mr Mortimer,' he says. 'What a dreadful day. You must be half-frozen. Our porter would normally answer the door, but all our staff are running round just now, what with the ball, and so we are all helping out.'

'Thank you, but I must first mention a young woman whom I have just encountered. I think she may have been trying to run away. Rosetti. Miss Titania Rosetti. She got into my hackney carriage for several minutes, then disappeared. She was in great distress and may well be ill.'

Friend frowns quickly, then resumes a bland expression.

'Oh, do not be uneasy, Mr Mortimer. Miss Rosetti does this sometimes. Let me take you inside and then we will fetch her and make sure she is safe and sound. I hope that she has not caught cold.'

Friend stands back and gestures for me to enter the building. I must do it. I step into a large wood-panelled entrance hall, brightly lit with oil and gas lamps. Several people, probably servants, or attendants, as the staff who take care of the patients are known, are stood very upright around the hall, smiling at me. I am not sure whether to be cheered or unnerved by this display. Am I in a lunatic asylum or a great country house? Now I think of it, I have read that the original model for public asylums was a sort of great house in which everyone has their place.

Friend instructs an older, male servant to find Miss Rosetti, and quickly, and to take one of the female servants, and be very gentle, mind, with her. He turns to me.

'Come along to our waiting room, Mr Mortimer, and I shall fetch Mr Rockingham for you.'

The small waiting room to the left of the main entrance is also panelled in wood and hung with several large portraits and what look like plans of the asylum buildings. I could be in my lawyer's office.

'Do sit down,' continues Friend, 'and make yourself easy if you can. These places can be quite intimidating for the uninitiated, I know, but you will soon feel at home. I will see you shortly at the ball, and we will be seeing a little more of each other during the week ahead. I am looking forward to talking to you about our work. One does not often get the opportunity. We are proud of what we do here at the Allingsford Public Asylum for the Insane, and hope you will do us justice, Mr Mortimer.'

'I will do my best, Mr Friend,' I reply, sitting down, 'though I must always tell the absolute truth, you know.'

I am not sure why I add the latter clause to my statement, as if I am suspecting the poor man of encouraging me to exaggeration or even lies. It is my nerves. He seems to take no offence, however.

'We would expect nothing less,' he says cheerfully, 'and we have nothing untoward to hide, I can assure you of that. Quite the opposite.'

Friend walks briskly from the room, smiling as he goes, and I am left to contemplate my surroundings in peace. I wonder if this is the first place in which lunatics find themselves in the asylum, sandwiched between two workhouse officials, who escort them here. Their initial assessment takes place in another room, I believe, known as the official receiving room. It is not so bad in this room, I suppose. I cannot imagine what it must feel like for the poor creatures on their arrival. What does it feel like to be mad? Do they know why they are sitting here? Still, I remind myself, I am not mad and am not about to be institutionalised. I am simply visiting for a week.

Nonetheless, there is nothing like being in a lunatic asylum to make one highly conscious of one's mental state, and so I adjust my ridiculous ruffled shirt, a concession to the evening's festivities, smooth my hair, and sit upright. Appearance is at least half sanity or insanity, it seems from some of my reading, and the last thing I want in my current state of mind is to come across as a likely candidate for admission.

CHAPTER 2

THE DOOR OPENS and a tall, large man with sloping shoulders appears, beaming at me with a big full mouth.

'Harris, dear boy - if I may,' says Rockingham. 'What a pleasure to see you again after all these years. Welcome to our home.'

His voice is a little high, his manner jovial, his clothing gawdy. I get up and shake his large warm hand, pleased by his drooping brown eyes, bald pate and high colour. He was my deceased father's oldest and dearest friend; they met at school and remained fast friends through life. He seems one of those benevolent characters straight from the pages of our Mr Dickens. I am a little cheered.

'You were a boy of ten last time we met, and only look at you know. But you are just as I imagined you from our correspondence over the years, and in person so very like your father.'

'Yes, so I believe,' I say, smiling. 'And here you are, all these years later, my parents' dearest friend. You used to give me gingerbread, you know, and a boy does not forget his oldest benefactor.'

'Ah ha, you see, it is proof of the long-lasting power of benevolence. It is what our whole system here is ultimately based on.'

'It is a wonderful notion, indeed, but it is difficult to understand how it leads to the management and cure of the insane.'

'You shall see how it works as the week progresses. The broad idea is to create the atmosphere of a well-ordered, virtuous home, where patients are taught the values of self-control, industry and moderation. The combination of authority and kindness has created an environment where the need for mechanical restraint is almost done away with.'

'It is still used in some cases, though?' I am aware that there are some padded cells at Allingsford, the thought of which horrifies me.

'Yes, sadly, but only in the most difficult cases. Of course, our overall system also includes medicinal and therapeutic treatments.'

'And that system also involves such things as balls for patients?'

'Oh yes; healthy recreation is an important part of any healthy home and society, and when our patients return to the world, they must be fit to partake in all its aspects.'

Mr Rockingham seems a charming companion, as he has been a charming and kindly correspondent over the years. When my father died two years before my mother, Rockingham took on the role of a sort of father-by-post, and his counsel over the years has been both compassionate and rational. We both sit down for a while. Rockingham pats my hand, and we chat pleasantly about my journey here and my life in London. We will get down to business tomorrow, he says, and he will put me in the hands of his most excellent staff. This evening, I am to be as an honoured guest at a family gathering, and to simply observe and enjoy. Of course, I am free to take notes, but, where possible, discreetly; it would not do to taint an evening of merry leisure with too notable a display of business.

We leave the room and walk along several cool, stone-floored corridors. I can hear the sound of a fiddle playing. I follow Rockingham into a large, long hall, noticeably warm, filled with what must be several hundred souls, of both sexes. I know that men and women are usually divided into two sides of the asylum but are allowed to come together for entertainments. I am overwhelmed. The sea of people, some standing, some sitting, some dancing, sways before me. The noise, of the fiddle, the voices and the stamping feet, crashes in my head. The flicker of lamps and candles on the faces of the mad, looking happy, dreamy, agitated, desolate, creates the impression of a ship of ghosts.

'There goes Mr Friend, whom you have met already,'

says Mr Rockingham, smiling and tapping his left hand on the side of his trouser leg. 'He is quite the musical man and runs our asylum choir, but you will hear more of all this during the course of the week. Come, come, let us enjoy the entertainment.'

We walk slowly through the hall. The noise gradually dies down and then the fiddle stops, as Mr Rockingham is recognised. People stand, smile, nod and bow at him. He returns the favour, saying, intermittently, 'how do you do, Mary?' and 'how is that leg of yours, Henry?' Apart from the odd sullen expression, he seems to be highly respected. I am stared at, too, and given the eye, I am sure, by some of the women, which is a little unnerving, though there are handsome faces enough among them. We stop, briefly, near a sort of stage at the side of the hall, where a band is positioned, including brass and woodwind instruments, and a piano. Rockingham shakes the hand of Friend, who returns the shake heartily, runs his fingers through his floppy black mane and, at the nod from the superintendent, strikes up his fiddle again. We proceed to the end of the hall, the noise growing again behind us.

'Harris,' says Rockingham, 'there is a pleasant nook here, where I thought you might like to rest and observe. Someone will bring you a glass of beer, and you may sit awhile, or converse as you wish with some of the staff and residents. Supper will be served at seven o'clock; we will sup together, and can have a little more discourse then.'

'Thank you,' I say, relieved to have an opportunity to gather my thoughts, 'that is very thoughtful of you, and this will do me very well.'

I sit down in a comfortable chair between two green, bedraggled-looking potted ferns, with which the hall is generously dotted. A servant soon appears with a glass of beer, which I accept gratefully. This is all rather pleasant, and I feel some relief. I have read quite widely on the life of an asylum, and particularly this one, but I have never been able to shake the feeling that they are terrible, cruel, dangerous places. One hears such horror stories, and then I always hold in my heart the idea of my poor mother, who suffered so dreadfully in a private asylum. I glance down at the beer in my hand, and have a sudden fear that it is poisoned. Perhaps the servant who gave it to me is a criminal lunatic?

But I must stay calm and rational, and be as objective as possible. I am here now and have begun my work. Things are never as bad as one's imaginings. I force myself to take a sip of the beer. I focus my attention towards the centre of the hall, where is taking place a country dance, some of the participants moving listlessly, some enthusiastically, and some bordering on the wildly.

'Good afternoon, sir,' says a tall, stately-looking woman to my left, as she sits down in the chair next to mine.

'Good afternoon, madam,' I say, a little startled, jumping up and bowing quickly, before sitting back down.

'Do forgive my bold approach, sir,' says the lady, 'but one so rarely finds refined company in here that one has to grasp at the opportunity when one can.'

'Yes, I see,' I say, not quite sure what to say. 'How do you do?'

'I am Miss Nightingale.'

'Like the famous nurse,' I say, smiling.

She nods complacently, and I observe her features, which are sharp and heavily lined, but rather striking. Her eyes are grey and her hair, brown, streaked with grey, is parted in the middle and folded over her ears, in that spaniel fashion that was favoured by the older women of my childhood.

'Are you employed here, Miss Nightingale?' I ask.

'Good gracious, no,' says she. 'I would do things very differently, I can assure you, if I was.'

'Oh; perhaps you are visiting a relative, then?'

She laughs suddenly, a light, tinkling laugh, which contrasts rather strangely with her croaky voice.

'Let us just say that I am here in an observatory capacity,' she says, and actually winks at me. 'One must keep an eye on certain women, you know.' She lowers her voice to a whisper. 'My rightful husband was ensnared away from me by a sluttish young baggage.'

'Oh, gracious.'

She nods vociferously. 'Yes, indeed.' Her voice becomes louder again.

'See that fat woman over there?' she asks me, nodding towards a short, round woman wearing a black lace collar, who is stood about thirty yards away near to a window. 'She believes that she is Queen Victoria.'

Miss Nightingale titters again. 'And the woman next to her, the brown woman wearing the yellow dress; she thinks that she is Mary Seacole, the other nurse.'

'Well,' I say, uncertainly, 'I suppose they are harmless enough delusions.'

'Not at all, sir, not at all; they can be quite disruptive, at times, I assure you. They frequently try to challenge my authority. The Queen is rather jealous of me, you know, being a timid, ineffectual creature quite enthralled to that German of hers. It is a little pathetic really. When once I called out for donations to help our poor dear soldiers in the Crimea, do you know what she gave? A supply of woollen scarves. One of the richest women in the world. How I laughed. I hear she is quite mad about bedchamber deeds, you know. And as to Seacole. "Call me Aunty", she says, "or Mother, like my darling boys in Balaclava used to do". It is really quite nauseating. She is trying to outshine me. Does she not know that there can be only one most famous nurse in the world?'

Miss Nightingale, who has been staring ahead, now flicks her head towards me and looks me in the eye. 'What do you think about it, sir? What should I do?'

I am again out of my depth. What do I say? Would such a woman become threatening? Or cause a scene? I abhor scenes.

'Oh, madam,' I say, 'I am not sure that I am qualified to advise.'

She nods and gives a small, pinched smile. I seem to have said the right thing.

'I suppose you are right,' she continues. 'It is gratifying that some people, at least, can acknowledge their limitations. Everyone is power-mad around here. There are several Napoleon the Firsts, Henry the Eighths, and Julius Caesars on the men's side, you know. At least I do not have to deal with them, generally, though no doubt they will be here somewhere this evening. Never mind; I will put my problem to Athena; she always sets me right.'

I think it best not to ask who is Athena, but see the lady now smiling and gently patting her left shoulder.

'My darling little bird,' she says, 'you always know what is best, do not you my beautiful little owl, bestest creature in the whole world?'

She turns to me again. 'Say hello to Athena, Mr Mortimer; she is quite the wisest resident of the house.'

I smile, look towards the woman's left shoulder, and say, 'How do you do, Athena?'

The lady frowns. 'To whom are you talking, sir?'

'Why, to your owl, Athena.'

'Owl? What owl? Do you really see an owl beside me? Good gracious, you are quite mad, quite mad. This place gets worse every day.'

She sighs, clicks her tongue, and says, 'I must be going, sir. I have not the leisure to sit talking idly with a mad stranger, gentleman or no. There is always so much work to do here with these people always fancying themselves ill. I do not believe in illness.'

The woman's face is now flushed, and she is tapping her left foot very quickly on the floor. I am getting anxious again, for her – and myself, I must confess - when a female attendant appears, smiles and nods at me. A large male attendant is standing behind her. I do hope she will not be harmed. I have heard of rough treatment occurring in these places.

'Come, now, Sarah, dearie,' says the female attendant, kindly, but firmly. 'It's nearly time for supper, and you know how it affects your nerves if you don't eat properly. Come and have a seat between me and Harry, here, and we'll have a nice bite to eat and then get you to bed.'

Sarah – her real name, I assume - is now looking quite angry, but her stomach is rumbling rather loudly, and she gets up and lets the two attendants each take hold of one of her arms and pull her slowly away. The male attendant smiles at me apologetically. Sarah turns her head back to me.

'You f*****g c**t,' she says, and plenty worse things besides, shouting more loudly as she goes.

I am shocked, a little shaken, though I have read that the most pure and virtuous women when sane can behave worse than the lowest street whore when mad, and curse quite as vilely too.

My spirits are sinking again. Poor Sarah; what it must be to come to that, and she clearly an educated person. I know that the majority of patients here are from the lower classes; it is a public institution, after all, and paid for by the public purse. But there are some patients who will have fallen in life's degree, and so fallen into a lower class; and then there are also a small number of private, fee-paying, patients admitted, who are usually of a slightly higher rank. Sarah must fall into one of these two groups. I must ask the superintendent about her.

How I wish I was back at home in my comfortable lodgings in Chelsea, with my books, cigars and brandy, resting in perfect peace and rationality. I may have been pleasantly surprised by this first exposure to the asylum environment, but now the reality of a lunatic asylum is creeping in, and the fiddle, the beer and the pleasantries feel like a sad satire. Still, it is only one week of my life, and I must see it through.

I am considering getting up and walking round the room, perhaps introducing myself to some of the residents and staff, but I do not have the heart for it following my encounter with Sarah. In fact, there is no need to do so as now Mary Seacole and Queen Victoria – as I am thinking of them – are approaching me, both of their faces combining a smile with an expression of tender concern. I get up and bow slightly, trying to rally myself for more encounters with lunatic women.

'How do you do, my dear?' says Mary Seacole, putting out her hand. 'As I am sure you will know, I am Mary Seacole, though you may address me as Mother Seacole.'

'How do you do, Mother Seacole,' say I, pressing her hand. 'I am Mr Harris Mortimer.'

I believe that the woman, a Creole, does have a look of Seacole, though I cannot be sure, having seen only a sketchy image of the original in a newspaper. She has an upright, dignified bearing, finely carved, even features, now sagging slightly with age, and brown eyes that have a look of intelligence. Her brown, curly hair, streaked with grey, is parted in the middle and pulled back from her face, and she is wearing a sturdy costume in a soft yellow colour, with a piece of white lace around her shoulders.

'How do you do?' I now address Queen Victoria.

'How do you do? You may kiss my hand,' says she, in a thick, Hampshire accent, 'then be at your ease.'

Not knowing what else to do, I obey.

This woman does not look much like the queen, apart from being short and round. She has squashed features, rough, sagging skin, and white wiry hair. As she is attired in the simple brown linsey dress of the asylum, she must be a public patient, and I imagine that she has had a hard life, perhaps of manual labour or the bearing of many children.

'We've come to warn you,' says the queen.

I manage an inquisitive look.

'Beware that Nightingale woman.'

Seacole nods. 'Aye, watch out my son. She is a tyrant, and likes to work men unto their death.'

'Ah,' I say.

'She turns up her nose at me,' continues Seacole, 'likely because my skin is a little duskier than her own, but I have done as much good as she has, probably more.'

The queen nods vociferously. 'I'm sure she believes she's the Queen, and gives out orders as if she were. Hoity-toity, hoity-toity. I've put up with it long enough. If it was the olden times again, I'd have her head chopped off – that'd teach her.'

The queen's face has lost its beneficent look and now looks quite angry. Seacole, however, remains beatific, but nods her assent.

'I go about my business, sir,' says Seacole, 'and she tries to prevent me. I build my shelters for the poor, wounded soldiers, I make my remedies, and there she is, pointing at me that long, bony finger of hers, and trying to prevent my dear boys from getting well.'

'Hoity-toity, hoity-toity,' says the queen.

I am nodding slightly, trapped within the world of these three strange women and longing to get out. I believe that the staff do not encourage delusions, but calmly turn the subject. There is clearly a knack to it that I have not acquired, and I remain struck dumb.

Thankfully, a change of scene distracts our attention. The lively tune ends; there is a pause, then Mr Friend begins playing a slow, light operatic tune on the piano. It is rather soothing for my jangled nerves. Now, a lovely female voice accompanies it, leaving me smiling quite involuntarily, though it is a melancholy number. The queen and Seacole move away from me towards the musician.

The singer looks familiar. No, it cannot be her, can it? It is, it is her; I am sure of it.

CHAPTER 3

THERE SHE IS, the woman who got into my cab, the woman who claims to be sane and to be held here against her will, the woman who asked for my aid. There is no denying her beauty, which is in no way diminished by the drab brown of the asylum uniform, trimmed very slightly with a little lace at the collar and sleeves, and her hair now tucked neatly under a simple, white cap.

The song stops. Miss Rosetti smiles shyly as the room applauds her, and I find myself clapping along enthusiastically. She now looks a little lost, and I wish I could go over and comfort her as I did in the carriage. She takes the arm of a female attendant, who escorts her to one of the benches at the side of the hall, where the meal will be served.

A man is coming quickly towards me. He has a short, slim body and a rather large head with a high, noble forehead. His hair is dark and curly, his eyes small and grey and his tiny mouth curves upwards slightly at each corner. He looks much younger than myself.

'Mr Mortimer?' asks he, smiling quickly at me to display slightly crooked teeth.

'Yes, sir,' I respond. He reaches out to shake my hand.

'I am Mr Cedric Jones, Assistant Medical Officer, come to take you to supper. I hear that you had an encounter with Sarah Barker? Not likely to be cured, I am afraid. Former governess. Monomania on reaching her climacteric, you know.'

Mr Jones wriggles his head as he speaks, which he does in staccato fashion, as if he is spitting out words, anxious to get rid of them. I will need to look at my notes again in order to fully understand the medical diagnoses here. I believe that he means that the woman Sarah Barker developed a form of mania, which focuses on one thing in particular, at the onset of the termination of her reproductive function as a woman. In her case, the mania must centre around her being the nurse, Florence Nightingale.

'Come, come, you must be hungry,' Mr Jones continues. 'Eating will settle your nerves. Must be strange. Visiting a place like this for the first time.'

He walks rapidly back up the hall. I hurry to keep up behind him. As we walk, everyone is being settled down onto wooden benches by various attendants. A few of the residents are resisting and some are shouting, which sets my heart racing a little, but they are either settled or escorted away. Overall, the process seems to be relatively smooth, and I cannot help but be impressed by the management of this whole thing, and on such a scale. I know there must be many patients here much worse than Sarah Barker and the women who think they are Mary Seacole and Queen Victoria. We arrive at the top of a table near to the main door through which I entered, where Rockingham is seated, looking quite at his ease, near a selection of smart-looking gentlemen.

'Mr Mortimer, Harris,' says he, his open, genial countenance a pleasure to behold. He gets up to shake my hand again, the red flowers on his garish waistcoat dancing in the light of a nearby candle. He introduces me to several of the well-dressed, rather over-fed looking gentlemen, who turn out to be members of the Committee of Visitors, the body that oversees the running of the asylum.

'What did you think of our songbird?' Rockingham asks me as we sit down.

'Enchanting, quite enchanting,' I say, perhaps sounding a bit doubtful. I feel a little nervous mentioning what happened in the carriage, as if I am telling on the woman somehow. And yet, did she not ask me to mention her case to Rockingham? 'However,' I continue, 'I must mention a strange encounter I had with her on my way here. The weather was dreadful, and my hackney cab came to a halt on the way up the hill to the asylum. Miss Rosetti appeared, as if from nowhere, and got into the cab. She said that she was ready to leave but that some terrible man was standing in her way. She disappeared again before I could ask more. It all sounds rather foolish now that I say it out loud.'

'Not at all,' says Rockingham, 'and her actions do not surprise me.' He looks round the table; the other diners are preoccupied with their own conversations. 'You are aware of the confidential nature of our work, and I know you will respect that. I can give you a brief summary of her case. It is a mild one of melancholia, triggered by a broken heart, you know, although I believe that she had other sorrows before that, the death of a father and a beloved younger sister. She has been with us only three months and has been progressing fairly well. Yet, it is rather early for a discharge, and we still have a few doubts about her. Mr Jones, especially, does not want to rush her release.'

'I see.'

'When she first arrived, she was constantly trying to run to her lover - a soldier who abandoned her long since - but always stopped short of trying to escape the asylum grounds entirely. She would stand at the gates talking to the imaginary man in a most poetic fashion and then the gatekeeper would bring her back to us, meek as a lamb. Her attempts to run gradually decreased, and then ceased after around six weeks. She has since been calm, rational, biddable, even charming. Her attempt to run again is a little disappointing, but there is often a small lapse before full recovery occurs. It is a minor setback, I hope; I am fairly confident that hers will be a happy outcome.'

'I am glad to hear it.'

'Her story is quite a common one, unfortunately. We have our fair share of Ophelias here at Allingsford, women's biological nature being what it is, and men, not always helping matters, by behaving in a caddish fashion. Well, well, this Ophelia will return to the world, and the bosom of her family, or perhaps resume her profession (she was a governess). No doubt, she will marry at some future point.'

I am, indeed, happy to hear this. It is pleasing to hear about hopeful cases, and that such a lovely woman can return to the world and serve her purpose in it. Still, I would not want to meet such a woman in everyday life. I am already on heightened alert regarding any propensity to madness in the female sex.

What I want for myself is one of those good, managing, pretty little women to preside over my table. I am thirty-five years old and in need of a mate, but I am so terrified about making the wrong choice, and bringing upon myself a similar life to my father's, of pain, suffering and scandal at having a mad woman for a wife. About five years ago, now, I became quite fond of a young woman of a very good family indeed, but she began to demonstrate an unnatural interest in those matters that are sacred to the marriage bed, often a sign of incipient madness. I was disgusted, and felt driven to mention the matter, with a deal of embarrassment, to her father. I do not think it did much good, for he merely laughed at me. Well, well; I did my duty.

Purity in woman is so important to me. I have led such an impure life myself – though, naturally, it is different, and expected, for men – that I want to start afresh, clean, when I choose a bride. I am not very proud of my past. I trained as a barrister and was one of those dreadful young chaps they called Jolly Dogs or Champagne Charlies. We used to create havoc up and down the Strand in London, destroying property, in and out of music halls and low haunts. We practically lived at Romano's, dining, drinking, picking up girls, and sometimes, I will confess, we resorted to the filthy back-alleys of the area to do so.

I was not happy, then, though I would have thought I was having a fine old time. I was nervous, anxious, hating my studies and not especially liking the company I kept, those crass, popular sort of young men with whom I never felt comfortable at school. I was intoxicated most of the time.

Of course, I still have my needs, and a woman who serves the purpose. She is a nice, clean, pretty girl, who lives somewhere in Soho, and we find a discreet little room not too far away to conduct our business. I am a little ashamed of it sometimes, but a man is a man, and I prefer to satisfy my needs in a business-like and separate fashion, rather than get myself entangled in a tawdry affair with an opera girl, as many a one has done before me. I only have occasional resource to the Cremorne Gardens in Chelsea. It is near to where I reside, and so a little tempting to a man fatigued after a day's writing labours, head and eyes aching, hands smudged with ink, and needing, as it were, to find some sort of release. I very, very rarely resort to the timberyard near Paradise Wharf; the women there are of quite the lowest sort – shameless, filthy, liquorish – and I know that I degrade myself.

'Your mention of the "Ophelias" interests me greatly,' I say to Rockingham. 'I take it that you are referring to a female type alike to the jilted lover of Hamlet, based on Shakespeare's play of the same name?'

'Oh yes; forgive me, Harris. I am guilty of speaking the cant of my profession; I am sure that you journalists do a similar thing. We use the Ophelia nomenclature as a shorthand for a young woman who develops a form of insanity after experiencing a disappointment in love. Women's minds and bodies are so delicately constituted, you know, due to their reproductive function as a species. Any shock to their system can cause irreparable damage, though happily most such cases can be cured. Our precious women must be treated with tender care, Harris; I am sure you agree.'

'I could not agree more, sir.'

What a benevolent, gentlemanly man Mr Rockingham is. We eat a meal, simple but hearty and not entirely tasteless, comprising roast beef and pudding washed down with a warm spiced ale. I am assured that beef is reserved for special occasions and that the usual diet for residents is somewhat less luxurious if still plentiful enough.

Rockingham now gets up to make a speech to mark the occasion, which is twenty-five years of Allingsford asylum life. I fear that I do not give it much attention as I am feeling somewhat tired, but it is over quickly enough. The sound of loud applause jolts me to my senses and Rockingham appears again beside me. His face is redder than the flowers on his waistcoat; his brow, which has two short, horizontal wrinkles in its centre, is moist and there are a few tears running down his cheeks. I cannot help but find myself deeply moved by this man and his cause. He settles down, takes a glass of water, then a brandy, and I ask him about Queen Victoria and Mary Seacole.

'The queen, in reality,' says the superintendent, 'is plain old Sally Wood, a former servant, wife of a farm labourer and mother of twelve children. Sadly, most of the family ended up in the workhouse, where Mrs Wood developed dementia. Fortunately for her, this was picked up by the medic at the workhouse and she was transferred here. Many sufferers from mental disease can languish in the workhouse, and be cruelly neglected, whereas here they are given comfort and dignity. She now remembers little about her previous life, though is lucid, in a repetitive way, about being Queen Victoria. Your Mary Seacole – in reality, Miss Clara Simpson – looks after her wonderfully. It is quite touching to see.

'As to Miss Simpson herself, she is half Jamaican, half Scottish – much like the real Seacole, I believe – and is a very well-educated woman. Her case, on the whole, is one of mania, from which she currently appears to be in a respite phase, saving the Seacole delusion. When in her manic phase, she barely sleeps, chatters incessantly, and takes things from around the building and grounds in order to build a hotel for the soldiers, she says, and gathers plants with which to make medicines to cure them. We have found a way to help manage her behaviour by letting her have her own plot in the kitchen garden, where she can indulge her fantasies in a harmless manner. Occasionally, when she is at risk of harming herself or she is quite worn out, we use a small amount of morphine, chloral hydrate or Indian hemp, to sedate her.'

'You have an impressive knowledge of your patients, sir,' I observe. 'There are about seven hundred residents here, are there not? How on earth do you keep track?'

Rockingham smiles. 'I confess that I do not. Sarah, Sally and Clara are well-known patients due to their very specific delusions, but it would be impossible for me to know everyone personally, though I would if I could, I assure you. As I hinted at in my speech, I fear that we are losing that family atmosphere that is so essential, I believe, to an effective asylum.'

Rockingham lowers his voice a little. 'We housed three hundred and fifty patients when we began, you know, and I felt at the time that even that sum was far too many. Those suffering from mental disease should really receive dedicated and unremitting individual care. Now we are at seven hundred patients, and are under constant injunction to cut costs. And there are some asylums forced to house several thousand people. No wonder abuses and wrongs can occur.'

Rockingham glances quickly at some of the Committee members sat at our table. 'Well, well, Harris,' he says, 'let us talk of brighter things.'

He tells me about some of the other entertainments offered by the asylum over the years, all part of the overall system of reward and rational recreation for residents. There is a summer fair, football and cricketing fixtures in the summer, and various types of musical, magical and theatrical events, though Shakespeare is now discouraged since one of the poor patients got a little overexcited during the murder scene in *Hamlet*.

It is approaching ten o'clock and the evening is drawing to a close. The national anthem will soon be sung, I am told. I smile a little to myself wondering how Sally Wood, or Queen Victoria, will react at this point, imagining her nodding superciliously as everyone around her sings, and expecting them to bow to her. I look across at the last of the dancers and notice some sort of commotion near the centre of the hall. The dancing stops and several of the dancers are huddling in a group around something. It looks like somebody has fallen, and is lying on the floor. Oh dear; this is very unpleasant. Mr Jones is rapidly approaching the scene from the other side of the room and my companion also rises and moves towards it. I, too, get up and follow.

It is our Florence Nightingale, or Sarah Barker, as

she really is, lying on the floor, her body on its back though slightly twisted, and blood running from the back of her head in a pool across the polished floorboards. Jones is now kneeling next to her. He pulls the shawl from around her neck, lifts her head very slightly and presses the shawl there, holding it with his left hand, presumably to stem the flow of blood. With his right hand he checks the pulse points, then turns to look up at Rockingham, his face very white and stunned. He seems to want to say something but his quickfire speech fails him, and he simply shakes his head. She is dead.

CHAPTER 4

'EVERYONE TO RETIRE now,' Rockingham says loudly, looking at the nearby attendants, who start to gather up the patients around them. 'Come, come, everyone to bed; off you go.'

A large man with a sagging face, who has witnessed the scene, starts to cry loudly. An attendant tries to pull him away gently, but he stamps his feet, refusing to move. Eventually, he is forcibly removed by two male attendants, which only adds to the distress of the scene. Otherwise, the room is cleared of people quite quickly and in an orderly fashion, and only a group of Rockingham, Jones, Friend, several attendants and servants, and a couple of Committee visitors, remain.

'Get a cart, please,' says Rockingham to the attendants, 'and something to cover her. We must take her to the infirmary and lay her out so that we can conduct the autopsy tomorrow.' He shakes his head. 'Poor, poor Sarah.'

'How do you think she has died?' I ask.

I must confess that I am feeling a little more anxious again, but I counsel myself to remain calm and recognise that deaths will happen here as they do everywhere else, including in the most benign environments.

'I cannot be sure until tomorrow,' says Rockingham, 'apart from what we see, that is the blow to her head, and brain.'

'She had a fit last month,' says Jones, standing up quickly, 'but seemed to have recovered. Perhaps it happened again, and she lost consciousness, causing the fall.'

'I hope we have not failed her,' says Rockingham, and I see a tear fall down his red cheek.

He looks at me. 'I still take all our deaths rather personally, Mr Mortimer, though you would think I would have grown accustomed to it after twenty-five years.'

I am touched by Rockingham's compassion and sensibility. What a remarkable man he is: affable, brisk in a crisis, tender.

Two servants arrive with a flat cart and a thick grey blanket. With the help of Jones, they lift Sarah's body, place it on the cart and cover it. The cart is pulled away, followed by Jones, who says that he will oversee the care of the body until the morning. My eyes are drawn to the pool of blood on the floor, and I feel queasy. I was never good with this sort of thing, and fared badly at school – Miss Harriet Mortimer, they called me – amongst the rough and tumble and easy violence of most of the boys. A number of staff are now clearing up the room after the evening's events and a woman in a large apron appears next to us and begins to clean up the blood.

'Tea, coffee, gentlemen?' asks Rockingham, looking at the Committee members and myself. 'We have had a shock, and what a dreadful way for our celebration to end. Still, death sits amongst us here as it does in every corner of this life; we must face it, and deal with it, then continue to focus our energies on the care of the living.'

'Thank you, sir,' say I, 'that is most kind of you, but I think I will return to my lodging. My driver will be waiting for me outside on this cold night and, I must admit, I am tired. Shall I come tomorrow, as planned, or will I be in the way?'

'Not at all; you must come all as planned. Our work goes on. We will expect you at about half after one o'clock, as agreed.'

I follow the porter back to the main door, where he gives me my overcoat, shakes my hand, and sees me out into the evening. The weather is even filthier than it was on my arrival, and I hurry over to the fly, on which the driver is sat waiting for me, wrapped up in some oilcloth. At least he has enjoyed himself; I can smell the beer on his breath from inside the carriage, and he is actually singing.

I try to settle back and organise my thoughts as we pass back down the gravel drive. The journey will last several hours, since I have missed the last train from Allingsford to Portsmouth, and will need to go all the way in this cab. The rain is battering the roof, and I can hear rumbles of thunder, quite an appropriate end to the evening. I withdraw my notebook and pencil from my pocket, with the aim of recording my initial thoughts.

What a day it has been. I have faced my fear. I have entered the asylum and left again. I have survived. Of course I have. As usual, when it comes to the subject of madness, I have allowed a sense of melodrama to overtake me. I should have trusted in the information I had and in the character of Rockingham, my family's oldest friend, for it seems that Allingsford asylum tries very hard to be the sort of benevolent place envisaged by those pioneers of the asylum reform movement decades ago.

And yet, my first experience of the place also ends with a death, with blood on the floor. I know that this asylum was built twenty-five years ago on the grounds of an old country house, which in the last century was used as a private lunatic asylum. As with the place that held my mother, it was unregulated, unsupervised, unchecked, and it is thought that all the worst horrors associated with those bad old times took place there. Instead of demolishing that building, the new asylum was built around it. This means that somewhere within the current building lies the old one. What is in there? What is it used for?

I cannot help but see my poor mother in that dark imagined place, and it pains me very deeply. She looks like a wild animal that has been tamed, cowed and humiliated. Her long brown hair is a nest of knots, her clothes are torn and filthy, her feet and face blackened by dirt. When I was five years old, she gave birth to another son, who died, and developed a dreadful monomania. For several years, my father devoted himself to her care, but she did not recover and, with great reluctance, he put her in the care of a private asylum. I was then seven years old. A year later, my father died suddenly; I am sure that it was from a broken heart. I was away at school at that time, and again, two years later, when my mother died in the asylum.

Rockingham looked into the matter, and had to demonstrate great perseverance and tenacity to break through the conspiracy of secrecy that then surrounded those places. There had been a change of management and staff at the asylum, and the new regime was driven mostly by profit and pleasure in cruelty. Following my father's death, Rockingham had continued to pay the fees, but was unable to visit my mother on the regular basis that my father had done. She was abused and neglected. Rockingham did not tell me the full story, by letter, until years later. He may never have done, for what son can bear to hear such painful things about his mother? But I, suspecting what had happened, pressed him to tell me the truth. He did so, without dwelling on detail, still hoping to spare me a little, I am sure. But ever since I have imagined every horror.

Tonight, I have met four female residents of the asylum. I feel almost sure that the older women are – or were, in poor Sarah Barker's case – in the right place for them.

But I am really not sure about the younger woman. Could Miss Rosetti really be quite well and ready to leave, but is being kept here by the will of a malicious male figure? Her actions on our first encounter were not those of a rational, decent woman, running out on a dreadful night in a state of dishevelment, to accost a male stranger in his hackney cab. And yet, if her story was true, then her desperation would be understandable. And what a figure of perfect beauty and serenity she made only a few hours later, at the ball.

The journey, though a little rough, soon passes given my distracted thoughts, none of which I have managed to commit to paper, and we arrive at my rather elegant Portsmouth hotel. I tip the driver, who grimaces at me for my trouble, and he agrees to collect me tomorrow at one o'clock at Allingsford railway station. I feel a little sorry for the horse, now having to drag itself back to the village, but cannot feel the same sorrow for the driver. So much for the friendliness of the countryside. Our London Hackney drivers have quite the fearsome reputation with their insolent temper and liquorish tendencies, but this man would make a better growler than any of them. The staff at my hotel are affable and obliging, however, my room is clean and comfortable, and I feel a little soothed by the sense of normality around me, however late the hour. I sleep well, surprisingly, given the turmoil of my mind, only dreaming a little of my mother, coming towards me through a field, then stopping, just out of my reach, her brown eyes full of concern.

CHAPTER 5

I WAKE UP LATE, and refreshed, my mind clearer. I am not sure that I will ever feel fully ready to face a day at a lunatic asylum, but I am feeling a little stronger than yesterday at least. I take a good breakfast of devilled kidneys and eggs, and stroll out of the hotel about half an hour after eleven o'clock to make my way to the railway station. The storm has passed, the sun is out, and I am enlivened by the bustle of the city, the sabbath though it is, and even more by the noise and activity of the railway station. After my father died, I spent school holidays with an elderly great aunt in rural Kent. She meant to be kind but a still, stuffed cottage governed by routine and chapel was no place for a grieving, growing boy.

My journey from Portsmouth to Allingsford is short, and my fellow passengers are looking quite as reassuringly morose and careless of their fellow men as they do in London. The driver is waiting for me, as promised, and even manages a slight nod in response to my 'How do you do today?' We arrive at the asylum with no hindrances, and he agrees to collect me at seven o'clock this evening.

Mr Rockingham collects me from the waiting room. His cheerful countenance has not returned, and he is looking pale beneath his natural reddish complexion. I get up and we shake hands.

'Are you well, Mr Rockingham?'

'Yes, I am quite well, thank you.' He lowers his voice. 'But I confess I am very worried about this sad business with Miss Barker. I can tell you about it because I trust you, and know that you are a good man, committed to writing fairly and accurately about our life here. I am determined to be absolutely truthful about all things.'

'I am honoured by your trust in me, sir, and will not betray it. What has happened?' I ask, curious but also uneasy.

'Come to my office, Harris, where we can converse in peace and privacy.'

I follow Rockingham down the corridor at the front of the main building and into his office, which is large and pleasant. The light from the two tall windows that look across the front grounds of the asylum highlights the dust specs on the heavy mahogany furniture and fern green leather of the chairs' upholstery. Some large portraits and landscape scenes hang from the walls in the gaps not covered up with shelves and cabinets full of books and files. Rockingham gestures to me to take the seat opposite him at his desk, and I note the silver-framed photograph of his family: Rockingham, his now-deceased wife, and two grown-up daughters, all the women short, round and exuding an air of benevolent kindness, much like Rockingham himself.

Rockingham smiles at me. 'I miss my dearest Catherine every day,' he says, with that air of manly candour and humanity that so distinguishes him. 'But I have my lovely daughters, who are very well settled in Portsmouth, and now three bouncing granddaughters to boot.'

'They must be a great comfort to you,' I say.

'Indeed, they are. Well, Harris, and so to business. I conducted Miss Barker's post-mortem this morning, for although we do not like to do such things on the Sabbath day, we must make an exception in cases of death, especially one so unexpected.'

'Do you always carry out the post-mortems here?'

'Oh yes, it is one of the important responsibilities of the chief superintendent.'

'Do you not require the permission of relatives? I know that some people still abhor the very notion of post-mortems, and some have religious objections.'

'In the sad cases where there are no relatives or friends to claim people, we need no permissions. But generally, yes, and I always like to respect family wishes. But post-mortems are useful to the medical profession and so we now ask the question of the family before a patient joins us, which saves time and upset. In Sarah's case, the family agreed.'

'So what did you discover?'

'Sarah's organs were remarkably good, and disease-free, for a woman of nine and forty, although her heart showed great weakness, suggesting that death could have visited at any moment near or far. However, my principal area of concern is that her body showed signs of poisoning. I will need to have her organs and stomach contents properly tested by a chemical analyst, but, in truth, I suspect cyanide poisoning.'

'Good gracious,' I say. I am shocked. 'How are you able to tell such things?'

'There was distinct corrosion of the gullet, and a couple of smaller signs such as a white tongue and dry, swollen, blistered lips. I may not have fully registered these things were it not that I came across a number of poisoning cases as a student.'

'But how on earth could she have ingested poison – cyanide, as you say?'

'I cannot be sure. We do use potassium cyanide to sterilise surgical instruments, a task generally the responsibility of Mr Jones, and it is kept in the surgery room. It is also used in the photography business, I believe, so I imagine there will also be a supply in Jones's photography room. He has a keen interest in the craft, you know, and takes all our asylum photographs. You are probably aware that we take photographs of all our residents on arrival and departure; it is a way of recording their progress. You will be able to talk to Mr Jones about it when you see him.'

'Do you think that Miss Barker wanted to take her own life and somehow managed to get hold of the cyanide solution?'

'It is possible. We go to great lengths to protect suicidal patients from themselves, though they can be extremely determined. However, Sarah was not diagnosed as at risk in that way.'

'She had a form of monomania, I believe?'

'Yes. In many respects, she would behave normally, and could fool people into believing she was entirely sane. But then, as you experienced, she would get onto this one fixed subject, this delusion, that she was Florence Nightingale.'

'How did she end up here at Allingsford?'

'She was a governess with a family in London when the symptoms began. She was there for years, I believe, and must have been valued; her former employer has been paying her fees. She was one of a small number of private patients we have here. They are allowed a few more freedoms than the rest; they do not have to work unless they wish to, and can wear their own clothes rather than those provided by the asylum. She could be a little disruptive sometimes but overall she was not too much trouble, though the prospect of a cure was unlikely.'

'Was she well liked here?'

'Neither liked nor disliked, I would say. She was a patient, and though the staff have often their favourites, we endeavour to treat everyone with fairness, dignity and respect.'

'I suppose I am wondering – though it is a terrible thought, I know - if any of the other patients might have tried to kill her?'

Rockingham sighs and looks very weary. 'It is not beyond the realms of possibility. We do have some violent patients, but it has never happened before. Our patients, if so minded, are much more likely to harm themselves than anyone else.'

'I see. What will happen now?'

'I must inform the local coroner of the case, and an inquest will need to be held. Inquests should take place on all deaths occurring in public institutions, including lunatic asylums. They are held here on the premises, rather than in a local tavern, and witnesses can be called.'

'I suppose if Sarah killed herself with poison, or something more terrible happened, it would not be good publicity for you?'

'No, but I remain committed to being open about the facts. We have a good reputation generally and the public understands that these strange, sad things will happen occasionally in such a place as this, where we are doing our very best to manage some of the most unfortunate, afflicted members of our society.'

I nod, not for the first time thinking about my mother. Rockingham seems to read my thoughts.

'Are you thinking of your poor mother, Harris?'

I nod again, flattered and touched by his sensibility.

'She was a fine woman, and your father was a very good man, who did his utmost for her.'

I nod yet again.

'Now,' he says, 'I am afraid I must get on with business. I will escort you to Mr Jones, who will begin your tour of the asylum. Mr Jones is aware of Miss Barker's post-mortem results. I will see you at the chapel for early evening service. Do ask whatever questions you wish. Everyone has been asked to be as candid as they can, bearing in mind the need for confidentiality with regard to patient records.'

'Yes, of course, Mr Rockingham. I am very grateful for the privileged access you have given me.'

'I know you will be fair, and I hope it will do us some good. My time here is nearly over, and I am greatly looking forward to my retirement, which I shall spend growing vegetables with my little granddaughters about my legs. But I care deeply about Allingsford – and its patients – and want it to have a successful future. Indeed, I care deeply about all public asylums. I deplore the fact that some have become merely large houses of detention, where abuses can go unchecked.'

'I can very much see that,' I say.

I hope this incident proves to be a sad accident and nothing more. In another place, on another subject, the journalist in me would be feeling a thrill of excitement at such a development. Now, I feel my horror return. The dead woman. The blood on the floor. And now the prospect of poison, and even murder. It is as if the bad old lunatic asylum's visible instruments of torture have been replaced by invisible, more insidious methods.

I think of Miss Rosetti and her rather wild claims. I would like to ask Mr Rockingham more about her, but it does not feel appropriate at the current time.

Mr Jones's office is adjacent but one to Rockingham's, and similar in style, if a little smaller, sparser and with much less of a homely feel. Apart from some glass cabinets, one filled with small bottles and the other containing indistinct objects, the only thing that really stands out is that there are collections of photographs on some of the walls. As I enter, Jones is scribbling intently, his head on one side. He gets up and shakes my hand.

'Are you interested in photography, Mr Mortimer?' he asks, noting me looking round at the pictures on the walls.

'Not personally, no, but I am interested in these photographs. I understand that you are the asylum photographer?'

'Yes, photography is a great hobby of mine, and here I can combine it with my work. I call that the Ophelia section,' he says, turning to the wall behind his desk.

On that wall, there are a number of before and after, insane and then sane, pictures of young women. The former show them in distress, their mouths drooping, their hair – sometimes crowned with flowers – loose and flowing. The latter show the same women looking much brighter, their hair tucked neatly into caps.

'Well, we had better make a start, Mr Mortimer,' says Jones. 'A lot to see. Big place. Busy day. Sad events. Do ask questions as we go.'

I follow him as he walks speedily out of the office, occasionally turning his head back towards me and sweeping his right arm forward, as if he is brushing refuse from the corridors.

'This is the principal block of the asylum,' he says. 'Somewhat grander than the other parts, as you will see, containing staff offices and the Committee room above us and so on. This enclosed corridor runs around the square core of the building and marks the dividing line between the male and female wings of the asylum.'

'But the sexes are not always kept separate? They were together yesterday.'

'Yes, they come together for entertainments, but that is the only time they mix. They attend the same services in chapel, but sit separately, and use the same dining room for mealtimes, but in different shifts. Otherwise, their lives are lived divided from each other. Modesty and virtue must be protected. Does not do to encourage liaisons. Harmful for physical and mental wellbeing.'

'But cannot the sexes have a beneficial effect on each other, as they do in normal life?'

'Yes, and that is why we encourage some contact, but not too much. Consequences can be dire when people with disordered minds become impassioned. Especially the female of the species – a specialism of mine. You would be amazed.'

'I see.'

We reach the hall where the ball took place, and I cannot help but see in my mind's eye Miss Barker's body, and the blood, as well as an image of Miss Rosetti singing.

'I hope the events of yesterday evening will not disturb the patients too much?' I ask.

'Perhaps a few of them. But on the whole, no; they do not tend to remember these things.'

'That is something, though the staff may take it hard?'

'Some do; that is true. But fact of life. Usually for best. Wasted emotions.'

I am a little taken aback by Mr Jones's matter-of-fact approach, especially in contrast to Rockingham's humanity. Still, he is young and has his way to make, and no doubt the job is burdensome and there is little time for sentiment.

'What do you think happened to Miss Barker?'

'It is difficult to say. No doubt there will be an inquest. Probably suicide. Women of a certain age, you know. Utility passed.'

Jones directs me through some sliding doors from the hall to the dining room, which is busy with servants clearing up from the one o'clock dinner and preparing for teatime at five o'clock. Then I am given a quick glimpse of the adjacent kitchen, with its gleaming tiled walls and two great oven ranges, the scullery, which contains another oven, and the cool grocery stores and meat and dairy larders. I am impressed, although it is hard not to think of the potential for a poisoner to be at loose here. I must concentrate.

Next, we progress to the female side of the asylum, Jones walking ever more speedily with me trying to keep up with him, and arrive at the convalescents' wing. I know that this is reserved for those just admitted, tranquil patients and those recovering enough to be soon discharged. One notices immediately the simpler design of the patient quarters. Most of the rooms and corridors are relatively bright and clean, if a little faded with patches of peeling paint, cracks and damp on the walls. Some are darker, dingy and a little bleak. The extensions to the building that have been added over the years to accommodate more and more patients are crowded and have a dismal, almost prison-like air.

The majority of the sleeping accommodation is on the two upper floors of the asylum, and after inspecting several of the dormitories, which house between ten and eighteen beds, we arrive at one of the dayrooms. Jones tells me that these rooms are designed for leisure, and gentle work, and help the patients to socialise during the daytime.

'Rather pleasant, is it not?' asks Jones, as we step inside. 'I must admit that this is my favourite part of the asylum. Good, quiet, obedient women. Preparing themselves to be both useful and ornamental in the outside world. Splendid, splendid.'

It is indeed much the nicest part of the asylum I have seen today, though there is something rather ghostly about it. The first impression is one of a faded drawing room of another era, as a group of quiet, quaint-looking women attend to their needlework, and the mid-afternoon sun streams in on them from a large sash window, which looks out upon the gardens, river and rising forest that is the view to the south. Some of the seated women glance at us briefly and smile, or lower their eyes with becoming delicacy. Some are muttering quietly to themselves. At least they are not shouting here. It is such a relief from some of the noise in other areas.

The walls are a slightly grubby white colour, divided horizontally by a chipped green rail. There is a variety of seating and some small broken tables. At the centre of the room, a large birch-framed mirror hangs above an oak mantelpiece.

'Mirrors are the key to sanity,' says Jones, noticing me looking in that direction, 'most particularly for women. I could put myself and all alienists out of a profession with one simple adage; women who mind their appearance are perfectly sane; women who do not mind their appearance are quite mad.'

He looks at me quizzically. I am not quite sure if he is being ironical or entirely serious. I note the expression on my face reflected in the mirror, which is a mixture of concentration and bewilderment. I note with satisfaction, however, my newly trimmed and oiled beard, whiskers and hair. Jones laughs, as he speaks, quickly. I am beginning to find the man a bit unnerving.

A bird screeches from a cage near the window, and a woman who has been looking out of it now turns her head to Jones and me. But I know who it is before she does so. It is Miss Rosetti. Jones notices me noticing her.

'Ah, yes, our beautiful songbird,' he says.

'What is her story?' I ask, keeping my voice low, though Rockingham has already told me.

'Oh, a typical tale in some ways. Governess. Jilted by lover. Melancholic. An Ophelia, if you like. But not that simple. Other things going on. More analysis needed.'

'So she is not ready to leave?'

'No, she is not. She will be disappointed. She wants to leave, and does not understand why she cannot. But that is madness for you.' He grins.

'She will be cured, though?'

'Oh, yes, probably.'

I would like to ask more about Miss Rosetti, but I am not quite sure how to go about it. A thought occurs to me. What if her story is true and Mr Jones is the sinister man preventing her release? He seems strange enough.

'Do you house a lot of former governesses?' I ask. 'Sarah Barker was one, too, was not she?'

'Yes, but we do not have that many. The majority of our patients are of the servant class.'

We approach Miss Rosetti; she puts aside her needlework and stands up.

'Miss Rosetti, this is Mr Harris Mortimer,' says Jones. 'Journalist. Here for a week learning all about us.'

She looks at me a little fearfully and glances at Jones. I think it best not to mention that we have met before.

'How do you do, Miss Rosetti?' I ask, touching her hand and remembering how cold her hands were in the carriage.

'Very well, I thank you, sir,' she says. Her voice is soft, melodious, I now remember.

I have a sudden vision of Miss Rosetti at the head of my table. She is dressed in vivid green or blue velvet, her auburn curls tumbling round her ethereal face and over her shoulders. She is making soothing noises and listening intently as I talk about the burdens of my day; then she sings a little, as she does every evening.

Good gracious, what lunatic visions are these? I shrug them off.

An elderly woman with a lopsided gait tries to interrupt by thrusting at us a large piece of embroidery. Jones presses her aside and says a few words. As he does so, Miss Rosetti looks at him, looks at me, and mouths 'it is he; please help me'.

'Must press on,' says Jones, turning back to me. He hurries to the door. I look at Miss Rosetti one last time before following him. She has the same imploring, frightened look that she had in the cab.

I follow Jones, though my mind is full of Miss Rosetti, and I do not know what to think. I must have a proper talk with Rockingham. I am so tired and deflated now. The northern wing is reserved for those patients who are harder to manage, and the rooms are very spare, any superfluous objects being potential weapons in the hands of patients prone to violence. I am shown a few of the padded rooms, and though Jones assures me that they are used only in extremis, and for the patients' good, I am horrified, for this is now my terrible vision of the asylum made real. I feel sick, my heart pounds, my hands are clammy. And now I must face the final stop on our tour, the deadhouse, which, I am now told, is housed within the old private lunatic asylum part of the building.

CHAPTER 6

WE MAKE OUR way back to the ground floor and to the southeast of the building, where we come to a long corridor running horizontally, that follows the line of a large wall containing several doors and some bricked-up windows.

'The old house is just through these doors,' explains Jones. 'Its structure is more or less the same as it was in the last century.'

He takes a bundle of keys from his pocket, selects the largest, and opens one of the doors. I have an urge to run, but manage to control myself, particularly as I sense that Jones is aware of my fear, and perhaps even enjoying it. I follow him meekly through to the other side, where he locks the door. Noticing my look of alarm he says, 'we have to be very careful not to risk patients accessing this area, which would distress many of them. Windows are fluted for same reason.'

'Yes, I see,' I respond, shivering. The building is icy cold, as is fit for its purpose.

I feel like I am in a ghostly vision of an old country house. We are in a small entrance hall, with a staircase leading up to who knows where and who knows what. The walls are a mixture of whitewash and faded beams, which gives the room an air of strange cozy menace.

'Come along, Mr Mortimer,' says Jones. 'Chop, chop!' He grins his unnerving grin. 'Just a little physician's joke of mine.'

I try to smile but it must be a more like a grimace, and follow Jones past the deadhouse and the laboratory. We stop at the dissecting room.

'Good size, is it not?' he asks, looking round proudly. 'Lucky to have this much space although we are sadly behind the times when it comes to equipment. I long for a slate table, a microscope and a weighing machine. Never mind. One day, I will be with one of the leading hospitals.'

'You do not plan to stay here long, then?'

'A few years, perhaps. These places have had their day, you know. We must move with the times. Rockingham is a dear man but old fashioned. Cannot accept realities. These places just get bigger. Cost to rate-payer increases. New methods needed. May, in future, be best to just stop the degenerate breeding.'

I am a little shocked and about to question Jones about this when I spot a series of holes in the walls, positioned about a foot or so from the ground.

'What are those holes for?' I ask, pointing at some of them.

'Oh, they are just marks from where chairs were nailed in bygone days. Patients were strapped in.'

I gulp.

'But I must show you my little museum before we go. It is my pride and joy.'

I am so sick at heart now that I fail to express my disbelief at the idea of a museum in a public lunatic asylum, but simply follow Jones, praying that this will soon be over. The museum is next to the dissection room, and is smaller in size. I gaze round.

From one long cabinet, a series of white motionless faces stare at me, as if they are questioning my presence. Jones chooses this moment to turn on one of the gas lamps, and now the faces are winking and grinning at me.

'The bad old days of phrenology,' says Jones, 'reading the character by bumps from the head and all that. Most of it ridiculous, really, but it still has many supporters. My predecessor was very fond of taking casts of the heads and faces of our dead.'

'And here,' he continues, moving past the cabinet, 'are a few of those chairs that I mentioned earlier.'

I stare at the strange, wooden contraptions.

'The box under the seat was used to trap the legs, and the board, a bit like the top of a bureau, trapped the thighs. Quite ingenious things really.'

Jones looks almost thoughtful. He moves on and his eyes light up.

'Now this is one of my favourite pieces, Mr Mortimer. You can keep your chains and gags and straw. Give me a whirligig any day of the week.'

I stare at a dilapidated-looking chair, covered in old leather straps, on wheels, which is placed on a round disk on the floor.

'They came in many varieties. This one is quite simple. You just strap the lunatic in and spin the disk. Fancy a go?'

I look at Jones, incredulous. Does this man think that he is humorous? All I can see before me now is my mother, her brown eyes dull with despair or alive with terror. The dark place of my imagining is real. There she is, crouching in a corner on filthy straw. Now she sits in one of those chairs chained to the wall. There she is, being force fed with one of those oval rings with handles. Now she screams as she whirls round and round and round.

'I have had enough for today,' I manage.

'Oh, yes, indeed. It is quite the house of horrors. We do get many keen visitors, you know, and I forget that it is not to everyone's taste.'

I follow Jones out of the building by a back door.

'Thought you might like a little air, Mr Mortimer. We will walk round the building and re-enter at the front, and leave the workshops for another time, perhaps. Some of the patients make the coffins for our dead, you know. It is most efficient.'

My head is still spinning as we enter the patients'

dining room and sit down to take some tea, which is a simple meal of bread and butter, the main hot meal being served at one o'clock. I am too fatigued and sick in body, heart and soul to take in any more of my surroundings, but the order and efficiency that so impressed me at the ball now strikes me as oppressive and machine-like, as the men slot into place like so many automatons. I force myself to eat and drink, though I might choke upon it, and it does fortify me a little. I must now get through the evening chapel service, then my driver will collect me. I cannot wait to see the old misanthrope, and his horse, and pray that nothing dreadful will happen between now and then.

We walk to the chapel through the dark that has replaced the bright winter day. I hurry along the gravel pathway after Jones, whose energy seems to be unlimited. Next to him, I feel like an old man. Several people are heading in the same direction, in small groups or singly.

'Are the services well-attended?' I ask Jones.

'Well enough, though attendance is not compulsory, as you might expect it to be. Practical difficulties in getting large numbers to and from. Also, some patients best kept away. Possibility of inducing or exacerbating religious mania. There are daily morning prayers for those so inclined and two services on Sundays. Usually get two hundred people at the latter.'

The chapel is a simple building with a sloping roof of grey slate tiles. There are two gas lamps near the entrance that highlight the different colours of the building's brickwork, and lanterns carried by the attendants escorting the residents cast a warm glow leading to the door. I feel a little comforted. I must confess that my church attendance has lapsed in recent years; as a bachelor, I only have myself to please and no-one to whom I must set an example, but when I do go to church, I feel the better for it.

My slightly warmer feeling continues as I look around the room, which is almost full, the men seated at ground level and the women in a gallery above and behind them. The asylum staff sit at the front, at right angles to the residents, and I follow Jones to this area, nodding to Rockingham as I reach my place. I look up to the vaulted ceiling, across to the stained-glass windows, then to the gallery, where I spot Miss Rosetti, her head bowed.

The chaplain preaches in a very firm, calm way, and his sermon is admirably brief. There is no terror and damnation, and the service lacks the strict formality and adherence to social convention that dictates your average Sunday service. The hymns, supported by a small organ, are uplifting, and some of the congregants sway and some hold out their arms as the spirit moves them. I am touched and humbled. This seems a more simple, unselfconscious and true way to God than I have witnessed before, and I feel a little peace enter my own heart.

The final hymn has just begun when a loud crash

invades my becalmed senses and jolts them into sharp reality. I hear some screams and shouts and see that somebody has fallen from the gallery down onto the male section of the church, though luckily, it seems, onto an area where nobody was sat. Some attendants get there swiftly, clearing space and attending to the fallen woman. I see that Jones is approaching and, for the second time this week, I find myself following Mr Rockingham towards a body on the floor.

CHAPTER 7

Miss Titania Rosetti

OH LORD, WHAT'S happening now, I think. I was in such a pleasant reverie. I quite enjoy these church services; they're some of the few times I don't feel anxious and constantly on my guard in this place. A loud noise and a cry has jolted me back to reality. I'm horrified to see that poor old bird, Sally, who thinks she's Queen Victoria, falling to the ground. I blink, as if dreaming, but a large blurred object to the right of my vision really has fallen through the air, and it is Sally, now flat on the floor near to the benches where the male worshippers sit. Her short, round body is on its side, her head at a strange angle, blood spreading all around her. I note one of the male residents staring, as if mesmerised, at a small stream of blood as it runs from her head across a groove in one of the stone floor slabs, and find my own eyes following suit, my stomach beginning to sicken.

My attention is turned when that worm in a suit, Mr Cedric Jones, appears, as he does at every evil scene. He crouches down next to Sally, checking for signs of life. I think I'd rather risk death than have his strange small fingers, like second-rate saveloys made of who knows what, creeping all over me. But poor Sally looks dead enough, to be sure. Oh, this is horrible. I can feel Clara, the kindly woman who thinks she's Mary Seacole, start to clamber down from the balcony. She must want to get to her friend. I follow. She might need my help. She approaches the body – I'm not far behind – and Jones tries to shoo her away.

'Off you go, Miss Simpson,' he says, waving one of his short arms towards the door, 'there is work to do here.'

'Work?' says Clara, kneeling down, her ample body seemingly stiff and supple at the same time, next to Sally.

I put my hand on Clara's shoulder while she kneels, hoping to comfort her a little.

'If there is work to do, sir,' Clara continues, 'then I am the woman to do it. There is nobody better qualified.'

She wags a finger at Jones, who looks a little shocked, staring at her with his small unblinking eyes. For a moment, he looks like an errant schoolboy, and I am almost tempted to laugh. It is a short moment of relief, for there is something about him that really does frighten me.

'Oh, my poor dear Victoria.' Clara touches Sally's head, and checks her pulse points. 'You are gone from here. But you are with your dearest Albert again. It is such a shame that I was not given the opportunity to nurse him in his final illness; things may have been so different.'

'Clara,' says Jones, sternly, recovering his power of speech.

'Let her be, Mr Jones,' says Rockingham, who now appears close to Clara, Jones and the body of Sally. 'Let her have her goodbye. It will help her and will do no harm.'

Rockingham reminds me of one of those dogs with drooping eyes and ears. A Bassett Hound. I think that's what they're called. He does seem a decent cove, I must admit.

Jones nods at his superior, but looks annoyed, his small mouth pouting slightly.

Clara's whole being seems to have sagged. 'And if only they had let me nurse you too, dear,' says she, a few tears falling. 'A mustard poultice, a little calomel and some sugars of lead would have set you right in no time, and made you ready to rule the empire once again.'

She strokes Sally's wiry hair and kisses her twice on the head. My heart goes out to Clara as I press her shoulder. She and Sally were fast friends, and that must have been such a comfort in here; how will Clara manage without her pal?

'Come now, Clara,' says Rockingham, bending slightly and taking Clara's right arm. He smiles at her kindly. She looks up at him, smiles back and wipes away her tears with her free hand.

'I must turn a bold front to fortune,' says she, 'as I have done before. My hot Creole blood will aid me.'

'That is right, Clara, dear; draw on your strength and experience, and be brave now,' says Rockingham.

Clara nods and smiles weakly at the superintendent. 'She was never the same since the passing of her dear Albert, you know.' She turns back to Sally. 'Goodbye, my dear, goodbye Your Majesty,' she says, looking intently at Sally's face, then kissing her on the head a final time.

Rockingham helps pull Clara slowly to her feet and pats her softly on the other shoulder a few times, then Mr Friend, the chaplain appears. Friend gives me one of his usual quick, penetrating looks. That man makes me nervous, but I am not sure why. He smiles at Clara, and takes one of her arms. A female attendant takes her other arm but Clara brushes her off and looks at me.

'You go with her too, Miss Rosetti,' says Rockingham, nodding at me.

I'm glad to go, though the close proximity of Friend is unsettling, and take Clara's arm. I notice that journalist staring at me. I hope I haven't gone too far there. I don't know what came over me. We walk slowly towards the door of the chapel, the female attendant following behind us. Our steps echo softly in the silent church; even the loudest congregants seem to have been struck dumb by this strange event.

Clara's body next to mine is warm and comforting in the cold night air. She's muttering to herself, and Friend makes soothing noises to her. We arrive at the main building and go into the entrance hall.

'Will you manage whilst I find Matron?' Friend asks.

The attendant nods, and takes the arm of Clara let go by Friend, who hurries off, soon returning with Mrs Annabel Christie, the Housekeeper and Matron, who is carrying a draught of medicine, I think, in her hand.

Mrs Christie is a tall, large, formidable woman with jagged facial features, as if she's been drawn by an angry artist.

Friend takes both Clara's hands in his own and says, 'God bless you, Miss Simpson.'

Mrs Christie and the attendant take Clara's arms and escort her to her ward. Friend turns to me.

'Miss Rosetti, you must be greatly distressed by this evening's events, and, indeed, those of yesterday. Thank you for your kindness to Miss Simpson; she was much in need of it.'

I wish he wouldn't look at me so intently. I feel like he sees right through my act, but I don't think that's the case.

'It was nothing, sir. I am little shaken, I must admit. I cannot really comprehend what just happened.'

'It is frightful. We will find out more in due course.' He pauses. 'I wonder, Miss Rosetti, if you have thought any more about joining the choir? You have such a beautiful voice, and I am sure it would do you good.'

'Thank you, sir, but I do not think that I will be here at the asylum much longer.'

Friend gives me an odd look; is it pity?

'Well, I hope you manage to get a good night's rest, in the circumstances, Miss Rosetti. Good night.'

'Good night, sir.'

I make my way to my ward. It's still quite early and not everyone is abed, but I'm glad to undress and get into mine, the rough blanket scratching my chin as I tuck myself in and close my eyes.

I think of Sally. Poor old girl. I suppose these things happen, but it doesn't smell quite right to me. How could she have fallen from the balcony? I suppose it could be in need of repair – some parts of this place are dilapidated enough – but I didn't notice anything. Or could she have jumped under the influence of one of those strange delusions that some of them have? Or even under the influence of the pills and potions most of them take? I suppose that's a possibility.

And now Clara has to get on in this place without her pal. It's so lonely and bleak in here. You can't really have relationships with others as most insane people just live inside their own heads. When they talk, it's either to themselves or at each other, rather than to each other. Not that I can get to know anyone in my situation. I can't be me, Miss Nancy Carter. I'm Miss Titania Rosetti.

Still, I'll be out soon. I'm so desperate to go know. I'm vexed with myself about my behaviour in the past few days, trying to run away and telling the journalist that I'm being kept here by Jones. I don't know what came over me. I've given the perfect performance so far, and then I do this. But it's harder than I thought it would be acting all the time, and my performance just seemed to run away with itself. I hope that I'm not starting really to go mad. It wouldn't be surprising in here. I must play the sane version of Miss Rosetti from now on and to perfection.

Will Jones find out about what I've said? He gives me the creeps and I'm sure there really is something sinister about him. He looks at me not in the usual way that men do, but as if he wants to chop me up and put me in one of his specimen jars. Well, it's done now. I can't have done that much harm after all my hard work over the past three months. I have an interview with Mr Rockingham tomorrow and I'll smooth over any errors. Another month at the most, I imagine, and then I'll be free. I don't know how much longer I can stand.

CHAPTER 8

I FEEL A LITTLE brighter today after the sadness of yesterday, and go through the morning routine feeling almost calm, although my stomach is fluttering a little at the thought of my interview with Mr Rockingham, and excitement that I'll be leaving here very soon.

I'm sat in the dayroom, where I almost die of boredom every day, waiting to be collected and escorted to Rockingham. I'm pretending to read some very dull volume of family sermons when Mr Friend appears in front of me. I'm surprised it's him but then, I think happily, perhaps he's been already preparing my discharge papers.

'How do you do today, Miss Rosetti?' Friend asks, his brown eyes full of concern. 'I hope you managed to get some rest last night?'

'Yes, a little, thank you,' I say.

'You have an appointment with Mr Rockingham, and I have come to escort you.'

'Yes, sir, I had not forgotten. Thank you.'

I get up and take his proffered arm, avoiding too much eye contact. He's tall and wiry, and his arm feels strong. We walk together very stiffly, as if we're about to enter a society dinner, and I have a strange urge to giggle.

'I did not have the opportunity to thank you for your performance at the ball on Saturday,' he says, 'with everything that happened. But it was delightful, and much admired. We performed rather well together, did we not?'

I turn to glance at him and he's looking at me quizzically. Why does he do that? What is he thinking?

'Yes, indeed,' I say, 'it was my pleasure.' I turn my eyes away from him. I don't like to look at him for too long as I get the urge to say something ridiculous.

We walk the rest of the way in silence and arrive at Rockingham's office. Friend knocks, we enter, and he departs, nodding and smiling at me. The office is rather grand, yet comfortable, a bit like the man. Mrs Christie is also present, seated near Rockingham's desk, and bids me in her low croaky voice to sit down. We exchange greetings and pleasantries, and I admire the picture of Rockingham's family. I'm the perfect lady.

'Well, Miss Rosetti,' says Rockingham. 'You have been with us just over three months now. I hope you are happy here?'

'Oh, I have been very content, on the whole, sir,' I say. My voice is soft, musical. I'm modest, humble, blush a little. 'Of course, I have missed my friends and family terribly, and am looking forward to our impending reunion. But I am so much better and back to full health, thanks to you all. I am very grateful.'

'You have made excellent progress,' says Rockingham, 'a model patient in many ways. However, we are not quite at the stage where we are confident enough to discharge you.'

'Oh, but you need have no concerns,' I say, smiling pleasantly. 'I am quite cured and perfectly well.'

'There has been the concerning incident on Saturday,' Mrs Christie says, her small dark blue eyes boring into me beneath creased eyelids. 'Your running out on a cold winter's night, accosting the carriage of our guest, Mr Mortimer, and claiming to him that a malicious man is keeping you here against your will.'

Stupid Nan. I must handle this well. I don't think they know that I've accused Jones.

'Oh dear. I do not know what came over me; it was so very silly. I think I was excited at the thought of the ball, and my singing at it, and also at the thought that I will soon be returning to my family. And then,' I say, pausing and giving them both a very nervous and scared look, 'I will be frank with you about something, if I may.'

'Go on, Miss Rosetti,' says Rockingham, his drooping brown eyes – I hope – full of concern.

'The man I was referring to was Mr Jones. I do feel very foolish about the whole thing now. It is just that I have found him rather frightening. He looks at one in such a peculiar fashion, and says very strange things. I realise, of course, that he is a physician of mental maladies, and simply doing his job, but he is so unlike other people. I can only express to you how sorry I am about the incident.'

Rockingham and Christie share a quick complicit look. I was right. I had an inkling that Rockingham didn't like Jones. But I've taken a risk, complaining about a member of staff in a place like this. I hope I've dressed it up so that it doesn't really feel like a complaint, yet explains my behaviour. Rockingham sighs and looks at me sympathetically.

'Mr Jones is a talented physician and my deputy medical officer,' he says, 'though I do acknowledge that his manner is not always a winning one. But rest assured, Miss Rosetti, that you are in the best hands here at Allingsford asylum. You have no other form of complaint, I hope?'

'Oh no,' I say, panic starting to rise within me.

'We have all come to the conclusion that you are not quite ready to leave us, but do not despair. I assure you that our decision is in your own best interest. And as a public lunatic asylum, we certainly have no motive to keep patients here who are fit to leave. There are so many poor souls needing our help, you know.'

'But when will I be able to go? Surely, it will not be long?'

'We do not know. Time will tell. But all will be well.'

'But, sir, my family need me. I must return to them.'

'And you will, Miss Rosetti. Do your duty and follow our instructions here and you will be home before you know it.'

I'm shocked, numbed. Although I was a little worried before the interview, I didn't believe that there was any real doubt about my leaving.

'Come, Miss Rosetti,' Mrs Christie says, touching my arm and helping me up.

Rockingham wishes me goodbye, his eyes sorrowful, the patch of wrinkles in the centre of his forehead deeper than ever, and I follow Mrs Christie out of the room.

'You may take a little fresh air if you like,' she says to me, unexpectedly, as we reach the entrance hall. She is probably testing me. 'But you must behave yourself. I will get one of the attendants to escort you.'

I nod, pitifully grateful, choking back my tears. One of the younger, livelier attendants appears, takes my arm and chatters away as we leave the building and walk slowly down the main drive in the afternoon sun. I'm not listening to anything she says. My head is swimming, my thoughts darting everywhere. I cannot believe this.

We arrive close to the gatekeeper's cottage. I think the flighty attendant says something about just calling in and is sure I'll be fine for a moment. She's breaking the rules, as a lot of them do, but I'm so relieved. I make my way to a small, wooded area near the cottage. It's not very sheltered at this time of year, but there doesn't seem to be anyone about. I sit down on a log and sob until I fear my heart will break. Then I rouse myself and silently scream, scream, scream, with rage.

Perhaps half an hour, an hour, later, I spot the young attendant coming out of the cottage with Mr Friend. I wipe my eyes with my handkerchief and walk towards them. The attendant nods at me and hurries off.

'Miss Rosetti,' says Friend. 'I hope you do not mind me accompanying you back to the house. I was a little concerned about you, following the bit of disappointing news you have had.'

So, he knows, does he? He looks genuinely sorry, and I feel the tears about to come again. I have the urge to run, shriek, dance, to be the maddest mad woman they've ever seen. I exert control over myself, and take Friend's proffered arm. It is pleasant to have someone to lean on. I wish I could tell him everything, here, now, just blabber, blabber, blabber. Of course, I do not. He smells nice, clean and lemony - I don't know what soap that is – with perhaps a sprinkling of dust from his office.

'I am sure that it is just a short setback,' he continues.

I nod, not turning to look at him. I should be using this opportunity to find things out, to try and help myself, but I can't. My mind is muddled, my body weak.

'Now, you are perfectly at liberty to throw a hymn book at my head, when I ask you this, but I promise you it will be the very last time I do so. Well, perhaps the last but one.'

I look at him and he gives me a sheepish grin. I cannot help but give a quick laugh.

'Perhaps you really might reconsider joining the choir?' he asks. 'I know that this is no aid to you in your current frame of mind, and please do forgive me for pressing the matter. It is just that music has helped me through the darkest times in my life, and I feel in my heart that it could do the same for you.'

I look at him, blinking back my tears.

'At least it may help you to endure the rest of your short time here.'

I note the 'short' and cannot help but give him a weak grin. He smiles at me warmly; we turn to face ahead and continue walking slowly towards the house. I'm half-relieved, half-disappointed when we arrive. I'd like to be in his presence longer; it feels like a respite from the horror of my situation. His strength, his warm voice, his humour, and the sense of normality he imparts. He does make me a little nervous, though. But I'm weak, defeated; who knows what I might do or say if I stay too long in his company?

We stand uncertainly in the vestibule for several moments, as if we've both just arrived separately at a grand house party and are not sure what to do.

'I must go now,' I manage.

'Yes. Please do let me know, at any time, if there is anything I can do to help you, Miss Rosetti, and try to take comfort if you can.'

I smile at him, turn and walk away.

CHAPTER 9

I WAKE UP EARLY, before many of the other inhabitants of my dormitory. My head is aching, my eyes are sore. I feel a dull ache all over and my heart is heavy. I don't know how I got through the rest of yesterday; I can barely remember. I slept well, though, having accepted a sleeping draught from one of the attendants. I can see how a person could get over-fond of those draughts, like getting a thirst for drink. I've only pretended to take my medicines so far. I didn't trust them. Who knows what they might do to me?

I'm so angry with myself, so very angry, and I kick myself under the bed covers. I was so driven to get here, I suppose, that I didn't think properly about getting out. And yet, I've played the Ophelia part beautifully on the whole. I did what needed to be done. I did mildly insane Ophelia, then sane Ophelia. Then I blew it at the last moment, the most important performance of my life, and it was arrogance, naivety, or – please, no – madness, to think that the lapse wouldn't make any difference to my release.

How I long right now to talk to and laugh with my older sister, Nel, and to snuggle up to my tiny, beautiful ma and bawl my eyes out. They don't even know I'm here.

How I wish pa was still alive, and here with me. He wasn't my real pa, mind, but he was such a good man, the best of the three. Us three sisters had different fathers. Nel's was a gentleman artist, and a useless, good for nothing. Ma left a very respectable family to elope with him, and lived to regret it. Mine was something in the city, who spent his days arguing over the price of indigo in coffee houses and exchanges. He abandoned ma, to return to his wife, when she announced that I was on the way; it was the first ma had heard that he was married.

The best pa was my younger sister's, Penelope's – poor Penny is also dead and gone - and he more than made up for the other two. He was French, and quite the armchair revolutionary, and found a home in Soho, London, as so many immigrants do. His surname was Cartier, which gradually became Carter amongst us daughters because no-one outside of Soho could be bothered to pronounce it properly. He died of a weak heart. He was a reasonable age by that time, though, being quite a bit older than ma, and we had time to smother him with love and laugh with him still. I remember him having the same thing for breakfast every day until he died, which was a small cup of the bitterest black coffee, a Holloway's pill, a Beecham's pill, and a good dose of cod liver oil. Clearly, these did nothing for him. It was a heavy loss. He was a cheerful, satirical, sentimental pa, who loved his wife and all of us with his whole heart, and it felt like the sunshine had gone from our lives along with him. But we had each other, and we muddled on.

Then I got the smallpox, and was brought very low, and our income as a family had already shrunk with pa's demise. Nel had to leave the dressmaker's where she was employed because she has a weak spine and the long, long hours of drudgery nearly killed her. Ma took in a little piece work, and we still had some money left to us by pa and also of ma's own that she's been spending so sparingly since she ran away from Sussex all those years ago. Still, it was becoming concerning.

Then Penny, at fourteen, the most spoilt of us all, announced that she would go out as a servant for a short time in order to make some extra money for the family. I can clearly remember the moment. We were sat around our old table, Pen looking very pleased with herself as she nibbled on some hot chestnuts we'd brought home from a stall.

I'd laughed loudly. 'What, you, Pen, go out as a little slavey?' I reached across the table to pinch one of the rosy cheeks on her olive skin. 'Don't be a simple. You'd hate it. You wouldn't last five minutes.'

'How do you know?' Pen said, petulant.

'Oh, little Pen, you're a baby.' I laughed again and pressed my right forefinger on her upturned nose.

'I'm not a baby. I wish you'd all stop treating me like one. Especially you, Nan' – she glared at me – 'and I bet I'd last longer than you.'

She's probably right, I'd thought, but I still laughed.

'Penelope, my love,' ma had said, 'you can do whatever you want. But have you thought about something a bit more genteel? You could work in a nice shop, or even in an office. To think of the jobs that girls can do now!'

'You could even be one of those telegraphists,' Nel chipped in. 'You're clever enough for anything. I wish I'd done something like that.'

'I'm happy to be a servant,' Pen insisted. Then she really was behaving like a child, being stubborn, determined to do something she probably didn't really want to just to prove a point, and likely to get back at me.

She'd been sulky and peevish for a few days after that, and then returned home one day announcing that she'd registered with a hiring office at the Soho Bazaar. I still didn't believe she'd actually take anything if offered it, but before we knew it, she was going off to work as the general servant/maid-of-all-work for a fairly well-to-do family in Bayswater. We all tried to dissuade her, but that only made her more determined, and so we thought it best to let it be, and wait for her to come crying home to us.

That was the turning point. The point I go back to over and over when I'm turning back the clock in my mind and making everything right. I should have tried harder to stop her. I should have locked her up, the stupid girl. No. I know it's not that really. I know that I should have been the one to go out and do whatever it took to keep the family afloat. I was too proud. I thought I was too good for it.

So Penny was a slavey in this so-called genteel house. There was a gentleman and his wife, a lady's maid, a governess, two children, a housekeeper/cook and Pen. She did struggle; I could tell when she came to see us on her half-day holidays, proudly pressing a few pennies from her meagre salary into ma's hands. She looked tired and worn and the light in her had dimmed a little. But she didn't complain. I was amazed at her courage and fortitude, though I suppose it was also another form of pride and stubbornness.

I remember the last time we saw her. We were sat round our table again, drinking cocoa. She looked thinner, and it pained me to see it, but she was quite cheerful that day.

'How is the mistress of the house?' ma asked. 'I hope she continues to be kind to my darling?'

'Oh yes, Ma,' said Pen. 'She's always giggling, like a child.' Pen eyed me at that point, still accusing. Us Carters certainly know how to bear a grudge.

'And she has all these queer sayings.' Pen mimicked her mistress, assuming a hushed, soft voice, and then giggling. '"One must practice self-control, my dear, and restrain one's appetite; it does not do to raise the animal spirits". She barely eats anything at table, and then the other day I came across her stuffing down bread and dripping in the kitchen. She just winked at me. She's a queer cove, but…'

'She is what, young lady?' said ma.

Penny had giggled, looking almost like the girl she was before pa had died. 'She is a little peculiar sometimes, but a very kind and genteel lady.'

'That is better,' said ma, smiling.

Apparently, the lady's maid was a little haughty, as is only natural, but not too unkind, the governess was cold, and the cook was cheerful and friendly. Poor Pen had to sleep in the kitchen, which was warm at least, but she was terrified at nights listening to the black beetles scurrying across the floor.

And so she was still vexed with me the very last time I saw her. And I've never been able to tell her how sorry I am for underestimating her. I'm trying so hard to make up for it now, Pen. I hope you know that somehow.

So, enough fear and misery. Enough self-pity and weakness. These things don't get a woman anywhere in this world. I must get out of here.

First, I won't put a foot wrong in my act. I'm Miss Titania Rosetti, former governess. I had my heart broken by my army officer lover, and as a poor, weak woman went through a bout of mental sickness, albeit in a very becoming, pretty kind of way. You can't be an ugly Ophelia; that doesn't work. Now I'm completely cured: humble, obedient, chaste, rational. I won't let any of my own – Nan Carter's – feelings and emotions spoil my act, however desperate I might sometimes feel.

Second, I must talk to that journalist again. Now that I've managed to mess things up by involving him, I can try and use him to my advantage. He's here for a week, so there's time, but not much. If I don't bump into him, I'll have to track him down. He could be susceptible. He's had that look in his eye in my presence that I've seen so many times before in men. A little lovelorn, I suppose, though he's not yet aware of it himself. He's rather vain, I suspect; he was really admiring himself in that mirror in the day room. Still, I'm in no position to condemn someone for that, being the vainest creature in the world, and I suppose he's handsome enough.

I must be careful about mentioning Jones again, though. I don't want to do anything that could further delay my release. Perhaps I could just drop very subtle, ambiguous hints. I'll improvise, as the performance dictates. I'm not fully sure why I mentioned his name in the first place. I suppose it's because he gives me the shivers and I really dislike the man. Could he really have any malicious intent towards me? I can't see why, but then he is so odd. I feel a chill as I wonder if he suspects my act, if he knows, even, that I'm not who I say I am. Maybe he's playing a game with me, goading me, and waiting for me to give myself away. If he is, I'm ready for it now.

I'm half tempted to try the truth on Friend. He seems so kind and charming. He likes me, admires me, even. But he's the man who holds the records here. How can I admit what I've done? He'd be horrified. What would he do? No, that's not the answer. If I did that, I might never get out of here again.

Third, I'll write to my dear pal, Connie, who's the only person who knows I'm in here, and why, and who helped me to do it. Poor Con's actually been in an asylum herself. I need to get her to visit me. She said she would if I needed her to. If it's still needed, we'll think of a way to get me out. She knows a few disreputable people - a few villains, even - to be sure; something can be done. I can't write a straightforward letter, though, because they read all correspondence here. I'll write her a note in the usual Miss Rosetti style, enclosing a pretend one for 'mama and my dear sister, Cordelia'. I compose it in my head.

Dearest Constance

I hope this letter finds you well.

I am doing very well indeed, and am quite ready to be discharged. Allingsford really is a fine institution and has done me a great deal of good. They feel here, however, that I would derive benefit from a slightly longer stay, but I hope it will not be for too long. In the meantime, I would dearly love you to pay me a visit if you are able to do so. How delightful it will be to have your company and hear your news.

Life here goes on much the same and I enjoy the fresh air and wholesome food. We are currently being visited by one of those gentleman journalists; he is writing all about us for The Times. Of course, patients will not be named, and everything will be done with the utmost discretion. What an honour for us all. I hope that we can read his articles together when I am home again.

I enclose with this a letter for mama and dearest Cordelia. I so long to see them but do not wish for them to visit me. I fear the goodbye afterwards would be far too painful for me to bear. Instead, I look forward with happy anticipation to our reunion.

God bless you, my dearest Constance, and bless my dear mother and sister.

Yours always affectionate and grateful friend,

Miss Titania Rosetti

That should do it. She'll get my hint of alarm about them keeping me in and will also be concerned about the presence here of a journalist. I'll write both letters today in the day room.

I feel a bit comforted and stronger now that I have a plan of action. They must not get the better of Nan Carter. They must not.

CHAPTER 10

I WROTE MY LETTERS yesterday and feel a bit better for it. That's one deed done. I also spoke to Mr Friend, telling him that I'd be very happy to join the choir. I need to show those in charge that I'm a meek, obedient little Ophelia, and willing to follow all their advice, advice which will apparently lead to my full cure. I suppose it might make me forget this hell for a moment or two. I love to sing, and can't resist showing off. But I'll be more in the presence of Friend. His company's too easy, and so too dangerous; I must be on my guard.

I eat both my own and my neighbour's breakfast of greasy bread and butter and weak tea. Some of them in here think they're being poisoned and won't eat. Their loss is my gain. That sounds cold and hard, I know. But my heart would break for them and many others if I let it. My heart's broken enough. That would be another route to real madness. I've got to take care of myself. I make my way to a rather dark, small room off the main hall/dining room, where the musical instruments and general bric-a-brac are stored. The choir practices here as well as in the chapel with the organ, I believe.

I am early and notice Mr Mortimer sat alone on one of the two-dozen or so chairs placed opposite a small piano. This is a much-needed piece of luck, to get him alone, but I must be careful. At the sound of my approach, he turns around, seems to almost blush, and gets up.

'Miss Rosetti. How glad I am to see you. I hope you are well?'

He comes towards me and takes one of my cold hands in his warm one.

'Oh, yes, sir, thank you,' I say, 'I have nothing to complain of, nothing at all.'

But I look at him with fear and desperation in my eyes, and it's not really an act, is it, for I am scared and desperate in many ways. He stares at me, then takes my other hand with his other hand.

'Miss Rosetti, I should tell you that I will do my best to help you,' Mortimer says, very quietly.

'Oh, thank you, sir,' I whisper, putting my hand on my heart.

Does he mean it? He doesn't strike me as the type to make rash promises to an apparently mad woman. I wonder if he's had a strange encounter with Jones, who fails to disguise his oddities to anyone, as far as I can tell. Perhaps, as a journalist, he's thinking of a possible story about him. All the better for me. Though I'm not sure what he has in mind in terms of helping me. It might be the usual sort of thing from his sort, a moral homily, a pat on the head. Still, he seems serious, and quite fixated upon me.

'Trust in me,' he says.

I drop my hands as I sense the arrival of Mr Friend. I'm not sure how I know it's him. I hope it's not a warning sign, as if I'm a dog with its ear pricked and hackles about to rise.

'Good morning, Miss Rosetti, Mr Mortimer,' says Friend, bringing his sunshine into the room. 'It is a pleasure to have you with us. Do pick up a hymn book from the side there and then take a seat.'

Other female residents, a few attendants and Mrs Christie now arrive. I forgot that there wouldn't be any male residents here; Friend must look after a separate male choir. Mortimer and I get caught up in the throng, and end up sat a few rows away from each other.

'Mr Mortimer is joining us today as observer,' says Friend, addressing the whole group. 'I know you will give him a warm welcome.'

He sits down at the piano and we begin by singing through the hymn, 'I love to steal awhile away'. I don't know it, but the words seem rather appropriate for my act and I adopt a slightly sad, humble face as I sing. One of the patients sitting directly in front of me, a silly giggling old woman who's a great favourite with everyone, drops her hymn book, and Mortimer gets up to pick it up for her. She's done it deliberately, I'm sure. She's clearly very excited to be in the presence of another man, and I can't blame the old girl. As Mortimer picks up the book, he stares at me, and I look back at him, wide eyed, as I sing, 'I love in solitude to shed/The penitential tear'. Would a few tears be appropriate at this point? Perhaps not. I lower my eyelids, fluttering my lashes a little.

We sing the hymn several times, Friend offering instruction and advice. I gradually find myself being a little moved by it, which surprises me; it's the sort of thing I usually laugh at. There are a few lovely voices around me and a few less so. There's one very loud, vexing person, who exaggerates the pronunciation of every word, as there is in every musical gathering. But I gradually forget the others and lose myself in the music, as I always do. We practice several more hymns, and come to the end of the session.

The female attendant choir members gather together the patients, and I get up too, ready to return to my usual day room.

'Wait a moment, Miss Rosetti,' barks Mrs Christie, directing her quizzical eyebrow at me.

I sit back down. I hope I haven't managed to do anything untoward already. Perhaps I've sung a bit too enthusiastically, and they think I'm becoming an hysteric or I'm developing some kind of religious mania. The other singers shuffle out. The silly old woman goes very reluctantly, and the great number of white ribbons on her cap fly round her head as she twists round her bony shoulders to giggle at Mr Mortimer. I get up as Mrs Christie approaches me.

'Mr Jones would like to see you,' says Mrs Christie.

I can't disguise the look of horror that appears on my face, and I notice Friend and Mortimer looking at me intently.

'Mr Jones?' I ask, 'but…'

'You can have no objections, I assume?' says Mrs Christie.

'No, Matron, of course not.' I bow my head.

'Wait a moment, then, and I will escort you,' Mrs Christie says.

She turns back to Mortimer, and they have a short conversation.

'I hope you enjoyed your first meeting of the choir?' Friend asks me, smiling a little wickedly.

'I suppose it was adequate,' I say.

Friend laughs quietly. 'I am deeply flattered.'

'I did enjoy it, thank you.'

'More importantly, how are you getting on?'

I look into his kind eyes. 'I find it hard, but I hold onto the thought of returning to my family very soon.'

I'm being honest, but I've said nothing to my detriment. Mrs Christie comes towards me and takes my arm. We say good day to Friend and Mortimer and leave the room.

I'm grateful for Mrs Christie's silence as we make our way to Jones's office. I'm readying myself for my meeting with him, which I'm concerned about. Does he know about my allegations against him? Mr Rockingham and Mrs Christie can't have taken me very seriously if they're happy to deliver me up to him like this. I really did think that Rockingham disliked Jones. Still, like might not come into it. They're all staff, I suppose, and so in this lunacy business together. I'm just one of the many mad female patients. I don't think Mortimer can have said anything, given what he's just said to me.

I can't help but think of my arrival at the asylum and my first encounter with Jones. I was taken to the receiving room, which is filled with books, boxes and bottles. I was greeted by the worm, who gave me what I know now as his usual cold, scientific stare. He gave out a slight chemical smell, which seemed to suit him. Then the aloof Mrs Christie weighed me and measured my height, before taking me through to the bathroom where I was asked to take off my clothes, get into the steaming bath and soap myself well. I'd known to expect this; Connie had told me everything that would happen. Still, I didn't like it, especially thinking of the worm in the room next door. Then I was given part of my asylum uniform to wear, some knee-length linen drawers, stockings, a pair of brown cloth slippers and a brown linsey gown, quite the ugliest garment I'd ever worn.

After a few days settling into the admissions ward, I was interviewed by Jones, with Mrs Christie sitting in, in the receiving room.

I sat in a chair in my too-hot, scratchy clothing – it was a warm day – occasionally looking at Jones from beneath my eyelashes. What a peculiar creature he is, I thought, with his small body, tiny eyes and large forehead. I could imagine him crawling into one of his specimen bottles at night and out again in the morning.

'Miss Titania Rosetti? Very poetic name, I must say.'

He looked at me quizzically with those cold eyes of his, wriggling his head from side to side like some strange kind of reptile. Was he suspicious, I thought? No, it was just his queer way.

'Yes, sir,' I said.

I went for soft, quiet and hesitant with my voice, and I occasionally gazed distractedly around the room. I knew broadly what to expect of this interview from Connie.

'Hair colour?' he asked.

'Auburn, I would say,' said Mrs Christie, as if I wasn't able to identify it for myself.

'Eye colour?'

Jones squinted at me with his head on one side.

'Light brown,' said Mrs Christie.

'Skin condition?'

'Fair, with the occasional very light, barely discernible smallpox marks,' said Mrs Christie.

I was delighted with the 'very light, barely discernible'.

Jones looked at his notes. 'I see that her weight is a bit low. How is your appetite, Miss Rosetti?'

'Oh, it has been very poor, sir, but it is improving,' I said.

They needed to think that I lost my appetite from love sickness, when dwelling on Eustace, my lost soldier. I did lose my appetite, and it was love sickness, but the object was my precious Penny. At the same time, I said that it was getting better because I wanted to eat while I was there.

'Are you a toper?' Jones asked. He grinned. 'Ha! Do you consume much liquor?'

'Very little,' I said. 'Perhaps a small glass of wine on special occasions.'

I drank more than that. I mean, I wasn't a lush; I could never take to gin, luckily. But I thought it best to play safe with that answer. Who knew what was the appropriate amount expected for ladies?

'Were your parents intoxicated or experiencing any form of illness during the time of your conception?'

How was anybody supposed to know that? Dearest ma and pa, when you were tupping each other to create me, can you remember how much you'd had to drink, or if you were feeling a little poorly? Mind, I suspect ma may have had one too many glasses of good claret. She barely touches liquor generally; how else would the stockjobber have got her to do the deed? I don't think he drank much himself as a rule; too busy counting his sovereigns.

'Did your mother have a difficult childbirth?'

'No.' I don't think so, though I believe Nel's was very hard.

'How is your menstrual flow, your monthly courses?'

'A little irregular,' I said, which was true.

'How was your puberty?'

I had no idea how to answer that one. 'Normal, I believe,' I ventured.

'And are you a maid, a virgin, Miss Rosetti? I should say that you do not have to answer this question if you do not so wish. However, I would advise doing so. The sexual development and life of a woman is fundamental to any question of female insanity.'

I'd known to expect this question, but I blushed a little. All to the good. I squirmed and lowered my eyes. No, I was not a maid, but I think that convinced them to the contrary.

'Bowel movements? Daily? More, less?'

'Oh, perhaps less. A little irregular.'

They were fine, really, but I thought irregular sounded more convincing for a mad, sick person with a poor appetite.

'Have you experienced any serious illnesses in the past few years? Illness can sometimes trigger insanity.'

'Just the smallpox, sir.'

Thankfully, I never got any other kind of pox. Poor Nel had a scare once, but it was a false alarm.

'Her emotions and symptoms seem to be consonant with the Ophelia type,' said Jones to Mrs Christie, looking again at his notes. 'Crying, hysterics, running round the village, when experiencing an episode in search of the lost love object; at other times, calm, compliant, mildly distracted.'

'Yes, that is correct, sir,' said Mrs Christie.

'Well, Miss Titania Rosetti, it is time to have your admission portrait taken.' Jones jumped up, like one of those devilish jack-in-the-boxes. 'I am the asylum photographer, you know. It is a hobby, and a talent, of mine.'

As I'd hoped and expected, I'd been diagnosed as an Ophelia-type, driven mad by love, and so on, and so I had to look the part. In the photography studio, one of the assistants loosened my hair and put some flowers in it. I made my features all droopy and sad and hoped my expression was suitably lovelorn and distracted. It was over, and my time here began.

I wasn't scared at that time. I really wasn't. Through the whole thing, trying to get into the asylum and then getting in, I was consumed by my goal, consumed body, heart and soul. There wasn't room for anything else. It's only since that I've started to wobble, that I've realised the incredible, terrifying and probably very stupid thing I've done.

CHAPTER 11

MRS CHRISTIE KNOCKS at Jones's door, and we go into the room after he shouts 'enter'. I'm hoping that Mrs Christie will be sitting in on the meeting; surely, that would be the appropriate thing? However, she simply nods at me and leaves. The room is similar to Rockingham's. It has a colder, bleaker air, though there are shelves of books and a few glass-fronted cabinets, the contents of which I can't make out. Also, the walls are covered in photographs.

'Well, Miss Rosetti,' says Jones, gesturing for me to sit down. 'I hope you are feeling better? You were naturally disappointed to hear of your delayed discharge.'

I take a seat in front of Jones's desk. 'Yes, sir, but I am quite well.'

'Good, good.'

He puts his head on one side and wriggles it twice. 'Your case interests me greatly, Miss Rosetti.'

I manage a look of polite interest. 'Oh?'

He glances down at a file on his desk, which I imagine must be a file on me.

'I am very interested in madness in the female species, you know. Particularly in relation to the reproductive function.'

I can't imagine Jones ever being reproduced and given birth to. He likely crept out of the slime underneath some mossy stone.

'Yes. The reproductive function governs a woman entirely, both her body and mind. It is her master, and she is its slave.'

I dread to think where he's going with this and how it applies to me, but I must try not to flinch.

'There are several crucial moments in a woman's life when she is most at risk of developing insanity: at puberty, then when the sexual urge is awakened but is not fulfilled in a virtuous way – these two often go together – and finally when her bleeding, and so her reproductive capacity, ends. In your case, disappointed love triggered your illness. Tell me, since the illness began, have you been having any unusual thoughts of a sexual nature, any urges and sensations that drive you to seek carnal pleasure with the opposite sex?'

I blush, which is helpful at least.

'I am not sure I understand you,' I manage.

Jones stares at me, then wriggles his head and sighs.

'Do you know, Miss Rosetti,' he says, 'I am not sure that I quite believe you. There is something about you, as opposed to the other Ophelias here, and in general, that is different from them. I suspect there is more going on. Are you prone to self-abuse?'

What? This beast wouldn't be out of place in some of the seediest stews in Covent Garden. The horror on my face must show.

'I hope the expression on your face indicates your innocence in relation to that abominable sin, Miss Rosetti. I will not press you on that. But I am very concerned about your behaviour on the night of the ball. The way you ran outside in terrible weather, in a shameful, dishevelled state, and actually accosted a member of the opposite sex by clambering into his carriage. That, I must say, is the behaviour of the harlot.'

I almost want to laugh. Little does he know. But if I do laugh, I would choke upon it, I know.

'But you need not be alarmed,' he continues. 'My aim is to cure promising young women such as yourself, so that they can go back out into the world and make useful, chaste brides. I have a responsibility to society, to the male of the species to ensure that they are not saddled with a bride prone to insanity, and particularly that species of it, erotomania.'

He wriggles his head again and stares at me, as if expecting a response. I'm not sure what reply would please him. He is quite insane.

'Should it prove necessary,' he says, 'there are many different cures out there. I know of a doctor in London who used to recommend leeching of the labia and cervix, then clitoridectomies, and then, in some cases, removal of the labia. This removal of the female genitals has cured several refractory wives, I can assure you, and their husbands are eternally grateful. Sadly, those methods have since been discredited; I am not sure why as they are based on very sound reasoning.'

I don't fully understand the medical language, but I entirely understand what he's saying. I cross my legs tightly underneath my skirts, and can feel the colour draining from my face.

'These procedures are nothing to be frightened of, Miss Rosetti; quite the contrary. But we are not there yet. For now, we shall increase the cold shower baths and introduce intermittent small doses of laxatives, tartarised antimony and camphor.'

He offers me a strange, placatory smile, as if, this time at least, giving a child barley sugar instead of the threatened dose of cod liver oil.

'What I would hate,' he continues, 'is to see you unable to fulfil your natural role in society, that is marriage and the bearing of children. Single women prone to erotomania can end up as the lowest street whores. Other women whose natural purpose is thwarted, and who become old maids, can turn into the vilest of insane creatures. And some of these are, or have been, governesses, you know. I have several fascinating writings on the matter. See here, this one.'

Oh, please let this be over soon. Jones picks up some papers from his desk, and starts reading from one marked all over in ink.

'"She becomes strong-minded; is masculine in her pursuits, severe in temper, bold and unfeminine in her manners. This unwomanly condition undoubtedly renders her repulsive to a man, while her envious, overbearing temper, renders her offensive to her own sex. [...] the 'Old Maid' is the pest and scourge of the circle in which she moves; and in extreme cases – verging upon, if not actually the subject of – worse insanity, she is little less than a she-fiend."

'And then, "Her whole life is devoted to an ingenious system of mischief-making; she delights in tormenting – corporeally and mentally – all that she dare to practise upon. She is intrusive, insolent, regardless of the ordinary rules of politeness; ever feeling insults where none were intended; ungrateful, treacherous, and revengeful [...]. Add to these mental characteristics, a quaint untidy dress, a shrivelled skin, a lean figure, a bearded lip, shattered teeth, harsh grating voice, and manly stride, and the *typical* 'Old Maid' is complete."

'Between you and I, Miss Rosetti, the late Sarah Barker was such a one. Not quite as ugly in her person, certainly, but in all other respects she was quite the she-fiend. And I suspect that a disappointment in love began it all. Well, well. I do feel that she is better off dead. All such women are. Women must be ornamental or useful, you see, ideally both, but principally the latter.

'I could lend you some reading materials, if you would like? You see, I see you as a special experiment. You are an educated woman, and mind in woman is not always a bad thing, if it is moulded in the correct way. I would like to bring you along with me, not just to cure you but to educate you on how and why I am curing you in such and such a way. It will be in an interesting deviation from the usual method.'

I feel weak, sick in heart and body, my rage numbed by shock.

'Would you like to see my photographs before you go? You will find them very interesting, I am sure.'

Jones jumps up from behind his desk and appears next to me, like a grinning demon, before I can protest. I don't have the will or energy to do anything but go along with it, and pray for it to be over soon. He helps me up and leads me to the wall facing his desk.

'This is my Ophelia section,' he says proudly, pointing at a selection of before and after pictures.

In the before pictures, the women are got up like so many actresses auditioning for parts in a Shakespeare play: loose clothes, loose hair crowned with flowers, a dreamy look. In the discharge pictures, they are more neatly attired and wearing white frilly caps tied under the chin with large bows. Even though I know all this, and I'm actually masquerading as an Ophelia myself, I can't quite comprehend that they really believe all this. If I wasn't so terrified and miserable, I could shriek with laughter. Don't they know that Shakespeare isn't real life? They just want to believe it. I'm not sure why. It must comfort and reassure them in some odd way.

'All being well, Miss Rosetti,' continues Jones, 'you

will be joining them soon, and I should like to put you in pride of place.'

I have an horrific vision of myself up there, not in photographic form but the real life me, my body skewered to the wall like a female Christ, the flowers in my hair my crown of thorns. Jones jumps to the side a little to point out some erotomaniacs.

'They can be an Ophelia or not, you know,' says he. 'Look here at this vile wretch. This is a sketch in colour as a photograph cannot quite capture the full effect. See the red and brilliant eyes, the flushed cheek and open lascivious mouth. Take note, Miss Rosetti, take note.'

'And see these old maids, these she-fiends. Look at their thin, sagging faces, screwed up with rage, the moustachios above their thin lips and their rotting teeth, their beards. Look at the bald patches on their heads, their hunched backs, their claw-like hands.

'Tate note, Miss Rosetti, do take note.'

CHAPTER 12

IT'S THE NEXT day. I took another sleeping draught last night; what else could I do in my petrified, shocked, sickened state of mind? But it didn't work. I've lain awake for most of the night seeing visions of Jones dancing before my eyes. Sometimes he was springing from a box, wearing a grubby lace ruff and a tall stove-pipe hat, his cheeks and lips painted vivid red. He grimaced, then laughed at me, grimaced, then laughed. Other times, he was dancing through the streets of London flourishing a giant knife, ready to attack my womanhood.

Jones is the maddest person in here; he has to be. But, then, what if he isn't? What if they all think the same as he? Rockingham, Friend, Christie and the rest. Rockingham defended him, after all. Would they really do, or condone, some of the things Jones suggested? I really don't know.

I don't think Jones can know about my accusations

against him, which I suppose is something. He suspects me of not being quite what I show to the world, or to them, at least, not that I'm an entirely different person. He thinks, probably wants, me to be some kind of sexually deviant female, possibly an 'erotomaniac'. Worse, he wants me to be a special case, a willing participant in his mad experiment.

But I still have time, I tell myself. I'll be given extra baths and tonics. The tonics I've actually taken so far – when I wasn't able to avoid it - have sometimes made me vomit or run to the water closet. But what if these new ones are more dangerous? What if he tries to poison me? Or gives me the sort of stuff that mad, sickly wretches would trample over their own grandmother to get their next dose of? I must fake taking all of them, whatever the situation. I'm an actress. I can do it.

And I'll be the perfect patient while I have time. Jones and his knife-wielding, physician devils will have to be disappointed. I mustn't allow myself to lapse again, to go mad momentarily in any shape or form. I'll work harder on Mr Mortimer. He's already said that he'll help me, and he's a little besotted with me. I must really use that now. I wasn't born pretty for nothing. You have to use the hand you've been dealt.

I think again of trusting in Friend. I feel like I could, and, oh, how I want to. But I can't take the chance. What if he believes the same things as Jones? It's hard to imagine, but who knows what's possible in here?

Connie, the best pal any girl could ever wish for,

will be here soon. She'll know what to do. If all fails, I could really run away. Oh Lord; I'm turning into the Ophelia I've been pretending to be. And where would I run to? And I have no money, no possessions. Oh, Connie, please come quickly.

After the one o'clock meal, I'm grateful to get out with a walking party, and I set off in procession with a group of around twenty women. I'm at the front marching behind Mrs Christie, and the group is being tailed by one of the attendants. We can't be trusted to do it alone; one of us might bolt. It's a little grey and misty and the greens and browns of the landscape are subdued, but it's fairly mild and the air is moist, almost wet, softening my skin rather nicely. I suppose it's a good sign that my misery isn't entirely affecting my vanity, at least.

It was unlucky that I got the smallpox, as I'd had the vaccine, though I was told that things would have been an awful lot worse without it. My mother and sisters thought I would die, but I thought living was worse than death when I saw the scars. I was jealous of Penny. At fourteen years of age, there was no sign of pimples; her skin was so soft and plump. And then Nel, a few years older than me, with her smooth, creamy, even skin tone. I would stare at their faces; in my worst moods, I could have almost scratched away their beauty.

It's a terrible thing for a vain girl to have her beauty taken away. You get used to feeding off the admiration and so you starve when it's gone. No more modelling or acting or singing for me. No more helping out in that fine photographer's studio on Regent Street, where the female customers like a pretty woman to help dress them ready for posing. Wear dark silks and satins (but not black velvet), madam; a little pattern is fine; avoid white, light blue, pink and lilac; a small amount of white trimming is acceptable. I had a knack for helping the fine ladies to come out well, and positioning their heads and bodies to disguise their worst features, without their being aware of my doing so. But no-one wants a woman who's cribbage-faced – however pretty she once was – helping them to look good. I tried to use stage makeup, but then I just looked like a streetwalker. I thought I might get back to the stage, as paint and disguise are natural to it, but I found that my chance had passed, and I was seen as damaged goods.

I avoided looking in mirrors, and it was a shock when I came to the asylum to have to do so several times a day. Vanity is the essence of woman, some of them say here; it is her downfall, but also, in a becoming degree, her saviour. They do talk a load of old poppycock here; though I'm vain, Ma and Nel must be two of the least vain people in England. But it did me good to face myself. My scars had healed a lot; I was pleasantly surprised. And now they're barely noticeable. It feels like a miracle when you think of those poor pock-marked wretches scarred for life, but then my case was mild, though I wasn't ready to listen to any blessings at that time.

We file past the portico, where the asylum porter is talking to Harris Mortimer. Mortimer gives me a kind look and I smile rather desperately at him. It's Thursday today so he must be leaving soon if he's only staying a week. I hope he meant what he said about helping me, but I can't risk talking to him now after Jones's comments about me accosting Mortimer. That would play right into Jones's hands. I must look out for another opportunity.

We've been walking for about an hour around the north side of the grounds when we arrive back at the portico, and go on through to the courtyard, to the right of the main building, around which sit the farm buildings, stables and dairy. A bit further on, the ugly brick chimneys of the asylum gasworks rise up, looking out of place in this country so-called idyl, making me even more homesick for the city. How I long for the smoke and the smog; a girl could quite choke on all this fresh air. Now we come to the southeast of the building, and to the edge of the pretty formal garden, a neat pattern of trees, lawns, beds and pathways, spotted with various chairs and benches.

We approach one of the kitchen gardens – there's one on each side of the south side of the asylum – passing fruit trees and bushes, the small orchard that produces cooking apples, and the patches of currently barren soil where root and sprouting vegetables grow. I can't remember their names. I've tried to learn a little of all this for ma's sake, who was brought up in the Sussex countryside, but I lose interest too quickly, and remain a stubbornly ignorant city girl. To me, food comes from the street sellers and chandlers' shops, or maybe a tavern or chophouse when I've been in funds, and that's as far as my interest goes.

I look across to the other kitchen garden, noticing a crouched yellow figure digging at the ground with its hands. It's Clara; there aren't many people at the asylum who dress in yellow. Poor old thing. She must be trying to soothe her mind over Sally's death. As we move closer, Mortimer, now alone, appears from the other side of the grounds. Mrs Christie comes to a halt and raises her right arm to indicate to our group to follow suit.

Clara's small brown boots are sticking out of her behind, giving her the look of a duck. Her yellow gown, especially the skirt, is covered in dirt and she's kneading mud in her hands, as if preparing a cake for the oven. Despite the time of year and her lack of outdoor garments, she's sweating heavily. She doesn't appear to notice us. She stands up slowly, a little stiff in her legs, moves several paces to the left, kneels down awkwardly and pats the hard lumps of soil in her hands into the ground. When they are quite neat, she picks them up again, straightens up, moves several more paces to the left, and repeats the exercise.

'Miss Simpson? Clara?' says Mrs Christie, moderating her harsh tone very slightly.

Clara turns to look at her, her face creased with worry, her brown eyes sorrowful, her right hand full of soil.

'How do you do, Matron?' she says, and also notices me. 'And Miss Rosetti.'

'Are you quite well?' asks Mrs Christie.

'Well, Matron, I do find that I am a little under the weather, now you mention it, much like my dear boys in Balaclava. But I soldier on, as they did. Onward Christian soldiers.'

'But you look very tired, Clara, and must take your rest. Come now, come with me.'

Clara kneels down again. 'Not at all, Mrs Christie. What is a little sacrifice for the greater good? For what else are we put upon this earth but to serve others? You, yourself, know this. Miss Rosetti, now, would make a fine nurse. Come to me, my dear.'

I step across to Clara, who is still kneeling, and take her hand.

'Will you not come back to the house, Clara?' I ask, 'and take some tea with me? We can talk about the Crimea. There are so many things I would like to know.'

Clara smiles at me. 'How kind you are, my dear. But I am not hungry or thirsty. I feel only sickness. It is everywhere in the Crimea, you know. My poor boys do not die in battle, but in the camp. I should have died myself, but then I was indestructible. It is only now that I am killed at last, here on English soil.'

'Clara, do get up and come with me now,' says Mrs Christie, moving to Clara's other side and reaching out one of her long, thick arms.

Clara does not respond, looks down at the ground,

and ignores further, repeated entreaties from Christie and myself.

Mortimer steps forward. 'Can I help in any way, Mrs Christie?'

'Thank you, Mr Mortimer,' Mrs Christie says. 'Indeed, perhaps if you are able to go and fetch a male attendant, that would be a great help. We need to get Clara back inside the house before she catches her death. It may be that she will need to be given some sort of sedative; please mention that to whomever you speak. Thank you. We are much obliged, sir.'

Mortimer nods at Mrs Christie, gives me a kind, concerned look, then turns and strides off towards the house.

'Stay with Clara, Miss Rosetti, whilst I just check on the others,' says Mrs Christie.

She takes a few paces towards the rest of the walkers, who are growing a little restless, and I kneel down next to Clara to make things more comfortable.

Clara looks at me, letting the mud fall through her fingers. 'He did it,' she says.

'He?' I ask.

'Yes, he who governs all.'

'You mean the Lord, Clara?' I ask, a little out of my depth when it comes to religious matters. I place my arms on top of hers as I slowly get up, bringing her with me. She wobbles a little but is now unresistant. I tuck one arm under hers and put the other around her shoulders. She is bigger and heavier than me, but I do my best to hold onto her. She is so hot that I can feel her heat pass through my coat to my body.

'No, no, not the Lord,' she says, 'for though He works in mysterious ways He cannot do such evil. It is him; he killed her; he's killed her, and he's killed me.'

'Please don't upset yourself, dear. We'll get you inside the house and to bed, and perhaps give you one of those famous tonics or salves of yours that serve your dear soldiers so well. You'll be right as rain in no time.'

'No, dear. I will make no more salves and soothe no more brows. I am very sick, dying.'

Actually, Clara is rapidly losing colour, and quickly turns her head to the left to bend it and wretch horribly, defiling her prized garden with the mess. She turns back to stare at me for a moment, her eyes watery and pleading, then falls away and down from me. I hear the sound of her head crack on some jagged soil or perhaps some stones; her body jerks for several moments, then lies still.

I put my hands to my mouth. This is too horrible. Another death of a harmless older woman. Mrs Christie appears next to me and bends down to examine Clara. As she's doing so, I see Mortimer with, of all people, Jones, coming towards us, the latter carrying a small bag.

'What on earth has happened here?' Jones says, also bending down over Clara's body.

Mortimer looks at me intently and mouths the words 'forgive me'. I'm relieved. He probably bumped into Jones first and had no choice given the urgency of the situation. He must trust me, and believe what I said about Jones. He must believe I'm sane, at least. I start to cry a little. I cannot help it. I brush my tears away with one hand and feel Mortimer grabbing my other. I look up at him through tearful lashes. I've seen that look on men's faces before. I'm not faking my misery, but I think I've got him.

CHAPTER 13

Harris Mortimer

I HAVE NOW BEEN visiting the asylum for one week, and much to my own amazement given the fearful state I have been in, I have decided to stay on a few weeks' longer. This story has become too big and involved to abandon now. I have a duty to the *Times* and to my profession to do a thorough job. I also have a duty to Miss Titania Rosetti – and, of course, to any others here who might be in a similar predicament – to protect her from Jones. For, indeed, I really do believe that the man is a lunatic, and a dangerous one.

I must talk to Mr Rockingham about him. Since my experience with Jones last Sunday, I have been thinking a lot about the man. I have tried to reason that he is just an odd, idiosyncratic character with a queer sense of humour, and a young doctor with some unorthodox views making his way in his profession, with little time for sentiment. But I find that this will not do. Jones seems to think that women of a certain age who are no longer useful – presumably the sort living in a place like this – have no value. Then what happens this week? Three women of a certain age, somewhere between their fortieth and fiftieth year, die. And Rockingham discovers cyanide poison in the body of the first woman, Sarah Barker.

And then we have the accusations made by Miss Rosetti. To be sure, I was rather doubtful about them at first. Here is a certified mad woman making what seem like mad claims that one of the men here at the asylum is trying to keep her here against her will. I rather doubt the sanity of many women in everyday life; I am unlikely to suddenly believe in the sanity of a mad woman in an asylum and in the saneness of her claims. Yet, given the man I have seen, and the events that have happened, I find that I cannot help but believe her. At the very least, I have a duty to investigate her claims and share my concerns with Mr Rockingham.

I have not sat down properly with Mr Rockingham since his disclosure about the poison in Sarah Barker's body. I wonder what he found in the body of Sally Woods, and, indeed, what he will find in Clara Simpson's body. Well, I will discover more when we meet this evening.

I have spent some of this week with the asylum porter, a very decent, amiable man, who has been showing me the remains of the asylum grounds and outbuildings, including the engine house, the various workshops and the blacksmith's forge. I even saw the carpenter's workshops, where, as Jones told me, coffins for the patients are made by some of the patients. It was a little unsettling, to be sure, but I imagine not quite as much so as it would have been if I had been in Jones's hands. The rest of the time I have spent at my hotel, making notes and thinking of the work here, often interspersed with thoughts of my mother. I have just wired my newspaper, telling them of my plans to stay on longer. Given the potential of the story, including the possibility of an insane mad doctor murdering his patients, they will not object.

Today, I am interviewing Mr Friend and Mrs Christie, having spent only small amounts of time with them thus far. Rockingham has given me use of the Committee room on the first floor, which is quiet and convenient. I am sat at the long mahogany table, watched over by various Committee members and local dignitaries captured in oils or by camera on the walls. It is a somewhat cold, characterless room, which suits me. It could be anywhere and so I feel less like I am trapped in a lunatic asylum and subject to all the horrors to which my imagination is prone. There is a tap at the door, and Mr Matthew Friend walks in.

'Good afternoon, Mr Friend,' I say, getting up to shake his hand.

There is a latent energy about the man, which I feel in his hand, and he exudes warmth. He is handsome,

I think, with his thick brown hair and beard, and his almost angular features and Roman nose. He does not seem a right fit for a clerk in a public asylum, or a clerk in any environment come, to that. He seemed more at home at the piano.

'Good afternoon, Mr Mortimer,' he says, taking a chair opposite to me and stretching out his long legs under the table. 'So, how are you finding us all?'

'Extremely interesting,' I say.

Friend smiles, showing white, slightly long teeth. 'Ah, interesting. That could mean any number of things.'

I smile. 'Yes, that is true.'

'I hope you are not put off by the sad events – the untimely deaths – that have taken place?'

'I am certainly not put off what the asylum does on the whole, though, I will admit, I have found the deaths a little disturbing.'

I am not sure how much Friend knows as to the circumstances of the three deaths. Does he know about the cyanide in Sarah Barker's body? Perhaps he knows more than this, and therefore than myself? Or it may be that he knows nothing at all. I must tread carefully; I do not want to put Mr Rockingham in a difficult position.

'Yes, they have been most upsetting,' says Friend. 'We are used to patients dying in the normal run of things, through illness, age, and, sadly, the occasional suicide, but not in this strange way over one week. You know that potassium cyanide was found in Sarah Barker's body? I know that Mr Rockingham is sharing everything with you so we can talk openly. It was found also in the body of Sally Woods.'

I knew it would be.

'That is very concerning. I suppose it is likely that poison will be found also in the body of Clara Simpson.'

'Yes, I fear so. Of course, the analysts are yet to confirm Mr Rockingham's conclusions about Sarah and Sally at least, but he has experience of this sort of thing and is unlikely to be wrong.'

'Do you think the women committed self-murder by poisoning themselves?'

'They must have done. Although, I cannot imagine how they acquired the poison, and how they conspired together in some way to make the deaths happen so close together.'

'Perhaps one suicide triggered another?'

'Yes, possibly. It is all so strange.'

'You do not think that some kind of foul play may have occurred?'

He sighs. 'That is such a terrible thought, and I cannot imagine it. I suppose one of our more disturbed patients could be responsible, but I do not see how. Again, how would they get hold of the poison? The life here is very well regulated.'

'I can only think that some lunatics can be cunning.'

'I suppose so.'

I pause. Can I risk pressing him further?

'Is there a possibility that a member of staff could be responsible?' I ask. I am hesitant. Have I gone too far?

Friend looks horrified. 'Of course not, Mr Mortimer. What do you take us for?'

'Forgive me, Mr Friend. Us journalists can get a little carried away, you know.'

'That is alright. And you are right, in fact, to think of all possibilities. But no, I am sure that could never be the case. What possible motive could anyone here have to murder one, two, even three, of our harmless women? It is unthinkable.'

Not if you are mad, I think. Not if you are Mr Cedric Jones. I cannot mention his name, though. I wonder what Friend thinks of Jones, whether they get on, whether Friend has noticed his peculiarities.

'There does seem to be a pattern in the type of women who have died,' I say, shifting tack slightly. 'They were all women at a certain time of life. Mr Jones might describe them as past their utility.'

Friend frowns. 'Yes, I have noticed that. Mr Jones certainly has some distinct views on certain things, though I would not like to criticise him. He is a colleague, and I am merely a clerk, dealing in paper rather than medical matters.'

I do not push the issue. I must first discuss the matter thoroughly with Rockingham.

'How long have you been in your position, Mr Friend? You do not strike me as a natural clerk. Do forgive me my bluntness; I do not mean to offend; it is just that you strike one as perhaps more of an artistic type.'

Friend chuckles.

'I am rather flattered than offended, Mr Mortimer. Your observations are quite correct. I am not a natural clerk and am, indeed, more of an artistic character. I grew up in the county of Herefordshire, a bit of a scapegrace younger son, I am afraid, and led a somewhat itinerant life trying to make my way in the world of music. It was not a success, as is often the case in such matters, and so I was forced to eat humble pie and resign myself to something more quotidian. Still, I find that I have facility for the work and do not mind it too terribly. As long as I can still have music in my life, I can rub along. I have been here three years now. It is not a place in which one would wish to spend one's whole life, but I have tried to do my duty, and have found the work rewarding in its way.'

'So you do believe in the work here, then, that all this is justified? Is the purpose of the asylum a good and moral one, and does it do its job?'

'I do believe in it. Societies should take care of their most afflicted members. As to curing the insane, that is a rather more complex matter.'

'Yes; there are many observers who do not fail to point out the lack of success in that area.'

'I can appreciate general concerns around the seemingly ever-increasing numbers of the insane.'

'You think, then, our world is, as it were, getting madder?'

'I am no medical man, but no, I do not believe that

our world is getting madder. It seems to me as if most people are much as they always were; it is just that the definition of madness grows larger and more all-encompassing. I have read my John Stuart Mill, Mr Mortimer, who suggests that the line between a little peculiarity, eccentricity or non-conformity and insanity is becoming ever more blurred, and thus our great British liberty is a risk.'

'Yes, I understand you, and it is rather an alarming thought. There have been cases of wrongful and malicious incarceration, I know, though they are usually associated with private asylums.'

'Yes, they are driven usually by a financial motive, whereas Mr Mill is concerned about ever stricter social mores that define anything outside of themselves as deviant, and therefore mad.'

He gives a quick laugh and continues. 'I can be quite forgetful, you know, and also, sometimes, I find myself talking to myself, and wonder if I, too, am beginning a bit way in that line, and it frightens me.'

I smile. 'You seem a very sane man to me, sir.'

Friend laughs. 'How can one tell?'

I do like this man a good deal; he is charming, intelligent and interesting. He would make a good dinner companion.

'Some believe,' continues Friend, 'that there is a blurred borderline between sanity and insanity, and that there exists a large portion of our population hovering around that borderline, little aware of what is to come.'

'Good gracious; that is an unpleasant thought. They do cure some of the people here, though?' I ask.

'Oh yes, very much so. I believe that if a person is not discharged before a year is out, the chances of their ever being so get lower and lower as time passes. But before that threshold, the picture is much more hopeful.'

'I imagine that those diagnosed as Ophelias are some of the milder, more hopeful cases? I believe that Miss Titania Rosetti, who sang at the ball, is one such a case.'

As record-keeper, Friend must have at least a general knowledge of cases. How much would he be willing to disclose about Miss Rosetti? I suppose he must maintain confidentiality. A faint smile plays across Friend's mouth; he has a slightly knowing look.

'Yes, I believe that she is almost well,' he says. 'She appears perfectly well to me but, again, I do not have a full grasp of medical matters. I believe that it is Mr Jones who has doubts about her fitness to leave us.'

This again corroborates what Miss Rosetti has said. Could I confide in Friend, and ask for his help? No, it would not be wise at this moment. Again, I must talk to Mr Rockingham first.

'Well, I am very grateful for your time, Mr Friend,' I say. 'Perhaps we could converse again in the coming days, especially once we know more about the three deaths.'

'I would be very happy to. Do just call by my office at any time.'

Friend gets up, shakes my hand, and leaves.

I have some time to think before Mrs Christie

arrives. The image of Miss Rosetti singing at the ball suddenly pops into my mind, and I remember Friend smiling alongside her as he played the piano. That was a rather peculiar look he just gave when I mentioned her. I do hope he is not setting his sights on her. That would be very improper. Perhaps I have been a trifle beguiled by his charm. He is a little mysterious, and a little swarthy in appearance, now I think upon it. He has the rather wild beard and hair that is currently fashionable among certain types, but is it entirely respectable? I wonder what his itinerant past consists of. I must be a little more guarded with him until events here are resolved.

Miss Rosetti's light brown eyes are looking at me and I can feel the press of her tiny hand. Perhaps, perhaps… if I knew that she was entirely sane, then I could even contemplate… No, no, I am being ridiculous. Have I not spent my life avoiding the taint of madness in women? A good, sensible little woman is what I need and that is what I shall have. There is a tap at the door, and I get up to let the housekeeper in and show her to a seat.

She is a tall, well-formed woman, though her face has a rather cruel aspect to it. The features are pinched, the mouth curls up slightly at one side, making it look as if she is snarling; the small dark blue eyes peep through creased lids, and one eyebrow curves in the shape of a sneer. But I must stop judging people's characters by their physiognomy; clearly, I am more in thrall to these scientists than I realise.

'Thank you for taking the time to see me, Mrs

Christie,' I say, pulling out a chair for her. 'I know what a very busy woman you are.'

'That I am, Mr Mortimer,' she says, sitting down, 'and I would be grateful if you did not keep me long.'

'I will try my best not to,' I say, and return to my own seat.

I look across at the housekeeper. I am beginning to feel like one of our new detective fellows. It would be quite a pleasant feeling, one mixed up with a slight thrill of power, if I was not so uneasy being in this place generally.

'As you know, Mrs Christie, I am here to learn about the life of a public asylum. I have seen a little of all you do but it would be helpful for me to learn more about your role in your own words and to hear your thoughts on the way our society cares for the insane. Perhaps you could begin with a description of your duties?'

'Yes, Mr Mortimer. I have an exceedingly busy and responsible role, being in charge of the female side of the asylum, and I have a number of attendants and servants under me. I must ensure that every patient is clean and is dressed neatly and appropriately, and that the female wards are clean and the beds fresh. I also have overall responsibility for the kitchen, the laundry, the sewing room and the female attendants' personal quarters. I do at least two tours a day, usually after breakfast and before bedtime and am present at mealtimes to ensure patients take their food, and at bath times to ensure the water temperature is correct.'

'With so much work to do, you must have to put a great deal of trust in your staff. Are good staff hard to find and keep?'

'They can be. Some young women these days are afraid of hard work, I am sorry to say. They are mad for amusements and sensations. I do not tolerate slackness, slovenliness or immoral behaviour. It can also be difficult in such a large place keeping an eye on them all. However, I do have some excellent women under me, and if they are interested and committed enough, they can study for qualifications in this profession. Women, you know, must try their best to be useful.'

Useful or beautiful. There it is again.

'I am sure there are few people here as useful as you, Mrs Christie.'

She nods.

'Do you have good relationships with the other staff here?' I ask.

This is, perhaps, too personal a question, but I am thinking of Jones. Perhaps I am also now thinking of Friend a little.

'Oh yes,' she says, but nothing more, as if she is shutting down the subject.

'What do you think of the overall purpose and utility of our public asylums? Are they a good thing? Do they do a good job?'

'Oh, most certainly. So many people need help, and what would they do without us?'

'But some might say that there are too many of these

people, and that rates of lunacy seem to be growing and growing.'

'I do not know about that. I know that life can be hard, and minds become disordered. It is not my role to speculate on these matters but to deal with what is in front of me to the best of my ability.'

'You are happy here, then?'

Mrs Christie looks surprised, confused.

'Happy? I had not thought. Yes, I am content. I have committed myself to this work. I am a widow, as I think you know, and my two sons are making their way in Australia. Here I am useful and occupied again.'

Being useful is clearly very important to Mrs Christie. I know that widows are valued in these kinds of positions, being free of other entanglements yet with all that domestic experience which is so invaluable for the role.

'Now, I know that this is a difficult subject, but I would like to ask you in a general way how you feel about the recent deaths. It must be very difficult for you and the other staff.'

A strange, indefinable expression crosses Mrs Christie's face.

'They are very unfortunate indeed. The safety of our patients is our highest priority and we do all we can to ensure it. Naturally, we are all grieved when this fails. Alas, sometimes things happen that are beyond our control.'

'Yes. Do you think that there is anything strange about these particular deaths? It seems odd, does it not, that these three women, all of a similar age, have died so close together, and seemingly in a similar way?'

Mrs Christie is looking nervous.

'I do not know,' she says. 'I think it is best to withhold judgement until the full facts are known. If then there are any lessons to be learned, we will learn them. For now, it is my duty to care for the living, and I must apply myself to it.'

'That is most sensible.'

Can I ask her about Miss Rosetti? How can I introduce her into the conversation?

'You care for your patients very well,' I say. 'I was so impressed by what I found in one of the female day rooms, which I visited with Mr Jones. It was the one near Miss Titania Rosetti's ward. The women were so well behaved, and it was all rather genteel.'

I am not sure if Mrs Christie's snarling eyebrow curls a little more. 'We try to maintain high standards, sir.'

'Is that the ward where those nearing discharge reside? I believe that Miss Rosetti herself is in that position?'

'Some nearing discharge do reside there, yes. As to Miss Rosetti, she will be with us a little longer. That is a decision for the medical staff.'

I do not push her further. She is clearly uncomfortable, and I am not sure that I will gain anything.

'Well, thank you for your time, Mrs Christie; you have been most helpful.'

I get up and open the door for her. She takes her leave, her thick blue skirts rustling as she goes. She appears to be around the same age as my mother would have been if she had lived, a few years above fifty, I would say. She must have great energy for a woman of her years. I cannot imagine my fragile mother ever performing such a role. Some of these women are remarkable in their way, and of course it is right and seemly that such personal care of women is put into the hands of women. Still, I would not like a wife of mine to have to soil her hands and mind in this sort of work. A woman of the style of beauty of Miss Rosetti, for example, would be cushioned in silk and velvet, and would stay clean.

CHAPTER 14

I STARE AT THE large stuffed trout in a box upon the wall, which is my only company whilst I wait for Mr Rockingham, who has invited me to dinner here at the Allingsford Arms, a rather pleasant country inn in Allingsford village. Our table is in a cosy panelled nook, nicely warmed by a flickering fire, and I am thinking about the strange events of the past few days. I could have stayed here this week, thinking about it; country inns can be so much better, more welcoming and less dear than their city counterparts. Even so, I prefer the life of the city.

The plump pretty servant appears, accompanying Mr Rockingham to our table. His whole self now seems to be drooping; there are dark shadows under his eyes and his skin seems almost grey.

'Mr Rockingham,' I say, jumping up. 'You look exhausted. Do sit down and warm yourself. Are you quite well?'

He smiles at me and takes his seat. 'I am perfectly well, Harris, thank you, just fatigued.'

'Can I get you anything sir,' asks the girl, whose soft, round accent suits her soft, round form.

'What do you have for us today?' asks Rockingham, his face brightening a little.

'Well, sir, we can let you have a nice bit of partridge if it takes your fancy, or perhaps some pork chops?'

'How about both? Would that suit you, Harris?'

'Certainly,' say I, pleased to see Rockingham's enthusiasm for his dinner.

'Thank you, dear,' says Rockingham to the girl, 'and please bring us a bottle of your finest claret.'

'Yes, sir.'

'And how have you passed your day, Harris? I am so pleased that you are staying on longer. I know that you will do us credit, despite all that is happening.'

'I assure you I will, sir. I have interviewed Mr Friend and Mrs Christie today. Perhaps we can discuss it in due course. Please do tell me how you are, firstly, and what has happened this week. I understand from Mr Friend that you also found poison in Sally Wood's body, and now yesterday, we had the tragic death of Clara Simpson.'

'Yes, this has been a most difficult week, perhaps the worst of my long tenure here. I found signs of cyanide poisoning in Sally's body, and from a preliminary look at the body of poor Clara, I suspect hers will be another case.'

'Good gracious. Do you believe that these are cases of suicide?'

Rockingham sighs, his large eyes drooping more than ever. 'I believe so. There seems to be a delay in arranging the inquests. The coroner's office is under a deal of pressure to cut costs, and I am not sure what is going on. I can assure you that you will be kept fully informed of developments. I wonder, Harris, have you ever witnessed an autopsy? Mr Jones and I are to conduct the one on Clara's body tomorrow afternoon. It might be interesting for you, and useful for your work.'

'That would be helpful; thank, you sir; and no, it is not something I have seen before.'

Now I can smell roasted meat, which brings the saliva to my mouth, and my rumbling stomach tells me how hungry I am. The pretty servant girl appears with a fellow servant, both carrying dishes loaded with the partridge and pork as well as vegetables, bread, butter, sauces and a large blue cheese.

'The food here always cheers one,' says Rockingham, serving some of the food onto our plates. 'Now, let us enjoy it, and you can tell me how things are going in your private life, dear boy, for I have known you so long that you cannot be offended at my impertinence. Is there a Mrs Mortimer on the horizon?'

I think I am blushing. Really, I fear that I am becoming quite womanish in my feelings and sensations. I am not offended, however, and smile.

'I wish there were, sir. I would very much like to settle down and raise a family, but I seem to be having difficulty finding the right lady.'

'Come, now; there must be lots of handsome single women out there vying for your attentions.'

'Possibly. It is just that I am so fearful of making a bad choice. I know you will understand me when I tell you that I am greatly concerned about marrying a woman with latent lunatic tendencies.'

'Dear boy; yes, I can understand that. But perhaps you are worrying too much and seeing things that are not there.'

'Yes, you could be right. But take a woman here in the asylum like Miss Titania Rosetti, now. In my usual daily life, I would not be able to see any of the signs in her.'

'Well, Miss Rosetti is almost well, so that is understandable, although, of course, you did encounter her on your arrival having one of her little incidents, which was just a week ago.'

'That is true. Mr Rockingham, may I confide something to you about Miss Rosetti? I am not sure what to do for the best.'

'Yes, of course you may.'

'You know that I told you about my first encounter with her, and her claim that a man was trying to keep her here against her will? She has since told me that that man is Mr Cedric Jones. You may think that I am foolish for believing her, and if she had accused anyone else, I would not. But I have to say that I have found Mr Jones to be a most singular man, and I am concerned that he could even be a dangerous one.'

Rockingham takes a sip of claret and looks at me with concern. 'Try not to make yourself too anxious, Harris. Jones is indeed a singular character, and I am not always fond of him myself. His ideas are not my ideas, and his methods are not my methods. But he has admirers amongst certain members of our Visitors' Committee, who do not entirely support what we do here, so we must keep him on board. It is a difficult balancing act. Jones's manner is also somewhat peculiar, I grant you.'

'But what if it is more than that? What if Jones has murdered Sarah, Sally and Clara?'

I am becoming flushed and my voice has risen. I can feel some of the other customers staring. Rockingham sighs gently and looks at me with great compassion.

'Harris, my boy. Take a bit of wine now and calm yourself. I do not like to see you like this. You are so like your poor mother, and have all her good qualities. But you must be careful not to let wild ideas and fantasies get the better of you. I fear I am to blame for bringing you here. It has been too much for you. I thought it might be beneficial in some way for you to see how the care of our mentally afflicted has changed so much for the better, so that those like your dear mother did not suffer in vain. But these dreadful deaths must be very painful for you. It might be better if you return to London now, after all, and I can keep you informed by letter or telegram.'

'Oh no, Mr Rockingham, and you must not blame yourself. I confess that it has not been easy for me, but I have been honoured to be part of all this, and wish to do a good job. I am glad to stay and see it through.'

'Only if you are sure, dear boy. I must admit that it has been a comfort to me having you here this week, but I do not want to see you distressed. I have a duty to look out for you in the absence of your dear parents, and I have neglected it terribly over the years.'

'Oh no, do not say that.'

'If you do decide to stay on, I wonder if you would like to move into the visitors' accommodation at the asylum? I know you were alarmed at the idea before, though you did not confess it – and I can understand why – but if you were close by, we could sup together each evening and talk through the day. Then we can look out for each other. The accommodation and the dining are good.'

Could I really stay at the asylum, with all my fears? Rockingham makes a good point; it would be helpful to be closer to him, in a way. Perhaps I have been getting a little overwrought and letting my imagination run away with me. But how could I bear it, with all my terrors, staying in the asylum at night, and hardly leaving? I would be closer to Miss Rosetti, and could look out for her. That would be one comfort. Have I, perhaps, been a little hasty about Jones? I do not know. But I still do not trust him. I could keep an eye on him too. I must do it.

'Thank you, yes, that is a good idea.'

'That is good news, Harris.' Rockingham pauses, and takes a bite of cheese. 'I wonder if you have become a little fond of Miss Rosetti? I could not blame you. She is a great beauty and is very plausible.'

I feel that I am blushing again. 'Oh, well, only in the sense that you say. She would be such an ornament to society if she were sane. But, of course, my future wife will be quite the opposite.'

'Yes, Harris, do take care; you need a good, practical little woman like my Catherine. I am sure that Miss Rosetti will recover in good time and lead a full life, but, even then, in those kinds of cases, there can always be danger of relapse.'

I nod. Of course, he is right. Have I not been wise to look out for this madness in all the women whom I have encountered? But then Rockingham fears that I am also looking too hard, and perhaps seeing madness where it is not, as if I have some kind of monomania. It is all very perplexing.

'Will you bring your things over tomorrow morning?' he asks. 'We can settle you into your quarters and then you can observe the autopsy.'

'Yes, thank you, that sounds like a good arrangement.'

'You will also be closer at hand if and when the inquests take place. You may be called as witness.'

'Yes, I had thought of that. I will be glad to serve if called.'

'Well, Harris, let us do justice to this fine cheese here, have a glass or two of port, and drink to a better time to come.'

CHAPTER 15

'ARE YOU QUITE well, Harris?' asks Rockingham, concerned as ever. 'Us physicians easily forget how disturbing these things can be to non-medical men.'

I smile weakly. I was very hot just a moment ago and now I feel an icy cold in my head, and a growing dizziness. I fear that I will not see much of this autopsy after all. The procedure has not even begun, and I am already nauseous at the sight of the corpse lying on a flat, wooden table, and of Rockingham and Jones, standing on each side in their caps and aprons, like so many high street butchers. The smell is dreadful to me; I cannot quite identify it, seeming something chemical covering something rotten and foul beneath. Dear oh dear, I really am weaker than a woman.

'Your reaction is nothing to be ashamed of, sir,' says Rockingham. 'Indeed, it is a sign of your humanity. It would be more disturbing if you were cold and composed. Many medical students take time to adjust before this sort of thing becomes second nature to them.'

Mr Jones nods at me and grins with that odd small mouth of his. Really, is this an appropriate moment for a grin? I do not feel at all comfortable in his presence, but I must persevere.

Rockingham gestures to a simple deal chair to my right, on which to sit down. 'Have a seat, now; you need not observe the minute detail of this thing unless you can manage it; take your time and simply observe what you can. Taking a few deep breaths should also help.'

I nod, grateful, as ever, for Rockingham's thoughtful attention, and sink into the chair before I faint into it, gripping its rough wooden arms, and composing myself by staring at the sawdust on the floor. I slow my breathing, as instructed, and venture to look up again, feeling slightly calmer and clearer-headed. It has been a bright day, and the light provided by the window, though now fading with the afternoon, is giving me too clear a view; perhaps I would fare better with an autopsy conducted by gas or candlelight, but daylight is recommended for ideal conditions.

Clara's corpse is laid out on a flat table, her head raised on a block of wood, and Rockingham and Jones are now removing her clothes. Poor woman, to think it comes to this at the last, all her dignity gone. Jones is brisk and rough, but Rockingham is respectful, tender, as if he is taking care of his own mother. God bless you, Rockingham. The yellow dress and other garments are laid aside, neatly and reverently by Rockingham, discarded quickly by Jones. I am moved by the sight of the naked body, so exposed, so vulnerable, unable to defend itself against the coming violation. Now I think about it, before this, I have only seen female flesh in situations of carnal desire, scraps of skin from loosened clothes of women at Cremorne or Paradise Wharf, or the neat presentation of bits of pretty body, soft and firm, of my woman from Soho, when we are together. I am very scrupulous and do not hold with the full intermingling of bodies. It will be altogether different when I am married, and can lie with my love in full cleanness and purity.

On a cabinet next to the autopsy table, there is a tray holding various implements. Rockingham now takes a knife from the tray and begins to cut Clara's body, from the chin down, over the throat, across the chest, around the naval to the pubis. I take some more deep breaths. I can do this.

Jones sneaks a sardonic glance at me. 'Still with us, Mr Mortimer?'

Really, the man is monstrous. Next, I believe, the organs will be removed, then examined and weighed. Rockingham puts the knife he has been using down on another tray and picks up a saw from the tray of instruments. Whether it is the sight of the saw, or my imagination of what is to come, or both, I do not know, but I faint and fall on the floor to the left of my chair.

I come to, lying on the floor, staring up at

Rockingham's gentle face looking down at mine with great concern.

'It is alright, dear boy,' he says. 'I fear the sight of our saw must have finished you off.'

He crouches down next to me, and gently turns and pats my limbs and head to check for injury, then he and Jones help me to my feet and back into my chair.

'No harm done, dear chap,' he says to me, then turns to Jones. 'Clean up yourself and Mr Mortimer a little, then take him to my office, where he must take a stiff brandy or two and lie down for a while.

'Dear Harris; I must complete my work here, but I will come to you when it is done, and we can have a talk.'

I sit quietly for a few moments, hoping that I will not further disgrace myself by vomiting into my lap, while Jones cleans himself up at a large basin. When he has finished, he pulls me up from my chair and drags me over to the basin to splash some cold water upon my face and wash my hands with carbolic soap. He brushes me down roughly with his hard, small hands to get rid of the dust and whatever dreadful sticky thing I am covered in from my fall, and we are ready to go. He is smaller than I, but I am forced to lean heavily on his right arm as we walk to Rockingham's office. He is cheerful, and is humming a tune; I am sure that this whole thing is a great entertainment to him.

'Never mind, Mr Mortimer,' he says, chuckling and wagging his head. 'Not every man can bear these things.

Better stick to wielding the pen rather than the sword, eh?'

We arrive at Rockingham's office, and I am comforted by its homely feel, its essence of Rockingham. Jones guides me to a low green settee and I sit down slowly, watching him bustle over to a small cabinet near to Rockingham's desk, on which sit a decanter full of brandy and several glasses. He has his back to me for a few moments, then turns round holding a full glass of brandy, comes over to me and tries to hand it over. I stare at the glass. Is it poisoned? I cannot help but think this, and he must notice the expression of fear on my face.

'Nothing to be afraid of, Mortimer. Gracious, you really have got the collywobbles, haven't you? A good old brandy will do you the world of good. But wait; you do not think it is poisoned, do you? I see.' He chuckles again. 'You should be afraid of me, Mr Mortimer, very afraid indeed. For I am the incredible, terrible, monstrous poisoner of Allingsford Asylum.'

He holds the glass of brandy next to his cheek, grins his strange, wicked grin, then roars with laughter. Really, the man is unhinged. I attempt a smile, trying to indulge him.

'You think these poor women have been poisoned, then?' I manage to ask, my hands shaking slightly on my lap.

'Oh yes, of course; certainly, they have.'

'By whom?'

I am really quite frightened now, but also a little

excited; will he confess? He stares at me, apparently dumbfounded, as if I am the one with a sanity problem.

'Themselves, of course; who else? Really, Mr Mortimer, I hope you will become a little more observant during your time here, and perhaps try to do some more research on our subject matter before writing your articles. I have a number of pieces I can lend to you that should provide some enlightenment.'

'But why would the women commit suicide? They seemed as content as anyone else.'

'In short, sir, it is a case of women of a certain age who are no longer useful or ornamental. I believe I may have mentioned the matter very briefly to you before. From my research thus far, I have concluded that when women reach this point in their lives, some instinct within them recognises their futility. Whether this instinct is prompted by organic matter in the reproductive organs or the brain, or both, is not yet clear, but howsoever it is engendered, it prompts the female of the species to self-murder.'

'That seems a very harsh view of life.'

'Not at all. It is simply nature's way of ridding society of its waste, you see, saving that society from having to impose its own measures for doing so. Have you read the works of Thomas Malthus? He is considered rather old-fashioned now, but I would add to his list of nature's ways of reducing the excess population – through famine, disease, war, and so on – the suicide of these kinds of women.'

'But I have not observed such a thing in the outside world. I see no evidence for this theory.'

'But have you observed properly? In any case, it is more likely to be manifest in a place like this, where we deal with lunacy cases. I am especially interested in female lunacy. The drive to self-murder is an aspect of the type of female lunacy experienced during their climacteric.'

Good God, I cannot keep up with this man's theories. I look over at the small portrait of Queen Victoria hanging to the right of the door. Unlike the majestic painting of a young queen that hangs in the asylum entrance hall, this is a small photographic picture of Her Majesty as she is now, one of those rather homely images where she is sat at a small table, dressed very simply, her admittedly rather plain and round face set off with a plain white cap. Jones follows my gaze. I point at it feebly.

'And at what stage in life would you say that our gracious Queen has arrived at?'

Jones smiles at the portrait, almost tender, and then turns that smile upon me.

'Oh, but our Queen is entirely an exception. True, she is not what one would describe as ornamental. I am sometimes tempted to draw onto that face a moustache and a beard.' He snorts. 'But she is still useful to society at large, you see. No doubt at home she is quite useless, and others will do the important work, but as a figurehead of our monarchy, she retains her utility.'

'I see.'

'And, of course, she has fulfilled her female purpose as wife and mother. I fear we could have seen a severe case of erotomania otherwise. She and her German consort were at it like rabbits, I believe. That is one of the other stages of female lunacy related to the reproductive system. Miss Rosetti, you know, is a possible case.'

Really, this man is vulgar beyond belief. And how dare he mention Miss Rosetti's name in such terms.

'Well, well, must get back to the autopsy,' he says. 'These cadavers won't chop up themselves, don't you know?'

He roars with laughter again, puts down the glass of brandy, which I did not take from him, upon the carpet next to the settee on which I am sat, gives me a quick bow, and hurries from the room.

CHAPTER 16

Titania Rosetti

IT'S BEEN AROUND ten days now since the death of Clara. At least there hasn't been another. I think that inquests are taking place somewhere in the building. They try to keep these things from us poor mad patients in case the sight pushes us over the edge. But rumours and sometimes truths slip out.

I've performed very well this week. I've smiled and curtsied, eaten my meals, walked and worshipped and sang, all with poise, elegance and simpering humility. My only concern on this front is that I feel I sometimes let my guard down in Mr Friend's company. I'm nervous one minute, too at ease the next, and feel that at any moment my fine lady accent might slip, or I'll give away something of my real life. He asks a lot of questions while giving me searching looks. Luckily, when I sing, I can hide within myself, and he can't get at me.

Mr Mortimer is now staying here at the asylum, which is a bit of luck, though I haven't yet made any definite progress with him. When our paths cross, he looks like he's trying to be a little more distant from me, or careful of me, somehow. But we always exchange a few words, and he keeps mouthing 'I will help you'. He has that soft look in his eyes. He's susceptible, and I need to press my advantage further and use that susceptibility.

However, I'm struggling to stay the rising feeling of panic within me. The letter I'm expecting from Connie still hasn't appeared. I know I'm being impatient and that letters take time, but it's so hard to control my fears after that interview with Jones. I'd really like to know what he has on me in his folio of papers, but how can I get at it without being discovered? I think I'm going to take a chance and try to look in the night. It's the only way. It's unlikely that someone like Jones would fail to lock his office door but you never know. It's a bit risky too, if someone finds me. But it's not like I'll be trying to run away, and I can have a convincing story ready. I've got to do something, and I'll do it tonight.

I look round at the other eleven ward inhabitants. All is quiet apart from a few soft snores. They all seem to sleep mostly soundly through the night; it's probably those sleeping draughts. I pull back the blankets and white counterpane and get quietly out of bed, stepping on the cocoa matting, which, I discovered, is one of the luxuries of the wards for milder cases of insanity. I wrap myself in the thick, coarse brown shawl provided by the asylum. I consider putting on the outdoor coat they also provide, but it might be more of a hindrance than a help being so big on me that I look like a child dressing up in its father's clothes.

I creep over to the window that connects the attendant's room with the dormitory. The attendant is nicely asleep and snoring. She keeps the key to the dormitory, which is locked at night, in a bedside drawer. I tiptoe through the connecting door into the room, across to the attendant's bed and pull at the drawer, which is a little stiff. The sound of wood scraping on wood as it opens seems deafening to me but the attendant snores on. The key is inside, I take it, shut the drawer, tiptoe out of the room and close the door. I look into the connecting window again and all is peaceful.

The sound of the unlocking of the dormitory door seems even louder than the attendant's bedside drawer, and I turn round anxiously as I imagine eleven awakened bodies crying out. Nothing. A few of the women are moving around a little but seem deep in sleep. I breath out, close the door and lock it as quietly as I can. I must do this now and be brave. If anyone catches me, my story is simple. I forgot to ask for a sleeping draught, and was missing my family terribly, particularly mourning the death of my sister. I did not want to wake the attendant, who is a dear thing, with my selfishness, and so thought I might try and get some of the draught from one of the offices or medical rooms. It's a bit flimsy but not entirely far-fetched and unconvincing.

It's very dark and cold in the passage, and I need to tread very carefully to avoid falling over or bumping into something. I've got a bit of tallow candle and some matches – pilfered from the kitchen at dinner time - in my nightshift pocket, but I need to use those sparingly.

I put out my arms to guide myself and realise that I must look like a wandering ghost. For a moment, I think about the ghost stories pa used to tell us all, always in a comical way and never really to scare us. Thinking of him now brings me comfort, and I try to shrug off any real fears about ghosts.

I creep along the ward corridor to the stairwell and descend the stairs to the ground floor, holding tight to the handrail and moving even more slowly as I go. Now I move through the covered walkway, and turn left into the central corridor. The large windows at each end of this corridor let in a very pale moonlight and guide my way to the front of the building, where the offices are. I turn right to reach them and approach the door marked Assistant Medical Officer.

I look round. All's quiet. I reach out to grasp the handle, twist it, and, I can't believe my luck, the door opens. I can remember the outline of the room, and shudder at the memory of Jones's words and his mad theories. I close the door behind me, feel my way to the chair opposite the desk, and sit down to light my bit of candle. I pull it from my pocket along with the couple of matches. The first one fails to strike. My hand is shaking as I strike the second and this time the candle's wick takes light, and the horrid smell of mutton fat from the cheap candle fills my nose.

I look about me, trying not to stare too long at Jones's gallery of mad women, the ghastly collection of apparent erotomaniacs and she-devils leering at me through the glow of the flickering candle flame. My eyes rest on the cabinet containing the various bottles. I shiver. Rumours have been spreading that the dead women have been poisoned. Not that you can generally believe the talk of mad people, but just because you're mad doesn't mean that everything you say is mad. I, for one, am beginning to think it could be true, and that the poisoner is Jones. He's mad enough for anything, and said himself that certain women of a particular age are useless to society, and likely better off dead.

I get up and carefully examine the desk, going through some of the papers upon it with one hand, careful not to let any wax drip from the candle I'm holding with the other. I can't see anything about myself. I turn to one of the shelves behind Jones's desk chair, pull down a few files from the shelf closest to hand, and sit down in Jones's chair to look at them. I can almost feel his weird fingers creeping through my hair. There's nothing of interest in these papers either. I'm starting to feel desperate, now; the bit of candle is running down and starting to burn my fingers. I look down and notice a few boxes on the floor to my right, pull out the first one and open the lid. My heart leaps. There it is. A leather-bound set of papers with my name on the front, Miss Titania Rosetti. I pull it out of the box, place it on the desk and open the cover. There on the top is my letter, the one I wrote to Connie, unposted.

I feel cold with sickness now, as if Jones is grabbing me around the throat, his grip getting ever tighter so that I can never, ever escape. Surely, he cannot do this? We're allowed our letters and there was certainly nothing untoward in this one. He really is trying to keep me here so that he can use me as one of his experiments and probably send me off to have my womanhood cut up and put in one of his jars. Oh, Pa and Ma, Nel and Penny, Connie, please help me now; please help me.

I must get out of here. I stand up, put the papers back in the box and make sure that the bureau top is in the same state as before. I blow out the last bit of candle, which I return to my pocket along with the used matches, and hurry towards the door.

'Not so fast, Miss Rosetti,' says a male voice. 'I have been waiting for you to do something like this.'

CHAPTER 17

IT'S HIM, CEDRIC Jones, coming through the office door. He's wearing a night shift, dressing gown, and a tasselled night cap, like some kind of mad, malicious jester. He smiles at me as if we are old acquaintances meeting at the opening of a new exhibition.

My heart is pounding against my chest. I want to run but I tell myself to stay, to stick to the plan. I doubt he'll buy my story, but I should at least try. If the worst happens, Mr Mortimer will help me; he must. Jones closes the door behind him.

'It is very dark in here for a student to study properly, Miss Rosetti. Let us have a little light.'

He fiddles with a nearby gas lamp, which finally lights up.

'Do not look so frightened, Miss Rosetti,' he says, wagging his head in that strange way of his. 'Sometimes, I do not sleep well. My brain is so full of ideas, you know. And if I am awake for long periods, I come down here to my office and read a little or admire my gallery of pictures.'

I'm still looking at the door, which Jones is blocking. He's a small man, not much taller than me, but I suspect that he's stronger than he looks.

'Will you not sit down?' he asks, gesturing to the chair opposite his desk. 'Or you may take my chair if you like. I suspect that you have been sitting in it. Admit it, now. You and I are alike, you see. Our brains are relentlessly active and curious.'

I'll go along with things. I'll sit down, but not in his chair, in the one opposite, then I'll have a free passage to the door. We both take our seats. Jones sits back in his, puts his head on one side, making the tassels on his cap shake, and stares at me.

'This is pleasant, is it not?' he says. 'Now, Miss Rosetti, what has brought you here this evening?'

'Oh, I was having trouble sleeping and came in search of a sleeping draught; I did not want to disturb anyone. Our ward attendant sleeps so soundly, you know.'

'So, you wandered out of your bed in the middle of a cold winter night, and in a most sluttish and unbecoming state, your hair all wild and loose. Only virgin young women and prostitutes display loose hair, you know.'

I want to scream at him. But I manage, 'I did not imagine I would encounter anyone, sir, particular a member of the opposite sex, also in an unbecoming state.'

Jones chuckles. 'Touché, Miss Rosetti. A rather bold and vulgar comment for a lady, but I admire your pluck. Now tell me truthfully, have you been driven by any urges or sensations this evening in certain parts of your body?'

This devil would put the whore of Babylon to the blush. I'm unable to speak, but manage a look of contempt.

'Oh, do not be alarmed, Miss Rosetti. I am not a man of that kind. I am more interested in your mind, yes, that slightly lunatic mind of yours. It is the combination of that mind and your possibly unnatural urges that fascinate me. I have not come across a case quite like you before.'

'I am a normal lady,' I splutter.

'I think I should be the judge of that, my dear. But let us not be at odds with each other. I simply want to learn about you, and you will also benefit. A mind like yours in a woman is a rare and fascinating thing if moulded correctly. Whatever prompted you here tonight, you could not resist seeking information; you are hungry for it, as your body may be hungry for unclean activities with men. Some of your type even crave these activities with their own sex. Can you imagine? Happily, I have not yet detected that depravity within you.'

Run or stay? Go along with it; keep going along for now. Run at the right time.

'You see, your mind is tainted by and dominated by your biological nature. Imagine what life could be for you if you were freed from the tyranny of your passions. You would become entirely rational, and could put your mind to good use. You could rationally embrace your role as wife and mother, or even become a rational spinster, serving those around you in some useful capacity.

'You see, I am a great believer in scientific progress. I do not believe in the inevitability of the erotomaniac or the she-devil spinster. In future,' – Jones waves his sausage fingers about – 'all this will fall away. Controlled breeding will more or less wipe out female lunacy in our species. Where any taint remains, new methods, or perhaps the revival of older ones such as the clitoridectomy…

'Do you know about our little museum of madness here, Miss Rosetti? It is rather a pet project of mine, and I am very proud of it.' He smiles boyishly.

I manage to shake my head.

'Come with me now and I will show you. It will convince you of the idea of progress.'

I'll go with him so far. I'll at least be away from this office, and then I'll find the right time to run. Jones springs up, his cap bobbing madly, and picks up a lamp.

'Follow me, my dear.'

I follow him out of the office door, which he locks, and round the central corridors towards the southeast of the building.

Help me, Pa. Help me fight this lunatic goblin with his cap and his lamp, more horrifying than any malevolent ghost or spirit.

Jones chatters away. 'The museum contains very interesting artefacts from the mad old, bad old days, and one day everything we do now will be in there. There are chains and chairs to strap people in and even a whirligig. Here we are. It's in the old part of the building, along with the dissecting room, laboratory and deadhouse.'

The deadhouse? He takes a set of keys from the pocket of his dressing gown and turns away from me for a moment to open the door. I should run. I should run now. But what if there is something in there he's hiding? Something that will prove to everyone how mad he is? I feel for the shape of the knife in my shift pocket. The man is strong, but I'm strong too. I've fought off men before. I can do so again.

Jones is smiling at me with evil benevolence as he gestures for me to step through the door and into the other part of the building. 'Come, Miss Rosetti.'

My heart pounding, I pass Jones, step through the doorway and take a few steps into an icy entrance hall.

'Enjoy yourself in there, my dear,' says Jones behind me, and slams the door.

CHAPTER 18

I TURN AND RUSH back to the door, just as Jones is turning the key from the other side. What have I done? Stupid, stupid girl. I bang and bang on the door, hurting my ice-cold knuckles. I hear a strange noise, like a poor old nag dying slowly on a London street. I think it might be me, trying to shriek. Am I in a play? Is this an act? It must be. I'm not sure I'm giving a creditable performance. And I've forgotten my lines, and what comes next.

I sit down on an old chair, which I stumble on to my right. My heartbeat begins to slow.

Help me again now, Pa, I think; help me dearest Pa.

Help me, Ma; help me, my Nelly. If I ever get out of here, I'll be better; I promise.

Help me, little Pen, wherever you are.

Help me, Connie. Even though you didn't get my letter, you have to know I need you.

At least Jones has gone. I realise I'm safe from him,

for now. There's no doubt that he's the maddest devil who ever lived. What on earth is he doing? Does he think he can get away with this? If he does, and none of the other staff care, then I'm lost. I could die here. They could just tell people I've died in some kind of natural way, and I'll never see my ma and sister again.

But I must try and think rationally. I will not become hysterical. It's what Jones wants. Surely, Mortimer, at least, will be on the alert for me and notice my absence. He doesn't like Jones; he'll become suspicious. And this part of the building will need to be opened up soon for its usual business. I think of the bodies of Sarah, Sally and Clara, lying in the deadhouse nearby. I will not end up lying there next to them, not without a fight.

I must at least try and get out. I know that there's a door to the grounds in this part of the building. If only I could get outside, I could try and sleep in a stable; anywhere but here. And I'm so cold now that I don't know how long I could last in here. I would freeze to death and be eventually moved from the deadhouse to Jones's museum as some ghastly relic of an erotomaniac.

I pull the bit of candle and the matchbox from my pocket and blow on my hands for a few minutes to warm them a little before attempting to light the candle. If I can only get a bit of light from this, I might be able to find more candles somewhere, and even a lamp. There must be plenty of sources of light in a place like this. The sound of the match striking makes me jump in this deathly quiet, and the wick of the feeble candle lights up.

I look around me at a small shabby hall, with several doors leading off it. I get up stiffly, carefully cupping my bit of candle, and approach one of the doors. I tell myself that I'm playing another part. I'm the leading lady in some ghostly melodrama, not the victim but a wicked lady of whom everyone is afraid; she's frightened of no-one and no thing. If I'm acting, I can do this.

I open doors and walk past several large rooms, possibly the deadhouse and some kind of laboratory. I'm no longer curious about what's in here – look what that brought me to. I simply have to get out. Finding the door is my only object.

I come across a room containing lots of peculiar objects. Is it a storeroom? My heart leaps momentarily as I spot a lamp on a shelf near the door. My frozen hands and fingers fumble as I attempt to light the lamp without spoiling my candle. It glows suddenly; relieved, I quickly blow out the candle to preserve the last bit. I notice that the room is more ordered than I thought and realise that it's the museum. I jump at the sight of some kind of black iron mask or muzzle in the cabinet nearest to me. Is that one of those scold's bridles they used centuries ago to quieten women? I turn away; I must not look at anything else in here.

Walking more comfortably, now, with the lamp in my hand, I continue on until I spy some windows and a door. Please, please, let the door be open. I almost dare not hope that it will be but what will I do if it isn't? I grasp the handle and turn it several times. Nothing. I keep turning and turning then shake it and shake it. Still nothing. I pull the knife from my pocket and try to tamper with the lock. I cut my finger in my frustration and scream inside my head. I approach one of the windows and try to prize it open with the knife. Nothing. I try another window. It's hopeless, utterly hopeless. I sink down on my knees and hug them. Think, Nan, think. The only thing I can do is go back to the connecting door and try that with my knife. The lock may be weaker. If that doesn't work, then I must find something to cover myself to try and keep warm and wait by that door until somebody comes.

I'm nearing the door when I hear noise; someone is on the other side and they're unlocking it. Oh, thank the lord, or the devil; I don't care which.

'Miss Rosetti? How did you enjoy your little visit? Just a little experiment of mine, you know, to shock you into realising your good fortune. Progress, you see. Progress.'

Jones is standing there, grinning as if he's just found me in a children's game of hide and seek. He steps through the door towards me.

'You are mad,' I say. I cannot stop myself. 'You are the maddest person I have ever met.'

Jones laughs. 'Do not be childish, Miss Rosetti; it is beneath you. And you were doing so well. Let us not have another relapse. Come now.'

I run past Jones, through the door and down the corridor, clumsily, breathlessly, back the way I came. I can hear Jones shouting something. I'm nearing some of the accommodation now. I fly at one of the doors and stop. I bang upon it, wincing with the pain in my fist, and I scream and scream and scream.

The door finally opens. A bewildered looking Mr Mortimer in a night shift opens the door. I throw myself into his arms.

I grasp his body, the tang of sleep and sweat on it, and cling to him. He is warm, he is human, he is not a cold, murderous reptile. He holds me for at least a minute, I think, and then I loosen my grip a little, look behind me, spot Jones not too far way, and cower behind Mortimer.

'He is mad beyond anything,' I say, pointing at Jones. 'He locked me in the deadhouse. I could have frozen to death. And he is trying to keep me here, and he wants to cut up my body, so that I am no longer a woman.'

Jones approaches, a look of placid tolerance on his face.

'Mr Mortimer, sir,' he says, 'I am so sorry that you have been disturbed in the middle of the night like this. It is intolerable. I am afraid that Miss Rosetti has been wandering again in a degraded state, as you can see. I hope that she has not been making any vulgar propositions to you.'

Mortimer stares at Jones. 'I beg your pardon? Really, Mr Jones, you astound me. I have tried to tolerate you and your peculiarities, for the sake of Mr Rockingham and the asylum, and for my work, but this is too much. You are monstrous, sir, an abomination. I am quite on the side of the lady, this lady here, Miss Rosetti, and I order you to keep your distance.'

'Really, sir,' Jones responds. 'You are deceived. She is quite the little actress. I fear that you have become a little attached and emotional. I have been noticing the signs and have been meaning to warn you.'

'Warn me against Miss Rosetti? The only warning that anyone needs in here is against you, sir!'

I can feel Mortimer's body shaking in front of me.

'What you will do now, sir,' continues Mortimer, 'is wake Mrs Christie and bring her to me. She will escort Miss Rosetti back to her dormitory. Then you will return to your bed. You will not go near Miss Rosetti again. I work for the *Times*, as you know, and if you do not follow my advice, I assure you that I have the power to ruin you. I will ruin your career and ruin you forever. I have enough evidence against you, believe me, sir. Now go.'

Jones stares at us gormlessly for a few moments, then turns on his heals and walks quickly away. I'm so thrilled, relieved, thankful. Thank you, thank you, thank you.

Mortimer turns round to look at me. I shrink away a bit now, embarrassed at his closeness. He takes both my hands in his. His tired eyes are shining, and he is smiling.

'My darling Titania, if I may call you by that name. You poor, poor thing. You are so cold. Oh, my love. You are safe now. Safe from that evil man. A change is coming. He will be found out. You will be released from here and all will be well. Trust in me. I will take care of you.'

He puts his face towards me and kisses me gently on my right cheek. His breath is a little stale from the night. He holds his cheek against mine, his small beard prickling my skin. He is murmuring, 'My Titania, my love, my darling, my beautiful girl.'

He pulls back and laughs. 'I am a changed man, my dear. And it is all down to you. I have been too severe, too cautious; I have not let love in. But now here it is, rushing upon me. My heart is full, so full, as it has never been before. We will marry, you and I, at some not-too-distant point, and will be happy, so happy. I think I always knew how it would be.'

Now he's leaning closer and slowly moving his mouth towards mine; he wants to kiss me properly. Oh Lord, this is awful; I can't do it. What have I done?

We hear the sound of footsteps close by. Mortimer lets go of me as Mrs Christie appears. She's in her night clothes and a bit dishevelled, though no less stiff and stern.

'Thank you for getting out of your bed at such an hour, Mrs Christie,' says Mortimer. 'I must explain to you this unusual situation.'

'There is no need at the present time, Mr Mortimer,' says Mrs Christie. 'Go you back to your rest and I will take care of Miss Rosetti.' She turns to me, offering me a blanket. 'Come with me, Miss Rosetti.'

Greatly relieved, I wrap the blanket round me and take her arm, glad to find refuge in her brittle bearing, more comforting now than Mr Mortimer's warmth.

She escorts me back to my dormitory. She doesn't ask me any questions, and I offer no explanations. She opens the door to my ward with another key, sees me to my bed and wishes me good night.

CHAPTER 19

Harris Mortimer

THE PAST COUPLE of days have been incredible to me. The inquests have finally been taking place on the bodies of Sarah Barker and Sally Wood and today, Clara Simpson. They have been done consecutively given the newly realised seriousness and therefore urgency of the three cases.

We are sat in the old side of the asylum in a room that looks like it may have once been a dining or games room in its original form, before it was turned to its lunatic purposes and now its third incarnation as an inquest/jury room for the modern lunatic asylum. It is adjacent to the dead room and feels almost as cold. The jurors, witnesses and local press – for word has got out - are seated on long benches, and the coroner sits at the top of this rectangle behind a table, on which his elbows rest as he scribbles away. I have been furiously scribbling myself, that is when I have not been giving evidence as witness. The coroner is bald, grizzled and frowning, and delivers stern looks over his horn-rimmed spectacles when addressing each witness.

The pale afternoon sun drifting in through the long, fluted windows might offer some small comfort, were it not that it falls on those indentations in the walls signalling the places where patients were strapped to chairs. The smell is very unpleasant. Many of the jurors smell of stale beer, spirits and tobacco, no doubt having adjourned to the Allingsford Arms following yesterday's proceedings. At least it is not compounded by the smell of dead flesh; the jurors have filed out to view the bodies in the dead room, and I have not had to endure the inquests in the presence of the corpses.

I am deeply uncomfortable in this place, but not as much as I was when I was alone here with Jones. At the same time, I am filled with a sort of dreadful excitement, for it turns out that my imaginings have not been as wild as I supposed; in fact, they have been vindicated. Rockingham became so concerned about the deaths, including the possibility that no inquests might take place, that he called in the police. A speedy investigation put Jones under suspicion of murder, and he has been detained here, watched over by a police guard, while the inquests take place.

There was a possibility that my lovely Miss Rosetti would be called as witness. For so-called lunatics – though I laugh at such a description of my darling – are considered valid witnesses when in their lucid states. Happily, this was not considered necessary, and she has been spared, though no doubt the dreadful details of these cases will reach her soon enough.

It has been strange to see the usually confident, dismissive Jones become increasingly weak and diminished over the course of the inquests. He seems smaller and thinner, his head larger, and the nervous energy that defined him has all but gone. At the same time, he seems in shock and disbelief; he cannot believe this is happening to him. For all his intelligence, he is rather dim-witted in some matters, or perhaps it is just arrogance or madness. For he has expressed his abhorrent views to witness after witness, and yet wonders why anyone could believe him guilty of the heinous crimes that would naturally follow from such views.

The jury has just returned and delivered its verdict on the death of Clara Simpson. Jones has been found guilty of her wilful murder, as he has been regarding the deaths of Sarah Barker and Sally Wood. The coroner did express some doubt about the sufficiency of material evidence pointing to Jones. However, given the overwhelming circumstantial and what he called 'moral' evidence against him, he felt compelled to direct the jury to the verdicts reached. This would both place Jones in custody, and so hopefully ensure the safety of all residents at the asylum, and commit him to a full trial at the next assizes, in advance of which more evidence may be available.

A deathly looking Jones now jumps up.

'This is madness. All madness. A malicious campaign against me. Due to my modern ideas. Jealousy. Stupidity. I cannot believe it. I will not believe it. This whole business. Intolerable. Monstrous. Mad.'

Jones stamps his feet and wriggles his head so violently that I can imagine it flying off.

'You are all mad,' he continues. 'I am the only sane person here. Don't you understand a fellow's sense of humour? A British fellow's right to express his views? This is tyranny! A mad tyranny! I will see you all dismissed, struck off. I will see this place closed down. I will burn it down myself. All such places will be burnt to ashes when I am in charge.'

Jones is forcibly held by an officer while the coroner delivers his summing up. Towards its end, in a weary but firm voice, the latter states:

'In all my long career, which will soon draw to an end, this has been the most strange and shocking set of cases I have encountered. And, to my great sorrow, I fear that it has been made worse by the delay that has occurred in the provision of coroner services. I would go as far as to say that at least one of these deaths may have been prevented by a speedier response on our part. My thoughts on these matters have been expressed publicly many times. I reiterate again my belief that to curtail the number of inquests we take for the sole purpose of saving money from the county rate will make it all too easy to avoid the detection of felonious killings.'

He sighs. 'There are some people who seem to believe

that some lives matter more than others in this world. I disagree. I applaud Mr Roderick Rockingham and all the good staff here who care so selflessly for distressed females like Miss Sarah Barker, Mrs Sally Wood and Miss Clara Simpson. Long may they continue.'

Jones is taken away, squirming, wriggling and repeatedly shouting 'mad' as he goes. No doubt, he will never see the asylum again, including his precious museum of horrors. I almost feel a little sorry for the man. I cannot explain why. He is guilty of the most heinous crimes, crimes driven by the most abhorrent of views. He is a monster.

We are sat in Mr Rockingham's cosy quarters taking a glass of port after dinner. The fire is burning and Rockingham, like the good, comfortable man he is, is clad in a shabby blue velvet housecoat and carpet slippers. I am feeling a great sense of relief, though my mind is still darting hither and thither on all that has happened. I am dog tired, and my eyelids flicker. Rockingham and I have only exchanged a few sentences in the past few days, when he quickly explained what would transpire, promising me a full explanation when all was over.

'Harris, dear boy, you must forgive me for implying to you that evening at the Allingsford Arms that your beliefs about Jones were completely unfounded. I did not want to further excite you after your recent experiences. I also wanted to be sure that you were as objective a witness as possible at these inquests, giving your views on these dreadful events without having had them in any way reinforced by my own or those of others. I have wanted to do everything with the strictest propriety and rectitude.'

'I understand, sir,' I say, and I do. 'I am sure you did right. I was somewhat taken aback, as you can imagine, when events took the course they did. How long had you suspected Jones?'

'From the first death. Even earlier, I believe, for I almost had a premonition that some such dreadful thing might occur. But I counselled myself against my thoughts. For I was always conscious of my own personal bias against the man. I never liked him. I did not approve of his appointment here, but I was overruled by the Committee of Visitors, some of whom care nothing for the insane, merely wanting to save ratepayers' money. It appears to be the challenge of my life to battle against such men.

'Well, well. The more I observed Jones, the more I suspected that were was more to him than an arrogant eccentric, that, in fact, he had criminally insane tendencies.'

'You think him criminally insane, then, rather than being simply an evil man?'

'I do think so personally, though the jury's view at the assizes may differ. It will be the difference between him spending the rest of his life in an asylum for the criminally insane and his execution. At least he will not be free to kill again.'

'But is there a chance that he could be found not guilty at the assize trial? The coroner has expressed some doubt about the strength of the material evidence against him.'

'I do not believe so. The coroner was right to express such a view, but I hope that more evidence will be forthcoming. Even without it, the overall case was very compelling. I believe that our recent jury was entirely convinced with it as presented. Let us count our blessings, for today at least.'

'I have so much to write about. I will be busy for the next year at least.'

'Indeed, you will. I regret that some of our local newspaper men will have stolen a march on you with regards to the story. But the coroner's office and we here at the asylum must show that we are not trying to hide anything.'

'Oh, yes. In fact, I have already sent someone off to wire my paper, and then, of course, I will have so much detailed information to report.'

'You will do us, and the story, great justice, I know.'

Rockingham and I converse a while longer. I do not tell him about my declaration to Miss Rosetti and my plans to marry her. There is too much going on; it is not the right time. I do fear a little that he will not approve, given his previous counsel to me. But I am sure that, when the dust has settled on all this and he can see how happy I am, he cannot fail to give me his blessing.

As I pack my things preparatory to my return to

London tomorrow, I am once again thinking of my mother. My time here has been painful, and yet, I feel that I have undergone some kind of baptism. My mother has been guiding me towards my future bride. My heart has been opened; I am a little less harsh and judgemental, and I have got my reward. I am fully ready, now, for the rest of my life.

CHAPTER 20

Titania Rosetti

I'M IN THE photographic studio waiting to have my discharge photograph taken. The kindly porter escorted me here, beaming with pride at my apparent restoration to sanity and fitness for release.

I can't believe it. I'm going home. My heart and stomach are dancing. I want to run round the asylum grounds in nothing but my drawers and frilly cap, shouting it to the world. But, of course, I won't do that. A few days after that terrible evening, I was called into Rockingham's office, who told me that they'd reconsidered my case, and that, after all, I was certified fit for discharge. I could leave the following week, on Monday 29th November, making my length of stay in the asylum just under four months. It was all very queer and mysterious, but what does that matter to me? Something is happening regarding Jones, I'm sure. I wonder if it's to do with the inquests. I hope something truly bad will happen to him – I'd put the noose round his neck if they asked me to - but right now, all I care about is that I'll soon be free.

'Good morning, Miss Rosetti,' Mr Friend says as he walks into the room.

'Good morning, sir,' I say, smiling broadly at him. I cannot help it. I'm a bit surprised to see him, though.

'I am afraid that I am your photographer for today,' he says, looking a bit sheepish, 'due to unforeseen circumstances here. I can only ask your pardon in advance; I have dabbled a little in the past, but photography is not my strong suit.'

'I do not mind,' I say. I'd be quite glad, in fact, if the picture comes out blurry, so that the trace of my presence here literally fades away.

I'm back in my old clothes, which have been cleaned up nicely, and it feels so good to be wearing something different again. They're a bit more snug on me now after nearly four months of the bland but decent enough grub, whereas they were hanging off me like the rags on a rail at Petticoat Lane when I arrived here. I'm wearing a huge ugly white collar tied in a bow, which I made myself, and a nice thin belt; this denotes my newfound self-respect and dignity. My hair is tucked under the usual frilled white cap, which shows that I'm not some common slut – or one of Jones's erotomaniacs - open to all comers. They don't say that, exactly, but that's what they mean. How Connie will howl with laughter when she sees it.

'Miss Rosetti, do go and take your seat,' says Friend,

gesturing to the smiling porter to escort me from my side chair.

We walk towards the centre of the room, and I sit myself down in the simple wooden chair. There are no fancy photographer's chairs here, no false pillars, no heavy draperies or backcloths painted with rustic scenes. But the chemical smell is strong enough, and I try not to breath in too much.

Friend is now approaching with one of those posing aids, or neck-clamps, as most people think of them, designed to keep anxious customers still long enough for a picture to be taken. It's a simple black device, with a pole that adjusts for height and a horseshoe-shaped prong at the top, that clamps the neck in place. I bet Jones loved using it; it reminds me of a toasting iron, and I can just imagine him toasting the heads of the patients and eating them up, washed down with a nice bottle of claret.

'I will be fine without that,' I say.

'Oh, that is good,' says Friend. 'They are dreadful things, aren't they? I know that some people struggle to stay still but you seem to have perfect poise.'

He stares at me for a moment, and I cannot help but stare back; we grin at each other. He turns, takes the posing aid away and positions himself behind the camera.

'I do not need to tell you to sit upright and straight, Miss Rosetti, for you are already doing so. Perhaps put your hands by your sides, and I believe that subjects are told to concentrate on that picture of the infant on the wall to the right of the window.'

He ducks under the black cloth at the back of the camera to make the necessary adjustments. He reappears and removes the cap from the lens, and I renew my focus on the photograph of a fat scowling baby piled on cushions, the fingers of a large hand – probably its mother's or a nurse's – gripping its right arm to keep it still.

This business is easy for me; I wasn't bluffing about my self-control. I've had a fair few photographic portraits taken in my time and in much more uncomfortable positions than this. Nothing too shocking, just those artistic shots that are fashionable in certain quarters. I never minded it, either. I don't feel like it's the real me that the machine captures; it's some other person or ghost. I don't think you can recognise me, the proper Nan. I remain my own private self. It's not like it is with paintings. I had my portrait painted once, by a very poor artist who was a little sweet on me, and I was shocked when I saw it; it seemed to expose my very soul. It's a good thing they don't paint portraits of people here; I would have been found out straightaway.

It takes a few moments for the exposure to take place, and now Friend is telling me that it's over and I can get up and make my departure.

'Let me escort you to reception,' says Friend, looking half-happy, half-sorrowful.

I take his arm; we look at each other again and laugh. I'm just so giddy because I'm leaving. He escorts me along the corridor leading to the waiting-room and stops just before we arrive there. He turns to face me.

'Miss Rosetti, please forgive this strange behaviour. I cannot tell you how happy it makes me to see you go.'

Is he blushing?

'I mean. That is clearly not what I mean. I mean that I am so happy that you are well again and able to return home to your friends and family.' He pauses. 'I will miss you.'

He really is blushing a little, and I'm feeling a bit flushed too.

'I was wondering,' he continues, 'if, perhaps, I could write to you now and again? I hope you do not think that untoward. You should know that I have mentioned the idea to Mr Rockingham so that it is all above board, and he does not see any harm.'

'I would like that, Mr Friend.'

Why did I say that?

'You would? And then I have a sister in London, you know. I visit her whenever I get the opportunity. Perhaps, one day, when I am there, I could take you to a music recital?'

'I would like that too.'

Oh, you silly Nan. I'm being very foolish. Really foolish. How am I going to manage this one?

Friend smiles at me in the way he smiles when he's just delivered a perfect performance on the piano, and I return the smile in like fashion. What am I doing? So much for my self-control. We enter the waiting room. A female attendant is sitting with the small bag of belongings I arrived with on her lap. She will be escorting me to the railway station.

I'm still giddy and smiling on the train journey back to London. I'm thrilled to be in motion; things are moving at last.

However, a few niggling anxieties surface.

The first one is what to do about ma and Nel. Although I can't wait to see them, I can't just turn up after all this time. What will they think? What should I say? I need to come up with a story. I think the best plan is to go to Connie first. I can stay with her for a few days, and she can prepare them for my return, tell them that I've written to her from wherever I'm meant to be and asked her to let them know that I'm well and ready to return home.

The second problem is Mr Mortimer, and I fear that it could be a serious one. He really does seem to have some kind of fixation upon me. I didn't like that look in his eyes and the wild things he said to me on the night I ran from Jones. But what could I do? I was desperate. And he must have helped me to get discharged, for which I feel so grateful. Thankfully, I've seen him only a few times since that night. The second time was in the asylum grounds when I was taking part in one of the walks. He grabbed my hands, regardless of who was looking, and pressed me to give him my address in London so that we could formally begin our courtship. I panicked, and nearly gave him Connie's address, but luckily thought of the post office at Charing Cross instead. Even that's a little close to home. I can only hope that once he returns to London and his old life, he'll forget this silly infatuation with Miss Titania Rosetti, a woman who doesn't even exist, a woman with a silly name from a story book or play.

And now, a third problem is Mr Friend, another man who likes a woman that doesn't exist. The problem is that – I admit it - I like him back. I mentioned the same post office to him; it just tripped off my tongue that second time. But I must put him off if he does write. I can't carry on pretending to be Miss Rosetti. Even if I wanted to do so, he'd find me out. I don't think he's as easily fooled as Mortimer. What if he realises that I've been pretending? What would he do?

Oh, Nancy Carter, you're really not as clever as you once thought you were.

But just for today, I can't let anything really dampen my spirits. I'm a free woman. I'm on my way back to the glorious, stinking city and to all the people I love. I'm going to begin again, and I intend, at the very least, to become a music hall sensation.

Above all, I've done what I set out to do. I can't quite believe that I did it, but I did, and no-one can ever take that away from me.

PART II

LONDON, ENGLAND

CHAPTER 21

Miss Nan Carter

OH, IT FEELS good, if a little dizzying, to be back in horrible, stinking, crowded London. When I first arrived at the asylum, I was so preoccupied by one thing that I didn't much mind the trees and hills and deathly dullness. But now my itch for life is back and here I am, at the heart of all life.

I'm sitting on the top of an omnibus on my way to the Strand. I avoided the interior, noting when I got on the exchange of a certain look between superficially well-dressed women, who then followed a real lady inside for the purpose of picking her pocket. Not that I've got anything for a pickpocket to steal - they wouldn't waste their time – but it's good to know that my street sense hasn't entirely deserted me. My knees are aching, though, squashed right together as they are by the two large coves on each side of me spreading their legs across the bench as usual. Not many women sit on the knifeboard. It's considered a bit undignified as well as hazardous getting up and down in skirts, but I'm ready for anything.

It's about three o'clock in the afternoon, I should think; it's gloomy and there are clouds of smoke in various colours – yellow, black, orange – hovering over the people and traffic in front so that they look like so many ghosts. It's pea-souper season; I forgot. As to the din, I can't quite credit it. All the shouting on the streets – the tradesmen, the news criers, the musicians; and is that a barrel organ playing? Then the noise of the carriages, the buses, the carts, the brewers' vans, the horses and other animals. Then the smell, which is of rotten everything, and overall pretty much of horse-shit, which you get in the countryside but it's sort of fresher there. And the hurry and speed and overall surge of it all. Now, this is my type of madness and oh, I'm so happy.

'Next stop, please, Conductor,' I find myself bawling at the appropriate moment, much to my delight. I throw down my bag onto the street, clamber down the iron rungs to the bottom floor of the bus, and pay the driver, who winks at me.

I'm immediately cursed at by a selection of passers-by for getting in their way, and retreat to the corner of a tobacconist's shop to catch my breath. I have a sudden horror of bumping into ma or Nel, but it's a chance I'll have to take. I make my way to Connie's lodgings, which is just off the eastern end of the Strand, above a bookseller of somewhat unwholesome reputation. It's a little off Holywell Street, which contains most of these types of establishments, so I don't feel too embarrassed. I lift the knocker, an iron cherub that's now bordering on the geriatric, and release it several times. My stomach's fluttering a little; I can't wait to see Con but I'm also a bit nervous about telling her everything. No response. I wait for about five minutes, then decide to pop my head into the bookseller's shop.

Mr Smith – I'd be surprised if that's his real name - the proprietor, a thoroughly respectable-looking man in a shabby but well-tailored suit looks up as I enter, and an embarrassed-looking customer pushes past me.

'Miss Carter,' says Mr Smith, smiling and running his right hand through his shock of white hair, 'if it isn't Miss Nancy Carter. How are you, my dear?'

'I don't complain, thank you kindly, and how are you, sir?'

'Oh, splendid, splendid. Still waiting for the revolution, but there's nothing new there. I suppose you're after Connie?'

'I am, sir, yes. She hasn't gone away anywhere, has she?'

'Oh, no, I saw her only this morning. She would have mentioned it if she was planning to be away.'

'Oh, that's good.' I'm so relieved. 'Perhaps I'll step over to the Shakespeare; she might be there?'

Con's a barmaid at the Shakespeare Music Hall. It's a good job; the Shakespeare's up there with the Oxford, Gatti's under the Arches and the Variety.

'It's a bit early, I'd say, but she'll be there this evening. Don't fret, you'll find her.' He pauses, appraising me with his intelligent grey eyes. 'You're not in need of employment, are you?'

'Oh no, sir, not at the present; but thank you.'

I squirm a little. Mr Smith helped me find a little artistic work a few years ago. I don't really want to do that again but if I have to, I will.

'A pity. You know where I am if you change your mind.'

The door opens and what looks like two students stumble into the shop, all hair oil and swagger. They spot me and giggle. I raise my eyebrows at Mr Smith, who winks at me and says, 'I'll tell Connie you're waiting for her; don't go far'.

'I won't.'

I leave the shop and spend some time walking up and down the Strand, standing outside the theatres and imagining my name on the billboards. It's getting dark now and the lamps begin to twinkle. I see myself dancing from lamp to lamp and up to the stars when they appear, singing a song to the whole of London. I'm not a simple, mind. I know that most people are more likely to end in the gutter, looking up at the stars, rather than the other way round. But I'm allowed to hope; I'm allowed to dream; and I'm going to try.

I head back to Connie's building. It's getting colder and I'm shivering. I'm just knocking at the door again, when Connie herself steps out of the bookseller's shop.

'Nan!' she shouts, and hurries towards me.

I drop my bag, and we hug each other. She's round and soft with a big bosom, and I snuggle into her cushiony warmth for a few moments.

'Why didn't you tell me you were coming home?' Connie says, in her mild Midlands accent. 'Is everything alright? But I'm so glad you're back, and safe.'

'I'll explain everything, Con, when we sit down. You won't mind if I stay with you for a couple of nights, will you?'

'Silly old girl; of course not. Let's get inside and get you warm.'

I feel a bit tearful now; I suppose I'm just relieved; I feel safe here, loved. We make our way to Con's rooms, which are on the third of four floors. The building's shabby, a bit damp, and relentlessly noisy, mostly from the sound of bawling babies crying for their pap. But it's decent enough, and Connie's bit is cosy, much like the woman herself. Connie insists on lighting a fire, wasting a few precious coals especially for me, and now I really do cry. I weep into Connie's hair for several minutes, before pulling back and sniffling. Connie's bright green eyes are full of concern, then she grins.

'Now, Nan, I know you've been out in public in the worst outfit a woman's ever worn – and you'll never be able to show your face again – but there's no need to blubber.'

I look down at my massive white collar and burst out laughing. 'I forgot I was wearing this,' I say. 'At least

I remembered to take off the cap they made me wear. I don't know which is uglier. I'll show it to you later.'

I begin to tell Con about my time in the asylum. When I get to the most important bit, she takes a quick breath and presses my hand.

'Oh, Nan.'

'I know, dear. I'll say more when I'm ready.'

I continue. When I get to the part about Harris Mortimer, she looks alarmed.

'It all just got out of hand,' I say, 'but I was so frightened and desperate to get out of that place.'

'It's not that, Nan,' she says. 'You did what you had to do. I can barely credit that devil, Jones. Poor Nan. It's just that the name Harris Mortimer sounded familiar to me, and now I know why.'

'He's a journalist working for a well-known newspaper.'

'No. It's Nel.'

Nel? What can my sister have to do with it?

'I think,' continues Connie, 'that Harris Mortimer is one of her gentlemen, her only gentleman, in fact.'

'No, he can't be. I would have recognised the name.'

'Did she ever tell you his name?'

'I don't know. Before I went away, I think she mentioned a gentleman of the press, who was very generous and undemanding; it was a nice job for her, after all we'd been through. But I suppose I wasn't paying proper attention. Oh Lor, is it really him?'

'I believe so. But there's no reason he would connect the two of you together.'

'No, I suppose not. But what if she loses that job because of me? And then, what if he tracks me down somehow? Oh, Connie, I've made such a mess.'

'You weren't to know, dear. Try not to fret now. I can't think what I would have done in your situation. I'm not sure I'd have survived it. It's like something out of a hellish melodrama. Thank heavens Jones is locked away.'

Connie's being so reassuring, as ever, but she looks worried.

'How are ma and Nel?' I ask.

'They're well, dear. Your ma's been a bit fretful and fidgety about you, and Nel hasn't said that much, but they're both in good health.'

'I need to go home to them soon. My heart's yearning to see them. But I need to think through what I'm going to say. Would you be able to let them know that I'm back, and well, and ready to go home? I don't want to just turn up. I wanted to ask you by letter but, as you know, that didn't work out.'

'I'll call in tomorrow and tell them gently. They'll be so happy, I know. Then you can go home the next day, maybe?'

Tears fill my eyes at the thought.

'Oh Con, what would I do without you?'

'Oh, you'd be in a terrible state,' says Con, smiling her dimpled smile. 'You'd be right up queer street, and no mistake. Though, Nan,' – she pauses and frowns – 'I do feel a bit responsible for putting the asylum idea in your head. I've been fretting about it. I feel like I encouraged you, even. I…'

'No, no; stop there, Con. Don't you ever say that. You're the best pal a girl could ever have. There was only one thing that made me do what I did, and I would have found a way if I'd never known you. Nothing would have stopped me.'

CHAPTER 22

ABOUT SIX MONTHS after Penny died, around June this year, I found out something very interesting related to Allingsford lunatic asylum in Hampshire, and I formed a vague plan in my mind. I fed on it over and over; I wasn't feeding on much else then, and barely ate. But I couldn't quite work out how to execute the plan. I just lay in my bed at home, my mind fretting, planning, fretting again, and my body fading away.

Then one day, Connie came to see me, as she often did.

'Won't you come out in the sunshine, Nan?' she asked.

She was sat on the edge of the bed I shared with Nel, and barely moved from, holding my hand and stroking my hair.

'I'm too busy, Con,' I said, managing a weak grin.

Con laughed. 'I can see that, dear, but if you could oblige your favourite friend just for an hour or so, you'd make her so happy.'

I could only answer by crying a bit.

'Oh Nan. Things can get better, you know. And they will get better. Listen to me now. I'm going to tell you a few things I haven't told you before, then you'll see how good things can come again to us all.

'You know I didn't have the easiest time growing up in Birmingham, with poor ma dying when I was so young and pa being a total beast. I had to slave for him day and night, you know, and he used to beat with me a stick. If I ever see him again – which I hope I never do - I'll take a huge stick to him, you can count on that.'

Con grimaced, which made me smile. You couldn't imagine cherub-faced Con harming anyone. She'd make a great rogue; no-one would ever believe she'd be capable.

'I tried a few different jobs,' she continued, 'trying to support us both. But I couldn't stick to them. I suffered fits of melancholy, and my mind got so distracted. I wandered the streets. Well, you know what I resorted to on occasion; we all understand that.'

I managed to nod and pressed Con's hand.

'I ended up in gaol once or twice, then one time, you can't imagine where I ended up instead.'

'Where?' I asked, having no idea.

'A lunatic asylum.'

'A lunatic asylum? No, Connie, no.'

'Oh yes, Nan. I barely knew what was happening to me, but somehow I got diagnosed as mildly insane, and I ended up staying in an asylum for six months.'

I lifted myself up on my elbows, so I could concentrate more.

'Well, it was a queer experience, I can tell you. Some of the staff in there were vicious witches, but I wasn't going to let myself be bullied again; I held my own, and I think that got the fight back in me. And some of them were kind, too. And, you know, Nan, I got better. At least I was away from pa and the streets. I got some rest and ate the bad food, and was discharged as recovered after half a year. Then, I think you know this bit; I got a bit of money from my aunt – my mother's sister – who hated pa, and headed to our big bad London, and here I am.'

I sat there, staring into Con's bright green eyes, unable to believe that cheerful, sparkling Connie could have been that girl.

'But what did they say was wrong with you? Why did you need to be in an asylum?'

'Oh, it was something about nervous irritability and melancholy, I think. But the queerest thing was that they labelled me as some kind of Ophelia-type mad woman. Ophelia from *Hamlet.* Can you believe it? They just loved this particular type, a pretty young woman – forgive my lack of modesty - driven mad when abandoned by a lover. I don't particularly remember even mentioning a sweetheart, though I suppose I could have done in my confused state.'

I laughed loudly at this - the first time I'd laughed in a while, I should think – and Connie laughed in return.

She was so happy to see me merry, if only for a few moments. Realising she'd sparked an interest in me, she continued to talk about the Ophelia thing from then on when she visited me. We got into the habit of her teaching me how best to pretend to be Ophelia-mad, as if we were writing a play together, and I was coming up with my lead role. Even ma and Nel joined in sometimes, just relieved to see a bit of life in me.

And then I knew that I could really do it; I could get into Allingsford Lunatic Asylum. And I knew that I would do it.

I told Connie about my plan; I couldn't tell ma and Nel. She tried so hard to dissuade me; she even pleaded. But she knew that I was resolute, and she understood why.

The plan was, you might say, mad, and it shouldn't have worked. But it did. I began taking the train to Allingsford to perform Ophelia. I was already a handsome young woman, thin, weepy and distracted. I just had to throw in a bit of hysterical laughing, singing of poetic love songs and murmuring of a lover's name. Eustace, I called him, a rather romantic name, I thought. I wandered the village and the area near the asylum, performing my act. I think I almost enjoyed myself, and it was soothing being Titania, with her empty head and lack of spirit, apart from the hysterics.

Anything dreadful could have happened to me. But I felt invincible somehow, as if I had some strange kind of power, and nothing could ever harm me. I did get held in a police cell one night, but was released the next day. It should have discouraged me; it didn't. I got leered at and jeered at and touched and pinched a few times. But I tried to keep near enough to where a few people lived so that I was never caught completely alone. A kindly woman even took me in, once, and fed me cocoa and broth while I told her all about my gallant but cold-hearted Eustace. I think they came to know me in the area, and so I remained unharmed, and someone must have alerted the authorities, for I found myself in the asylum at last. I'd done it.

'Oh, Nan,' says Connie, 'I still can't believe you did it. It was so brave and…'

'Stupid?'

'Yes, bleeding stupid! The most noodle-headed, stupid thing anyone's ever done!'

'I know. You're right. I can't quite believe it myself. But I don't regret it, despite what I've put myself through and the mess I've created. I can't ever tell ma and Nel, though. They'd never understand, never forgive me. I couldn't bear that.'

Con looks thoughtful. 'Nel might, dear, perhaps one day, at least.'

'I'll never tell them. But I must try to put things right now.'

Connie gets ready for her shift at the Shakespeare. Before she goes, she nips out to get me two hot potatoes from a nearby stall and gives them to me with some gin in a cracked glass.

'I know it's not your favourite tipple, Nancy Carter, but it'll help put you right, and I'll make sure it's champagne next time.'

She's so truly good, I begin to cry again. She wipes away my tears, kisses me on the head and disappears. I eat and drink, feeling a nice fire in my throat and stomach from the spirit, and snuggle up under a blanket on the old settle. The dying embers of the small fire spit companionably and I listen to the noises in the building – there go the bawling babies - and the dimmed sounds from the street outside – shouting, music, traffic. I'm safe and cocooned in the heart of the city. I'm home.

CHAPTER 23

I'M MAKING MY way to Gerrard Street, where ma, Nel and I live in lodgings at the top of a rickety, four-pair building, where most of the inhabitants are a bit dissolute, I suppose, or artistic, as we prefer to think of it. I'm delighted by the old, familiar sights of French shop signs, restaurants and cafés, in which people are playing dominoes. And the whiff of garlic and oil, sometimes mild, sometimes strong, tells me that I'm really back.

As I approach our building, I see a figure standing near the door. It's Nel, waiting for me. I get closer and she smiles, though she looks a bit hesitant. I drop my bag and give her a hug. She's a little bit stiff at first, not just from the cold, but gradually relaxes. She steps back and looks at me.

'You've added a good layer of padding there, to be sure,' Nel says.

'I know, and don't I look well? I should be modelling for Pears soap.'

'You look like the cat that's got the cream, and fair eaten too much of it as well.'

It's our usual mode of chatter but not quite right. I feel like Nel's vexed with me about something. She can't know about Mortimer. What is it? Isn't she pleased to have me back? I expected a little happy crying at the very least.

I stare up at the dark mildewed building, then turn back to my sister. We look a bit alike, having the same snub nose and small mouth, though are different enough for people not to know that we're sisters unless they see us side-by-side. She has a heart-shaped face, dark blue eyes and perfect skin, a little darker in tone to my own. Her figure's more womanly than mine, which I was always envious of.

'Stop gawping at me,' she says, 'or you'll have me thinking my complexion's gone off, and that won't do me much good. Yours has come on a treat, though.'

'Hasn't it?' I say, placing both hands on my chin and tilting my face up for inspection. 'Oh, Nel, I could fair eat you up, I'm so happy to see you. As to going off, you're as pretty as a picture, if not more so.'

She laughs, but not quite wholeheartedly.

'Is ma home?' I ask, my stomach aflutter and my heart yearning at the thought of seeing her soon.

'She should be, if she's not still out shopping. She's not great on her legs at the moment but she was determined to go out herself and choose us a nice bit of supper. She'll be so glad to see you; she's quiet these days, but when she has talked, it's been all of you. I'm surprised she hasn't strewn the streets with flower petals like that painter who was mad about you, the one who wrote all that terrible poetry.'

'Oh, but ma could never write terrible poetry,' I say, grinning at Nel as she turns to push open the battered blue door of the house.

I follow her up the creaking wooden stairs. I'm tempted to pinch bits of her flesh as I go, just like I used to as a child, but think better of it. We pass the different floors, where reside the Italian waiter and his Irish wife, the Polish revolutionary and the old German watchmaker who's a little sweet on ma. Now we're on the small fourth floor landing and I can see our door.

'Ma!' I shout, running over to the frail-looking woman stood just outside it.

Ma is stood up, as straight as she can, like a soldier on duty, a small smile quivering on her thin lips, her eyes anxious, expectant. I look into her face, then wrap my arms around her; she's shorter than me and all bones, but it's still the delicious smell of my ma. In better times, she used to smell of orange blossom from her eau de cologne, and the sweet, spicy gingerbread I so loved as a child, and still do; now she's just clean skin and hair, but I can still smell the cologne and the gingerbread. I step back finally, and ma laughs with delight, looking years younger.

'My Nan,' she says, 'you're bonnier now than you were when you were ten years old and won that dancing prize dressed in that terrible pink frilled outfit I made for you.'

'Aren't I just, Ma?' I say. 'And I'd look divine in that outfit now, I'm sure.'

There are happy tears, tears of relief, in ma's eyes. She can see that the lamp has been lit again, however feebly, inside me.

It's strange, but so comforting at the same time, to be back in the old place. It's a good set of rooms, though it is high up, with a large room we use as our living area and kitchen, and two additional small rooms that serve as bedchambers for ma, then Nel and me. It's looking brighter than it was when I left, when it was stripped back to its bare bones because we'd sold or pawned a lot of things. Now there's a new floral bit of fabric nailed onto the architrave of the main window, a pot plant and some more books.

'Oh no, Ma, not the dogs,' I say, spotting a pair of cheap pottery spotted spaniels on the mantelshelf.

Nel giggles. 'You can't escape them, Nan; as soon as we were in clover again, ma asked me to get them back.'

'They're even uglier than I remember,' I say.

Ma smiles sheepishly, then laughs. 'They were a present from my naughty little girls and so I'll always love them for your sakes.'

'I know, Ma. I can't promise to love them too, but I'll try not to be too tempted to accidentally drop them on a hard floor.'

We sit down to a dish of tea. The old round table with the wobbly legs is covered in a fresh white cover and quite the feast is spread out upon it. There's bread, butter, boiled eggs, some sardines and a bit of Gruyere cheese, and even some cold meats, no doubt donated from the old German watchmaker, whose rooms are on the ground floor, and who is the kindest gentleman in London.

'I'll pour, Ma,' says Nel, 'you take the weight off, and sit next to Queen Nan here.'

Nel flashes me a slightly sarcastic look. Nel, sarcastic? No, I must have imagined it.

Ma smiles, and we sit down in chairs snug next to each other, ma kissing my cheek and patting various limbs as if I'm a prize bull at a country fair.

'Are you well, Ma?' I say, looking into her light grey eyes and pushing a lock of grey hair from her forehead back under her indoors cap. She was once a beauty, ma, but is wrinkled and sort of drooping now. She's most like Nel in looks, I think.

'Of course I am,' ma says. 'How could I not be? My nerves are a little excited with the return of my darling girl, that is all, but how happy I am to see you well, and your spirit is up again, too.' She pauses, a bit hesitant. 'How was your time away?'

'Oh, it did me a great deal of good, as you see. Connie's aunt in Birmingham is so kind. She's like an older version of Connie, you know, the same green eyes and large chest.' What am I saying? I giggle stupidly. 'I helped her with the household tasks, and I've improved so much, you'll be glad to hear.'

'I'll be glad to see it in action more than hear it, Nan,' says Nel.

What is up with her? I give her a quick scowl and turn to ma again. 'I'm better now, Ma,' I say, 'and I'm set to amaze and conquer the world.'

'If you want to conquer the world, my dearest Nan, we might have to do something about your outfit,' says ma, with a touch of her old humour. She always had such a fine way of dressing, and I like to think I take after her, when I have the means, of course. 'That old dress is very shabby and a bit snug on you.'

'If you think this is bad, you should see what I wore…' I stop. I nearly say, 'in the asylum'. I continue, 'when I was doing my chores at Connie's auntie's house. Anyway, Ma, I shall now put you in charge of my appearance. Nel can write the songs, as she has such a knack with words' – I glance at Nel, hoping she's softened by this, at least – 'and I shall do the rest. Soon I'll be the biggest music hall star in London; then I shall leave all that behind and take to the fancy theatre and opera. I might marry a lord in Belgravia or a nabob in Tyburnia, or even the Prince of Wales, and stroll down to Lombard Street every day to count my thousands. Or maybe I'll just sail my way across the whole world, in first class, of course. I'll see how the mood takes me.'

'As long as you're happy, my Nancy, that's all that matters to me.'

'It's all that matters to her, as well,' Nel mutters quietly.

'Nel; not now,' says ma, almost fierce, 'can we not enjoy your sister's return, just for an hour, at least?'

'Yes, Ma,' says Nel, in a flat voice. She gets up and begins to clear away. Where has my affectionate, amiable sister gone?

Ma presses my hand. 'Things will get better, dear; give her some time. Well now, as I said, the happiness of both my dear girls is all that matters to me, whether you become an international music hall star or settle down to lead a very dull and respectable life instead. Though I suppose I have not set the best example myself in that regard, and it is too late now to hope that you will become dull and respectable.'

'You followed your heart,' I say, patting ma's cheek. 'It's just a shame that your heart made you follow some rather useless men, to start with. Still, we wouldn't be here if you hadn't done such foolish things, now would we?'

'No, dear, and that is unimaginable,' says ma, looking at me lovingly.

Ma comes from a very respectable gentry family in Sussex, and her father was a gentleman parson. He took a cold, unrelenting view of his religion, which didn't endear him to his parishioners, and so ma, who was an only child, was lonely. Her mother tried to give a little softness and warmth, but was ineffectual, being sickly and afraid of her husband. No wonder ma eloped with her drawing master – Nel's pa - when she was seventeen. He was a tall, pale namby-pamby type, could spout a little verse and some long passages of Shakespeare, and told ma she was his muse. He brought her here, to Gerrard Street, which was renowned at the time for its artistic residents. But he turned out to be a terrible artist. Luckily, ma had managed to save an allowance she got from her mother, which she used to support them both. Finally, he got such an unquenchable thirst on him that he wouldn't have been able to spot a hole in a ladder, and spent his final days shouting at people at the Royal Academy, before dying of delirium tremens. Poor ma.

'Have you agreed to marry Herr König yet?' I ask her, smiling and nodding at the cold meats on the table.

'Not yet,' says ma, laughing.

Herr König, the old watchmaker, is very fond of ma, but not in the way of really wanting to marry her. He must be pushing seventy years old by now and ma runs errands for him when his legs are bad. He watches over us all, and would give us everything he has if we would only let him.

Ma and I spend the next few hours nattering and laughing, with Nel proffering the odd word or two but mostly sulking, it seems. Ma tires easily, and I escort her to her tiny room, help her undress and get her into bed. I tuck her up so tightly that she can barely move, as she did us as children, and kiss her on her cool forehead.

'Would you like me to read something to you?' I ask. 'Or maybe sing a lullaby?'

'No, dear; you get back to Nel and try and have a good talk with her.'

'I'm not sure why she's behaving so coldly to me. What's happened to her?'

'Talk to her. You will smooth things over.'

'Night, night, ma; don't let the bedbugs bite.'

'Nothing can bite me, Nan, now that you are home. God bless the days that brought me all my daughters.'

She stares at me for a while, smiling, then closes her eyes and looks peaceful. She seems younger like this, though there are a few more white hairs on her smooth head than I remember. I look at her awhile, making sure she's there, that this is real, and I'm home. I get up, kiss the top of her head within its bed cap, and reluctantly return to Nel.

Nel's pouring some wine from a fancy bottle into two pewter mugs. She hands me one, as if in the manner of a challenge. I take it, sit back down at the table, opposite her, and take a few sips.

'This is very nice wine,' I say.

'Yes, it's good stuff, much nicer than that vinegary stuff from the Bull and Bottle. My gentleman gets it for me. He's very generous. How else could we pay for all this?' She gestures round the room.

'I'm glad to hear that you're comfortable.'

'That *I'm* comfortable? Don't you mean ma and me? Oh, and you, Nan, now you're back. Who do you think has been paying the bills and looking after ma while you did a flit to make your poor little self better?'

I gulp. 'I had to do it, Nel. I was going mad.'

'And we weren't? What would ma have done if I'd decided to swan off as well? Did you think about that?'

I feel a bit sick, and shake my head feebly.

'No, of course you didn't. Because all you've ever thought about is yourself. Have you any idea what you've put us through? Forgetting about me, think of poor ma. How could you do that to her? Didn't she suffer enough? She needed you here. We both did.'

'I wasn't thinking straight.'

'And now you just turn up, with your pretty, artful little speeches, and ma's beside herself with joy, and it's all about bloody you again!'

I'm stunned. Not by what my sister's saying, really, because I know she's got a bit of a point; I've just never quite acknowledged it to myself. I'm shocked by the change in my sister. She was always so sweet-tempered, soft, forgiving and gentle, so like ma, I suppose. Now, looking closely at her, I can see her forehead tensed up with anger, and sad drooping lines descending from the corners of her mouth. Have I done this? No, that's not fair. It was the terrible things that happened to us did this. I suppose I just didn't bother to pay it attention; I put my own pain first.

'Oh, and didn't Connie's aunt have any ink and paper?' continues Nel, though her voice is more deflated now, a bit less angry. 'Could you not have written one word to poor ma all this time?'

Nel tips the rest of her wine into her mouth in a most un-Nel like fashion, pours some more into her mug, spills it all over the clean tablecloth, then bursts into tears.

I'm so heart sick and my throat hurts. I reach out my hand to Nel's. She pulls hers away. I get up, move closer to her and put my arm on her shoulder. She pushes it off and shrinks from me.

'Don't give me one of your acts, Nan; you're not in the bleedin' theatre now. I'm going to bed.'

So much for my perfect arrival home.

CHAPTER 24

Harris Mortimer

HERE I AM, a few weeks into the new year, 1876, with the world before me. The incredible events at Allingsford have made my name, and I am the writer of the moment. I rise early every day with renewed purpose and relish for life. I either go into the office of the *Times* on Fleet Street, on foot or by omnibus, or set to work at home on my research and writing. At the end of a fatiguing but satisfying day, I dine with friends and acquaintances or take my ease at home. It has been so pleasant to be back in my comfortable lodgings in Chelsea over the past six weeks or so. Mrs Hodgkins, my domestic, keeps it spick and span, with everything in its place, which is so soothing to mind and body, and she cooks me up some tasty little dinners. It is not generally advisable to become overfamiliar with one's servants, but I have become really quite fond of her.

This evening, I have been dining with some of my friends and colleagues from the newspaper; I have become rather popular. The ladies have adjourned to the sitting room and we gentleman are taking our brandy and pipes.

'Mortimer, old chap,' says one of our sporting writers, Dickie Dodds, puffing away at his pipe. 'We have a little gift for you.'

The other chaps round the table are smiling at me and I smile back, contented. The candlelight is flickering over the array of faces, bald or bearded, pale or rosy, collars stiff or slack, waistcoats neat or bursting at the seams. We are full of turtle, brandy and good cheer. Dodds produces something from under the table, a small parcel wrapped in brown paper and string. He hands it over to me, and I deftly undo it and laugh heartily.

It is a small pottery figure of Cedric Jones. The head is much bigger than the torso and the face creased up in half-grin, half evil leer. The tiny legs are bent slightly, and the arms are outspread, as if he is about to bow to an audience. He holds a yellow poison bottle in one hand and a surgical saw in the other. The figure is glazed to perfection, and remarkably like the original man, so that I can see him before me as he was that evening in Rockingham's office. I shiver. Undoubtedly, the whole thing is tasteless, vulgar, even obscene, when one considers it, but also rather wonderful.

'We thought you should have a little reminder of the man who made you,' says Dodds. 'I would not put it on your bedside table, though; it will surely give you nightmares.'

'Oh, I am immune to such things now,' I say, 'after spending so much time in his company. Although there was a time at the asylum when he stood before me proffering a glass of brandy, and I thought that if I accepted it, my end would be nigh. It shall take pride of place on my bureau at home. Thank you, everyone. I shall cherish it.'

A little cheer goes round the table.

'The world is going Cedric Jones mad,' says Harry Jenkins, a popular author of cheap novels. 'I cannot pass a news stand without seeing his name in large bold type and garish colours, or sketches and photographs of his diabolical face winking at me, as if he's ready to jump from the pages and murder me. And not just that. His face follows one all around the city, from hoardings, cabs and sandwich boards.'

'Oh, but the general public must have their insatiable appetite for murder satisfied,' says Charlie Austin. He's a rather pompous fellow, a veteran reporter from the Crimean war, who clearly thinks all this a little beneath him. I fear that he has become a little jealous of me.

'That is true, sir,' says Monty Smithwick, editor of the newspaper and good-natured host of the evening, 'but, you know, I fear that I have to count myself amongst them. It is all rather gruesomely fascinating. Only yesterday, I could not resist purchasing a ballad and a pamphlet on the man, and I am sure that my wife is desperate to see that opera about him. She has not quite admitted it yet, but when she does, I confess that I will likely accompany her.'

'It is something in our human psyche,' says Alfred Mortlake, a ponderous poet, stroking his long red beard.

This is rather an artistic gathering. As well as journalists and the red-haired poet, we have several novelists, a painter and even an actor. Our host's wife is known to go in for women's rights and even eschews the corset occasionally. Of course, I cannot condone such things myself, but I try to respect most views. My own nature is artistic, after all, and how at home I feel here, in this charming, colourful, welcoming house.

The mood becomes a little sombre as the poet and I discuss insanity and the various methods used to detect and cure it, but is soon lightened, as ever, by our jovial host.

'Do you know,' Monty says, 'since the advent of Jones and all the scientific humbug that is being written about him, I am seeing criminal lunacy everywhere around me. My dear one and I were only dining at Simpson's last week, when I noticed that the waiter's head seemed to be disproportionately large for his body. We almost fled the restaurant in terror, with the reckoning unpaid.'

Chuckles flow and ebb around the table.

'And my dear wife,' says Phillip Pitt, a parliamentary expert, catching the theme, 'is all for dismissing our dear old charwoman, whom we have always thought so good and cheerful, because of a slightly cackling laugh she gave in response to one of my very poor attempts at a witticism.'

'Never mind the charwoman,' says Willy Bingham, a well-known gothic novelist, 'this morning, I almost accused my own dear wife of murdering the butcher, and of an intention to follow up with the baker and no doubt the candlestick maker, simply because she mentioned that he was not a very useful man, nor even a particularly handsome one for that matter.'

We are all roaring with laughter.

'I feel that I should be noting down the measurements of your heads,' I say, 'and I am really not sure that we should be sat here in such conviviality when any one of you could be poisoning our victuals in plain sight.'

I am rewarded with further laughter. I have become rather charming and even humorous in these times. My acquaintances say that I am a new man, and have sloughed off my old skin, which was a little stiff and formal. They jest that I must be in love, or that I have taken to smoking something much more interesting in my pipe than my usual tobacco.

'Well, well, enough of this jollity,' says our host, 'we must join the ladies, who will be wondering what we are about. Some of them, indeed, will be pining most dreadfully for our Mr Mortimer, who is quite the bachelor of the day.'

'Oh, I am not sure about that,' says Dodds, 'I suspect that Mortimer's heart is already taken.'

I smile mysteriously, and we adjourn to the sitting

room, where I perch a little precariously on the edge of a velvet divan, admiring the glorious paintings by Rosetti. The subjects are too sensuous for some tastes, but I am a man of the world. Not that any wife of mine would ever degrade herself by modelling for such things.

I am accosted immediately by Augusta Dodds, wife of Dickie.

'Mr Mortimer, do let me introduce my dear daughter, Miss Adelaide, who is such a keen follower of your work.'

Mrs Dodds's bulky physique suggests that she would not be out of place in some kind of sporting arena herself, perhaps a rugby field. Miss Adelaide, on the other hand, is a simpering, bony, round-shouldered creature.

I get up to kiss her skeleton hand.

'Mr Mortimer, I am so interested in your subject, quite enthralled to it.'

Her voice is thin, dry, a little rasping. That cannot be a good sign.

'Indeed?' I manage.

'Oh yes, I read nothing else but madness and make copious notes. I would make quite the amanuensis, you know.'

She goggles at me with her fish-like eyes, and I wonder if they are symptomatic of any latent female neurosis.

'I am currently quite the slave of Andrew Wynter's "The Borderlands of Insanity".'

Good gracious; how does she even get hold of these

things? I have a vision of her sat at the top of my dining table, covered head to toe in ink. After the cheese course is cleared away, she smokes a cigarette and delivers to me one of her evening lectures on the madness and neuroses of modern life.

Next up is a tall, masculine-looking woman with cropped hair and – good gracious – is that the hint of a moustache? She is Maud Bishop, a friend of our hostess.

'Mr Mortimer,' she says in a loud, deep voice, and shaking my hand rather vigorously, 'we really must talk properly. I have an ambition to become a surgeon, you know.'

Good God.

'And at the moment,' she continues, 'I am simply passionate about post-mortems. I believe that you have observed one first-hand? Will you not share with me all the glorious details?'

This is abhorrent. To think of one of the fairer sex meddling in such things. Imagine my darling girl in such a position; it is unthinkable. No wonder some of our alienists are concerned about the unsexing of the fairer sex in our age. This one would surely be incapable of breeding, and perhaps it were wiser that she should never make the attempt.

In relief, I turn to the two fair, pretty daughters of Phil Pitt, Mabel and Maryanne. This is rather bad form on my part as I was sat between them at dinner, but I really cannot face any more claimants. They are softly spoken, gently humorous and rather engaging. I am somewhat concerned now, however, to notice Mabel giggling rather too much and slurring her speech. Good Lord, a possible dipsomaniac; imagine the hereditary consequences of that.

I am weary now and decide to make my departure, rather to the dismay of some of the ladies. Monty escorts me to the door.

'Thank you to you and your good wife for a delightful evening, sir,' I say. 'I have not enjoyed myself so much in ages.'

'Glad to hear it, Mortimer,' – he winks at me with one of his large grey eyes – 'though I think you do well to make your escape now before you get eaten alive by the ladies, eh?'

I laugh and we shake hands and make our farewells.

It is all rather flattering, I suppose, I think, as I sit in the hackney on my way home. Indeed, I do believe that I have acquired more manliness and assurance since my return from Hampshire, and no doubt this is having its effect as well as the fact of my general eligibility. I should really try to be more open. But how could these vastly inferior creatures compare to my Titania Rosetti? It is laughable. The more I see of the world, the more I appreciate what a jewel amongst womankind I have found.

Unfortunately, I have not yet had a response to the three letters I have sent her. I hope that I have not embarrassed her with their enthusiasm. I am not too troubled, though, only a little impatient for a response. It is natural that Miss Rosetti should want to have some time of repose in the bosom of her family after her dreadful ordeal at Allingsford. It is also seemly, and maidenly, of her to delay a while. She will write soon.

I bang on the roof of the cab.

'Driver,' I shout. 'Change of direction. Drop me off at Cremorne Gardens, if you will.'

I must say that I was rarely tempted by Cremorne on my first return to London, being so fully occupied by my new, fuller life. However, I have slipped a bit this month. It is a cold January, and one needs a little comfort. Still, I mostly try to stick to my little Nel, who is really such a good, decent girl, for one of her sort. Of course, I will dispense with all this when Titania and I are formally engaged.

I arrive home from Cremorne in the early hours, a little grubby, a little sticky, a little disgusted with myself, as I often am after one of these jaunts. Still, Mrs Hopkinson is terribly discreet as well as efficient with my laundry, and all traces of shame will be scrubbed away. With my frozen fingers, I quickly flick through the letters on the silver tray in my entrance hall, sighing at the recognition of the handwriting of various matrons trying to sell off their daughters. I stop; I do not recognise this handwriting. It is elegant, dignified, that of a real lady. I rip open the envelope and look at the signature. It is from her, from Titania Rosetti.

CHAPTER 25

I AM SAT FIDGETING at the table, waiting for the arrival of Miss Rosetti and her companion, a Miss Millais, I believe. I must confess that both my heart and stomach are fluttering like those of a romantic schoolgirl. They will be here at any moment. At last. I knew she would respond soon. Her letter was brief but to the purpose. She apologised for her tardiness of response and said she would be very glad to meet me again, with a chaperone. Oh, she judged just right. She is delicacy itself. To think, I once had those doubts about her wild behaviour at Allingsford. Of course, that was quite naturally driven by the dreadful torment that she was forced to undergo.

Here she is. I get up, shaking a little. She glides towards me, a vision of loveliness. See how the winter sunshine, which can be so harsh to poorer complexions, or emphasise those tainted with paint, only heightens the perfection of her own. She is wearing a simple fitted gown in sapphire blue. I am dazzled; I realise that I have only seen her previously in that dreadful asylum uniform.

'Miss Rosetti.' I take her hand and put it to my lips. She nods and smiles, then steps aside to reveal her companion.

'Mr Mortimer, this is my dear friend, Miss Millais,' she says.

Miss Millais is a fresh-faced, comely creature with bright green eyes; she has the air of a genteel milkmaid.

'Delighted to meet you,' I say, kissing her hand also.

'Charmed,' she says, flashing her dimples and dropping a curtsey. How idiosyncratic. It is like Miss Rosetti to have such an original, delightful friend. It is her artistic soul, no doubt, which makes it the perfect match for my own.

I help the two ladies to their seats, fussing a little over their comfort, then take my own. I'm struggling to take my eyes off my Titania but manage to order tea and cakes from the waiter, which soon arrive.

'Miss Rosetti,' I say, when we are all settled, 'I do hope that you are recovering well from your terrible ordeal in Hampshire. Indeed, I would not want to upset you by referring to it too explicitly, but you do look so much better.'

'Thank you, sir; I feel very well and am quite recovered. I must thank you, properly, for all you did to help support my discharge from that place.'

'Oh, it was nothing, I assure you. I am only happy if I can aid you in any way, small or large.'

I am smiling like an imbecile, I fear. She is becomingly reticent, looks down at the table, and fiddles with her napkin.

'I am very grateful,' she says. 'Of course, I have so much support from my dear family and friends that I do not need anything else.'

Miss Millais smiles at Miss Rosetti and squeezes her hand.

'Yes,' I say, 'they must be a great comfort to you. I am greatly looking forward to meeting them all, in due course, and naturally, Miss Millais' - I glance in her direction, then smile shyly at Titania – 'when the time comes, you shall always have a second home with us.'

Miss Millais seems to splutter a little and then spills her tea, which forms a large puddle in her saucer and makes a stain on the white tablecloth.

'F… fiddlesticks,' she says. 'I do apologise, Sir Mortimer; I mean, sir, Mr Mortimer. I am all fingers and thumbs today.'

'Not at all,' I say, as the tall, bandy grinning waiter appears to wipe the tablecloth and present Miss Millais with another dainty cup. He goggles at the ladies – the devil. I glare at him, and he canters away.

'Where are your family from?' I ask her. 'I cannot quite place your speech, which is a little unusual to my ear.'

I really cannot place her accent, and she pronounces her words in a very slow and drawn-out way.

'Oh, I come from a military family, sir. God save the Queen, and all who sail in her!'

She smiles and then salutes me with one of her pretty plump hands, looks quickly at Miss Rosetti, who mumbles something and turns away, then looks back at me. She takes a sip of tea from her new cup, sticking out her little finger in a rather exaggerated manner.

'Well,' she continues, 'we travelled all over, don't you know. I fear that along the way, I may have picked up a few peculiarities in my, er, lingo.'

'Oh, it is most charming. You will have to teach me some of your dialect words. I do love the diversity of the English language.'

Miss Rosetti gives a charming little giggle and puts her handkerchief to her mouth.

We share some more pleasantries as we consume our tea. I am delighted to see how they both enjoy it. Most of the ladies I know take very little at table. I cannot imagine that either the Rosetti or Millais families are in affluent circumstances, and this must be a treat for them.

'Do you have a profession, Miss Millais?' I ask.

Miss Millais is eating a cream cake, her fourth, I believe; she has an astonishing appetite. She makes a strange, hiccupping sound.

'I can only apologise, again, sir,' she says. 'I fear all this sugar has made me a little, er, bilious.'

She composes herself. 'Oh yes, Mr Mortimer, I am a lady's companion.'

'That is such a worthwhile thing to do. Is it to anyone I would know?'

'I do not believe so, sir. She is a very private old girl, and it would not do to, er, peach on her, so to speak.'

'Oh no. And, Miss Rosetti,' I say, smiling at my love – I wish she would look me in the eye a little more, though I know her modesty is becoming - 'I do hope you are not thinking of returning to your profession? There will be no need for you to do so once we are married, of course, and I would not like you to risk your health before then.'

Miss Rosetti looks at Miss Millais intently and nods. Miss Millais gets up.

'Ain't it hot in here, Mr Mortimer?' she says, wiping her brow. 'If you have no objection, I must just take a bit of that fresh, frosty air, forthwith. I shall not tally long.'

She smiles at me and walks away from the table. How perfectly in tune and discreet these friends are. Titania knows that I have been longing to be alone with her and her original friend reads her mind. I reach across the table and put my right hand on Titania's right hand. How small and delicate it is.

'What a lovely friend you have,' I say. 'She is the perfect companion for my Titania.'

Titania looks around and pulls her hand away.

'Mr Mortimer…'

'Will you not call me Harris, my love? Mr Mortimer is a little formal for one's fiancé, you know.' I chuckle.

'But, Mr Mortimer, Harris, I am not your fiancé. This is all a little too much. We hardly know each other. You have been so kind to me, and I am truly grateful, but I do not wish to marry anyone at the current time. My priority must be my family.'

I knew it. I have been carried away, trying to rush her. No true lady could respond in like fashion. I have become a little tipsy with my new freedom and openness of heart, and have gone too far the other way.

'Do forgive me, Titania. You are quite right to be cautious. If I could only make you see what a wonderful change you have wrought in me, you would understand my behaviour. But there, I have checked it. You must take all the time that you need. Ours can be a long, luxurious engagement. We have all the time in the world, after all, and the rest of our lives to spend together.'

'But I have never agreed to marry you. I do not know if I will ever wish to marry. You must not waste your time. You do not know me. Find yourself another lady who is worthy of you.'

I laugh. 'Worthy of me? What woman on this earth could be more worthy than you? How you would smile if you saw some of the so-called ladies who set their cap at me.'

Titania takes a deep breath. 'You must understand that I do not want this. I have had a terrible time with him, with Mr Jones. He is not yet truly gone from us. I cannot think properly, or be at my ease, until that happens.'

'Oh, Titania, now I see. Can you ever forgive my selfishness? Us men are such hardy creatures that we forget the true, sensitive nature of a woman's mind and heart, especially one of such exquisite sensibility as yourself. Let us have no talk of engagements until that devil is gone for good. He will be brought before the assizes in March, where he will be sure to be condemned to meet his end. It is an unpleasant subject, I know, but then you will be entirely free.'

'It is not what I want. You must understand.'

My poor darling looks close to tears. Miss Millais now reappears, looking at her with great concern.

'Well, Mr Mortimer,' says Miss Millais, 'I think I should be taking Miss Rossetti home now. She tires so easily, you know. It has been such a pleasant outing; you have been so good, so very kind.'

I am alarmed. I have scared them away.

'Oh, yes, of course, Miss Millais,' I say. 'You must both go and take your rest. Can I do anything for you before I go? Perhaps if you give me your home address, Miss Rosetti, I can send you some flowers to cheer you and some tonics or delicacies to fortify you?'

'No, I thank you, sir,' says my darling. 'I must go now.'

I stand next to the table, thoroughly dejected as I watch the ladies leave, Titania leaning on the arm of her friend. Should I follow them, discreetly? No.

Oh, Harris, you insensitive, oafish bear. Badly done, old fellow. You must slow down. You must give her more time, particularly until Cedric Jones is gone from this world.

But how beautiful, how perfect she is. She came

today. She loves me, I know it. She has the chaste soul of a true lady, that shrinks from anything indelicate, bold or vulgar. Only imagine how some of those dreadful Misses from my editor's dinner party would have reacted today if I had mentioned matrimony. No doubt, they would have shrieked with delight, and their monstrous mamas would have dragged me to the nearest church. I could not love Miss Rosetti more.

CHAPTER 26

IT IS DONE. Yesterday at the March assizes in Portsmouth, Cedric Jones was found guilty of the wilful murders of Sarah Barker, Sally Wood and Clara Simpson. He is due to be executed next week. It will take place behind the walls of his Portsmouth prison, thankfully. We are past the time of public executions, though no doubt there will be some tumult in the city that day given the notoriety of Jones. I will not attend. I will send one of the newspaper's younger staffers, who will enjoy the excitement. These events are far too vulgar for me now.

I have received a letter from Mr Rockingham – dear fellow. Journalists are still swarming round the asylum. But he is very well, and busy, and congratulates me on my work. He informs me that Mrs Annabel Christie is leaving the asylum after all this time. He is disappointed but can understand her decision after all the recent turmoil at Allingsford, and wishes her well. In fact, I am to interview her today. I thought it might be an interesting piece. I do not know how enthusiastic she is about the prospect of our interview; I suspect that Mr Rockingham encouraged her to oblige me. She did not give too much away when we last met, but perhaps now that she has left the asylum, she will feel able to be more candid. These first-hand accounts from staff who worked alongside the infamous Cedric Jones will be so fascinating for my readers.

She is coming here, to my home in Chelsea. I could not imagine where best to conduct the interview. Nowhere seemed appropriate, somehow, and then when I discovered that she would be on her way to the county of Surrey, I thought about meeting her here, with dear Mrs Hopkinson's reassuring presence close by, and she accepted my proposal.

She sits, a little stiffly, but also looking oddly defeated, in my best armchair. She is thinner than I remember her, which only further emphasises her sharp features. I suppose this big change of life has been a difficult decision for her to make.

'Mrs Christie. Welcome to my home. I am so grateful to you for taking the time to come here and talk to me.'

'It is no trouble, sir.'

Mrs Hopkinson bustles around us with tea and biscuits. Mrs Christie smiles at her; it is a somewhat frigid smile, but a smile, nonetheless. I suppose she approves of hard-working older women. She accepts a cup of tea; her hands shake a little.

'You must be looking forward to your retirement, and after all your years of service?' I ask her.

'Yes. Well, it will not be quite a retirement, just something different. My eldest son is returning home to England next month, bringing with him a young wife. She is delicate, he says, and so he has asked me to live with them, and to be their housekeeper, and, if it so please God, and children come, help in that capacity also.'

Her voice is shaky, like her hands. Her shoulders are hunched; what happened to her proud, upright bearing?

'I hope it will be a great source of comfort and pleasure to you.'

'Thank you. I hope so too. It is a decision I might not have made some years ago. I am not sure that a mother living with her son and daughter-in-law is a recipe for perfect domestic harmony. New wives must have dominion in their own households, and I fear that I will be too apt to interfere given my own experience as a mother and manager of a household and, perhaps more significantly, at Allingsford. Still, I will make the best of it.'

'I am sure that you will. I cannot imagine anyone more competent. Your son and his wife are very lucky. You will miss Allingsford, I think?'

'Yes. I was content with my life there. I was independent; I served a good cause, and earned my own income. I had a true respect for myself, and felt proud.'

'That is gratifying to hear. Though you do sound quite regretful?'

'In some ways, I am, but it was time to go. I could no longer be easy in myself.'

Indeed, I feel a little sorry for Mrs Christie. She was so formidable. Now she looks like a wounded bird. She seems relieved in some way, as if of some burden, but also weaker and even, perhaps, a little frightened.

'I am very sorry to hear it. Is that because of the terrible things that took place?'

'Yes. And I have not been able to speak. To say what I wanted to say.'

'Ah, yes; you had to maintain your decorum all that time whilst working alongside Mr Jones.'

'Yes. Well, no, not quite.'

'Oh? Would you like to say more, Mrs Christie?'

'I, I cannot. It is such a burden to bear.'

Her colour comes and goes. This is dreadful; I had not anticipated seeing her like this. I hope she is not on the verge of some kind of nervous collapse; she is of a certain age, after all. I am so glad of the comforting presence of Mrs Hopkinson.

'It might do you good to relieve yourself of it. I assure you that I am discretion itself.'

'No, it cannot be. May God forgive me for my sins.'

Mrs Hopkinson gently pours her more tea, and presses a biscuit into her hand. Then she puts one of her stout arms on Mrs Christie's shoulder, and a few tears actually drop from the latter's eyes. This is dreadful.

'Do excuse me a moment,' I say, getting up, nodding to Mrs Hopkinson and leaving the room.

I return ten minutes later. Mrs Hopkinson is sat in my chair, holding Mrs Christie's hand, who seems a little more peaceful. 'There, there, dearie,' Mrs Hopkinson says a few times, before getting up, smiling at us both and taking her leave. God bless Mrs Hopkinson. It is not quite appropriate for my char to be so familiar with a guest of mine; still, I really think that it was the right thing in this instance. One must not be too rigid about these matters. And the more I think upon it, the more I have come to realise that Mrs Hopkinson is quite the angel.

I manage a little more conversation with Mrs Christie about her work at the asylum and her life in general.

As she is preparing to depart, she says, 'Mr Mortimer, I am mortified by my unseemly behaviour, and yet, I find now that I cannot help it. My will is collapsing. I hope that you will not judge me. Indeed, I feel that you may understand, perhaps being a little prone in that direction yourself.'

I am shocked, and my face must show it.

'Oh, do forgive me, sir, if I offended you.'

'No, no, not at all, Mrs Christie.'

'It is just that I noticed when you were at the asylum that you seemed to have fits of distraction, and then today you are displaying a slight involuntary movement of the right side of your mouth and cheek.'

I put my hand to my cheek, and can feel a movement.

'I am so sorry for my impertinence, sir,' she continues. 'It is as well that I have left the asylum for I must be seeing signs of mental incapacity everywhere I go. I must keep a check upon myself in my new life or I will greatly confuse and alarm those around me.'

'Pray, do not think of it again, Mrs Christie. And, please, do let me solicit a private carriage to take you onto your new home in Surrey, at my expense. It is the very least I can do for you kindly incommoding yourself to call upon me and share some of your life experience.'

I step out to arrange this while Mrs Hopkinson waits with Mrs Christie.

When she leaves, she is all gratefulness and begins to weep again. Really, this whole thing is so unforeseen and quite heartbreaking.

What could she mean about my fits of distraction at the asylum? I was very preoccupied with Jones, I suppose, as I had reason to be. And I was full of fear in that place, and ever thinking of my dearest mother. That is enough to make anyone a little fretful and preoccupied.

And then, naturally there was my darling. Darling Titania. Darling Tatty. That was a little pet name for her they used sometimes at the asylum. Darling Tatty. My batty Tatty. Ha. I keep writing to her. Just one letter a week. I am trying not to rush her, and am being very moderate. Though I may have written two last week. She has not yet responded. She is counselling me in patience, and rightly so. How she governs me, and all for my good, even though she is not here with me. Tatty, Tatty, I am so batty, for you.

As to my facial twitch, I confess that it has been

mentioned by other people. Sometimes I can feel it physically but much of the time I do not think I notice it happening. Some of my chaps at the paper rather teased me about it but then became very gentle with me. The other night, I heard a filthy whore call me 'that twitchy cove'.

I return to my comfortable chair while Mrs Hopkinson prepares me a bit of dinner. I think of poor Mrs Christie and burst into tears.

CHAPTER 27

Nan Carter

I'M FEELING A bit sick with nerves. Tonight, I'm seeing Harry Visconti, manager of the Shakespeare Music Hall. It turns out that Connie has started walking out with him, and she's persuaded him to see me. It's unlikely that he'd suddenly book me as a performer; I'll have to start again somewhere smaller and less central. Still, it's Mr Harry Visconti himself, and I can't help but quake a bit.

Connie and I have managed to see a good few acts, in theatres, clubs and taverns, over the past few months. I hope I can match them, if not do better. In the asylum, I spent most of my time thinking about my reason for being there, and then how to get out. But there were occasional moments when my mind wandered to my hoped-for future, and I would try and think about a new music hall act. I was stumped at first, wondering what on earth could inspire me in that place. Then it struck me that I could base the act on what I was actually doing, pretending to be a mad woman. It all came quite quickly after that and it was such a relief and an escape to lose myself in that, either practicing in my head, or sometimes, even, in my ward in the middle of the night.

Nel, ma and I are sat round the table at home having a nip of wine. The floor is covered in all sorts of fabrics, bits and pieces. There are washed-out bits of silk, velvet, lace, muslin, ribbons, tassels, bows, braid, buttons, stockings, garters, and a variety of butterflies, birds and insects that make up quite the menagerie. Ma and Connie have been building up a stock while I've been away, and we've added it to since my return. It feels like we've been to every OldClo man, slop-seller and market in London. Ma hasn't looked this alive in a long time; she's waving a bit of violet ribbon in one hand and a butterfly ornament in the other. I think she's a little tipsy.

Nel and ma are wonders with the needle. Ma still takes in a bit of piece work now and again when she can manage it. Nel doesn't mind taking care of our needs at home but hated having to do it to earn her bread. She used to supplement her income with some gentleman friends – as did I – and found that she'd rather risk violence and the pox doing only that than continue to endure pain, misery and grovelling servitude in a dressmaker's.

Nel hasn't forgiven me. But she sometimes forgets

that she hasn't, and I have brief experiences of my old Nelly. She's agreed to come tonight; she couldn't resist the chance of free champagne, I'm sure, and she loves Connie.

'Are you sure you can't see any scars?' I ask my mother and sister, staring at myself anxiously in the cracked mirror hung on the living place wall. I've been using lemon juice to fade the skin a bit, and then olive oil to soften it. I think I look well enough, but I need reassurance. I'm wearing a bright blue silk dress with short puff sleeves and cut low on the shoulder, so my skin is very much on display.

'You look fresher than a bunch of spring flowers from Covent Garden, Nan, and ten times as pretty,' says ma.

I look to Nel, who doesn't have a mother's partiality, and she smiles and nods, if a little begrudgingly, to agree. We no longer have any curling irons, but wet rags overnight have done a good-enough job, and Nel assures me that dress improvers are no longer considered necessary as a more form-fitting shape is fashionable. I've made my own hair rat, or piece, from the hair left in my comb over the past month, and with that in place and a little square felt hat in scarlet covered in pigeon feathers I look quite the dazzler.

'See, Ma, not too much paint,' I say, pointing at the bit of home-made lip and cheek rouge and powder Nel has dabbed on me. Ma's a bit old-fashioned like that. In her day, only blatant and brazen whores wore face paint

– and she could never think of us in that way – and lots of folk still think that. But you have to enhance yourself a bit in the entertainment business. People want an escape from their drab lives. Ma tries to look disapproving but can only smile. Her eyes are bright tonight, and not only with the wine; she's clearly so happy to have all this life and colour around her.

I put on my old boots, warm jacket and muffler, which spoils the look a bit, but I don't want to catch my death and add to ma's troubles. Nel does the same and we're ready to go, ma telling us to enjoy ourselves but to take special care, as she always does. We've packed a bag with the costume and props for my act, though I might not get the chance to show it to Mr Visconti this evening.

'Are you sure I look well, Nel? And my scars have quite gone?' I ask as we walk, trying to tread daintily amongst the usual horseshit, dust and vegetable refuse. I'm not usually the nervous type, but this evening my stomach is jumping around like fleas in a pit.

Nel pats my left hand. 'Oh Lord, Nan, stop fishing for compliments.'

'Sorry,' I say, grateful for the hand pat, at least.

We arrive at the Shakespeare and are shown through to the bar.

'Nel, Nan!' shouts Connie from a table in the corner across the room.

We hurry over and she jumps up to give us both a hug. I notice some of the customers eyeing her bosom, though she doesn't stand for any insolence and, as Harry's girl, most men know better than to try and maul at her.

'Look at you tonight, Nan,' says Con. 'You're quite the stunner.'

'Aren't I just,' I say, laughing, and Nel rolls her eyes at Connie.

'But sit down, sit down, ladies,' Connie says, 'champagne all round.'

'What a treat,' says Nel, as we take our seats.

'Oh, it's nothing but champagne, champagne, champagne in this business,' says Connie, the dimples flashing in her plump pink cheeks. 'Well, for some people at least.'

She picks up the opened bottle and splashes some of the pale, gold liquid into two slim glasses for Nel and me, and I feel dizzy with excitement already.

'Thanks so much for this, Con,' I say, 'and for coming into work on your night off.'

'Oh, it's nothing. I love being on the other side of the bar. And Harry's happy to advise new acts. He likes to keep up with the times. It's easy to get stale, he says.'

Harry started his career very young as a music hall performer. He was once known as the Flying Viscount due to his comical dance routine involving very long leaping steps with his very long bandy legs. When his glitter started to fade and people stopped humming his tunes, rather than take to drink, despair and the workhouse, he became a music hall chairman, using his booming voice and poetic patter to introduce other acts.

Then he reinvented himself again as an impresario, and he's a successful one at that.

'Just a quick warning about Harry,' continues Connie. 'He's going through one of his melancholy phases just now so don't take it personally if he doesn't seem impressed with you. I'm used to him now and try not to mind it. It soon passes.'

Just as Connie finishes speaking, the man himself appears. Connie looks up and smiles at someone behind my head, then gets up to kiss him.

'Harry, dear, this is Nan Carter and her sister, Nel.'

I turn round and begin to get up, but Mr Visconti stops me.

'Sit down, ladies; do not trouble yourself. I'm honoured to meet any friends of Connie's.'

His voice is very deep and rather nasal. He kisses my left hand then moves over to kiss Nel's right hand, before sitting himself at the table, his long legs flayed out to his left, ready to trip up passing customers.

'Take a drink, Harry,' says Con, picking up the bottle again and emptying it into a glass for him.

'Thank ye, dear,' he says, looking at her warmly; they do seem very fond of each other.

I don't think he's much above thirty years old, but he looks older. He has large ears, a long nose, a wide, mobile mouth and short tufts of red hair, but his most noticeable feature is his huge brown eyes, which at the moment are looking extremely mournful. He's still got the flash of a chairman, sporting a large waxed moustache, diamond cuff links and shirt studs, rings on his fingers and a crimson silk handkerchief.

'So, what do you think of our music hall?' he asks. He speaks very slowly, his words drawn out as if each one costs him a huge effort to deliver, and life is not worth the candle.

'It's dazzling,' says Nel, in her soft, pretty way, smiling and looking round the bar, then back at Mr Visconti.

He nods at her, gratified, and turns to me.

'I couldn't agree more,' I say, 'and I'm thrilled to be here.'

'You have performed before, Miss Carter, I believe?' he says.

'Oh, yes, at a few smaller venues a few years ago, but I became unwell, sadly, so had to take a break.'

I glance at Connie a little nervously, but she smiles at me encouragingly.

'Well, you certainly have the beauty, dear,' says Visconti, 'though, as I am sure you know, it takes a lot more than that. One of the best and most successful acts I knew – Mabel Ball was her stage name – was as ugly as sin.'

We're all silent for a few seconds, then Visconti chuckles, displaying very good, long teeth, which turns into a loud laugh. Relieved, we all start laughing too.

'Well, I am very happy to advise you on your act,' he continues. 'Connie will bring you through to my office in two hours' time, and we can use the props room. Not as good as the stage but it will give me an idea.'

'I can't thank you enough, Mr Visconti,' I say.

Visconti gets up slowly, nods at me, kisses Connie on the head, and walks away, dragging his legs as if they are filled with iron bars.

'Poor dear,' says Connie, looking after him with concern, then turning back to me and pressing my hand, her pretty, green eyes lit up. 'Well done, Nan; he liked you, I'm sure, even with his low mood.'

We smile and laugh and raise our glasses. Even Nel is looking a bit pleased for me. We spend the next couple of hours like proper lushes. I'm desperate to talk to Connie about Mr Mortimer and his endless letters, and not least the recent hanging of Cedric Jones. But we can't do any of this in front of Nel, and I can't really complain about that. Finally, Connie looks over at the clock behind the bar and says, 'It's time to see Harry'.

My stomach jumps a little, but the champagne is damping the worst of my nerves and I'm ready.

CHAPTER 28

IT DIDN'T GO well. Or, at least, I got what I'd pretended I wanted – advice. Really, I'd wanted him to hire me on the spot and say that it was the best act he'd ever seen.

He said that my act was too risky, for a start, and that it would close any respectable theatre down. But if I made it respectable, it wouldn't quite work. He did give me the name of a man who runs a somewhat smaller, more disreputable place in Whitechapel, who might give me a chance. If I could build up a following, then who knows what might happen?

I'm talking to Nel about it the next morning. We're sat at the table in our nightshifts, our hair wild and loose, our eyes a bit red, our skin a bit grey. Ma laughs and calls us her two darling scarecrows, before stepping outside to call on Herr Konig. We're also somewhat parched from drinking too much champagne. Still, that's not a problem we have to deal with much these days, so it's a price worth paying. I've drained a ginger beer and two mugs of cocoa. I feel a little tearful, too; no doubt, that's also partly the consequence of last night's thirst.

Nel is impatient. She's tapping the long fingers of her right hand on the table, as she does when she's irritated. 'So, Nan, the famous Harry Visconti said you were talented, and that there's certainly hope for the future, but that you'd need time to make your way a bit, feel out an audience, attract them and so on?'

I nod.

'So why are you being so self-pitying? This is your dream; there is hope. Just get on with it.'

Lord, she's brutal. Right, but brutal. She used to deliver harsh wisdom wrapped up in a silken glove. Now, she just goes for my jugular with a gnarled, bloodied hand. I start to cry in earnest. I'm not sure I can take any more of this raw honesty.

'Nelly, you don't love me anymore,' I say, aware that I'm whining and sounding just as self-pitying as she thinks me.

Nel looks at me sternly with her dark blue eyes, then softens and sighs.

'I can't go on like this,' I say. 'Can't you forgive me? Nelly, I'm so sorry. I missed you so much when I was away. Didn't you miss me?'

'Oh, Nancy Carter,' she says. 'Of course I missed you, I love you, and I can forgive you. But you've got to show me and ma that you mean business. You need to earn some money, for a start. For my part, Mr Mortimer won't last much longer, and then what will we do? Did you think that you'd become an overnight sensation and move us all into the Savoy?'

I smile sheepishly. 'I suppose I did, just a little.'

'Well, maybe you will, one day. But in the meantime, you know what you need to do. You haven't brought half a penny into this house since you came back. You've been swanning round town like you haven't got a care in the world, wasting precious money on ribbons and glitter, and frolicking round here like it's a ladies' dance academy.'

'I had to prepare for my act,' I say, a bit pathetically. 'You're right.' I cry a little. 'I will work, I promise. I'll make everything up to you and ma. I'll shovel shit; I'll collect pure; I'll scavenge in dustheaps.'

Nel raises one neat eyebrow and laughs. 'You'll really collect pure, dogshit, for us?'

I laugh too. She's coming back to me, just a little bit more. 'Well, maybe not pure pure, exactly, but certainly horseshit.'

She laughs again. 'That will be a sight worth seeing.'

'It will. I'll wear my best stage outfit while I'm doing it, with a top hat and red bloomers. I'll be the most dazzling purveyor of horseshit in London.'

I reach out across the table and take her hands.

'Seriously, though; I know I've talked about becoming a sensation and all that stuff and nonsense, and I'm really going to try do that. But I'll also do anything to help look after us, anything at all. I mean it Nel. I'll work and you and ma can put your feet up. You can have your own water closets and bathtubs, with the softest, most luxurious towels, the most expensive perfumed oils, pomades, soaps and lotions, in the world. And a whole army of servants.'

'I'm glad to hear it. I've acquired some fine tastes during my time with Harris Mortimer.'

I wince slightly but manage to keep my facial expression bland and pleasant.

'Honestly, Nan,' Nel continues. 'He's the best thing that's happened to us all in a long time. Not in a sweetheart's story kind of way, or anything like that. It's just so easy. I see him once a week usually – though he's been away for a while recently investigating some story in a Hampshire lunatic asylum, of all places – and he takes me for a nice meal or to the theatre. Then we go to a lodging house and stay over for the night. Nothing dreadful happens. He even insists on using a rubber. Can you believe that? I wouldn't have to use the sponge, but he wants me to do that too as an extra precaution. He talks a lot about cleanliness and purity, actually, which is a little queer in the circumstances – he could be a peculiar husband for someone one day – but it suits me. Sometimes, he doesn't even want to do the deed; he just wants to talk. And he's so free-handed with money and gifts. I've even managed to put by a bit of money for when it ends.'

'I'm so glad, Nel.'

Oh, I hope I haven't brought that time forward.

Nel's had a couple of bad experiences with her gentleman friends in the past. She still limps a little from when she was hit and pushed over, and she's got scars on her back from when one of them thought it would be an uncommon lark to play with a knife. What with these, and her spine trouble, she's hardly had it easy. I feel another rush of tenderness towards her and lift her hands to kiss them.

'Thank you so much for looking after us, Nelly.'

Nel smiles at me; it's almost one of her old sweet smiles.

'Does ma know about Mr Mortimer?' I ask, tentatively.

'No; well, I haven't told her in straight language. I just tell her that I'm spending the evening with friends and staying over with one of them. But she knows.'

I nod. Ma's not stupid. She knows that sometimes me and Nel have friendships with men, and they give us a little money and gifts in gratitude for the pleasure of our company. After all, we have to eat. But she would never think of us as fallen or impure, or even as whores.

Nel looks a bit wistful. 'Nan, don't you want to get married and have a family, one day?'

I think for a moment. 'I don't know. Possibly, one day, but I have things to do first.'

'I want to, and soon. But how can I ever meet anyone respectable? I'm getting older; I'm seven and twenty, already well past the marrying age according to some. You should see some of the looks of pity I get sometimes. And then, Nan, what if I'm damaged inside, after the life I've led, and could never get in the family way?'

'Oh, Nelly.'

What can I say to comfort her? I look at her handsome heart-shaped face and notice again how tired she looks, and not just from last night. She's only three years older than me but at the moment, I have to admit, she looks older. She must be fretting all the time and has likely been fretting all these years. That's enough to steal anyone's youth away.

'Ellen Carter,' I say, 'there must be hundreds of respectable gents setting their cap at you, only waiting for you to give them the nod. You just need to pay more attention. Why, you're the loveliest, sweetest woman in London.'

Nel grins. 'Hardly sweet, at the moment.'

'Well, you've got a bit of spice, along with the sugar, in there too, just now. And we both know that's my fault.'

Nel squeezes my hands. 'Oh, Nan, why do you always say the right thing, just when I'm set on being really angry with you?'

I get up to hug her tight, and she lets me.

CHAPTER 29

'OH, CONNIE, WHAT should I do?'

'Well, you could marry him, and that would solve all your money worries, at least.'

'I'd certainly be earning it, spending the rest of my life pretending to be Titania Rosetti. And you'd have a permanent, walk-on part as Miss Constance Millais, the woman with the strangest voice in the country.'

'Oh, it wasn't that bad.'

'Ain't it hot in here? I'm feeling a bit bilious. I wouldn't want to peach on her,' I mimic.

Con giggles. 'I was truly terrible, wasn't I?'

'You don't even act or speak like that normally.'

'I know. I don't know what came over me. I was trying so hard to act like a lady. I was telling Harry about it and he laughed so much. He said I should turn it into an act. I don't know how you did it for all that time. It shows that you're a born actress and I'm best suited to what I already do, serving drinks.'

'And eating cakes.'

'Oh yes, I've a talent for that.'

Me and Connie and are sat in her room, snuggled up in a blanket, drinking cheap cha that doesn't taste quite right, and looking at Mortimer's latest letter. They started off all politeness and consideration and have descended into this one, which is so emotionally strained it would put Ophelia herself to shame. I haven't responded to any of them. I thought it might encourage him, but it seems to have had the opposite effect.

'Maybe write one letter,' suggests Con, 'being very cold and clear. And then leave it well alone. That's all you can do.'

'I will. I do feel bad because he did help me. But this isn't normal. And I can't go on feeling bad for ever.'

'You can't, and you don't owe him anything. He's just a really queer cove; I saw that. He's one of those men who'd want to keep you at home in a cabinet, a pretty ornament for display.'

'You're right. Much like Cedric Jones, in a way. But Jones would have kept me in a specimen jar and Mortimer would keep me wrapped in silk and velvet. It's frightening.'

'They both make me shiver.' Connie suits the action to the word, then pauses. 'And what about the other one?'

I try to look innocent. Con tries to look stern, which she never can quite achieve with that angelic face of hers.

'Nancy Carter, have you been writing to Mr Matthew Friend?'

I nod.

'Oh, Lord save us.'

'I know, I know. But his letters are so delightful. And he sends me little poems.'

'Another bleedin' poet. Just what you need. And you write back as Titania?'

'Yes, sort of. I'm getting a bit muddled.'

'I'm not surprised!'

'And I may have agreed to meet him when he comes to London next.'

Connie puts her head in her hands and tugs hard at the curls on her forehead, then looks up. 'But, Nan, promise me you'll be careful. Can you trust anyone associated with that asylum? What if he's another queer one? What if he's a murderer?'

'Well, three rum coves at once would be an achievement, even for me.'

I grin and pinch Con's cheek. 'I'd better get going.' I swallow the rest of my tea and get up. 'I'm on again tonight.'

'Well done for persevering with this, Nan; I know it's not easy.'

'Thanks, Con. It's horrible but it's money and experience.'

'It'll all be worth it, dear.'

'I hope so.'

I bow to the audience. If audience isn't too dignified a word for them. I've got through another performance of my act. I'm so hot and I'm feeling a bit sick. The smell of this place at the end of an evening would knock a tanner off his feet. Sweat, grog, piss, vomit, and the stale, musky tang of bodies getting over-familiar with each other in corners. Lord save me.

A man reaches out to pinch my leg. 'Show us your drawers, my girl; better still, what's underneath them.'

'We'll have less of that!' bawls Sailor Bill, the manager of this fine establishment.

Bill, a stout, raven-haired, bulbous-nosed former sailor from Liverpool, could project his guttural growls across the Atlantic if he was minded to do so. And the clientele of the Parrot and Bottle know better than to disobey him. The Poxy Parrot, as it's known to its less respectful customers, is an old-fashioned public, with a small room on the side used for entertainments. It's rough, by most standards, I suppose, but just manages to stay on the right side of respectability.

I step down from the small stage area to make my way gingerly over the broken-glass strewn, slippery floor to Bill. I'm waylaid briefly by one of those toffs who like to tour the East End when they're not touring Greece and Italy.

'Miss Carter. May I present you with this rose; a rose for a rose, ha ha.'

I take the rose and smile sweetly at the thin, shiny faced, lisping fellow in front of me. He barely looks old enough to have ventured out from his mother's apron strings.

A few more young gentlemen of a similar mould

beg kisses on the cheek; I let them kiss my hand. Finally, I get to Bill. He hands over my paltry wages, which I pocket, trying to feel grateful.

'Keep your pecker up, Miss Nancy. You're doing well.'

'Am I?' I ask.

'Course you are. The house is getting fuller every night. Haven't you noticed?'

I hadn't really. After the first few nights, I've tried to block out the audience.

'And, old girl, you've raised the quality of my clientele. You can't take a step these days without tripping over a member of the Quality. There's not a lot between the ears of these lords, is there? It's like stealing Godfrey's Cordial from a babby. Though I suppose their money's as good as anyone else's, even if it is likely robbed from the meek and the poor who will one day inherit this good earth of ours.'

I can't help but laugh. I think he's exaggerating a bit to cheer me, but I appreciate it. I like Bill. He's a real gent and I feel safe with him, which I wasn't really expecting. I suppose Connie did say that Mr Visconti would never have put me in the hands of a villain.

'Thanks, Bill,' I say, and manage a small, tight smile of goodbye.

Bill escorts me to the back door of the side room.

'Keep yourself safe on the way home, and remember to mention the name of Sailor Bill if anyone threatens trouble.'

'I will, Bill.'

Bill watches me until I'm out of sight. He reminds me of pa a little, which is comforting. Connie says he's got a wife and eight children in Dublin, and two other wives somewhere in America. It wouldn't surprise me if this were true; it wouldn't bother me either.

I step out into the night air with relief, bracing myself for the long walk home. I'm determined not to take cabs; they would eat up my earnings. But it's risky. I wear the top hat from my act and a long black coat, which hopefully suggests to most passersby that I'm just some gent heading home after a night of jollity rather than a lone woman. I've even been propositioned by streetwalkers a couple of times. When I see women like that, I can't help but think, that could be me one day. But I push the thought away. I keep myself erect and on the alert, fighting my tiredness, and hold my right hand on the knife in my pocket, ready to wield it at a moment's notice.

I'm not sure how long I'll be able to keep this up. And even if I do, we still need extra money. I think I'll have a chat with Mr Smith and see if I can pose for a few more photographs. And I could try to find a gentleman friend. One like Mr Mortimer, ironically, who doesn't expect too much. One of those toffs might do. Or maybe Mr Friend? Oh Lord, Nan, pull yourself together. The one good thing from all this is that Nel is nearly coming back to me. She can see how hard I'm trying. She can see how drained and miserable I am when I get home, peel off my stinking costume and scrub myself raw with stale water and carbolic. And she hasn't heard me complain, not once. I can always have my little whine to Con, who doesn't mind. And the next day, I fight my fatigue and am as fresh as I can be as I take ma tea in bed.

I arrive home and Nel is waiting up for me. She hands me a mug of cocoa and a bar of heavenly rose -scented soap, both of which I inhale deeply. She pushes a strand of my foul-smelling hair away from my face, and says, 'Oh Nancy Nan, I don't expect you to kill yourself on our behalf, but thank you for trying'.

CHAPTER 30

Harris Mortimer

SHE HAS SENT me the coldest letter. I cannot credit it. She says that she is determined to remain single for the foreseeable future and that I must find somebody new. She will not respond to any more of my letters. This is more than maidenly hesitancy, I am sure. There must be something going on. I wonder if she has found out that I am not quite pure. I cannot imagine how but then, one never knows. Not that such a revelation should upset her. I am a normal man, after all, and my current mode of life is normal and expected. Still, it may have shocked her delicate sensibilities. Ladies, as they should be, can be terribly sheltered from the everyday facts of life.

Happily, I am seeing Nel this evening and will put an end to things. In fact, I have been meaning to do this for some time. Ellen – I believe that is her full Christian name – is such a good clean girl; she is pretty and gentle, and in another walk of life might have made a respectable lady. But she is a creature of the lower classes, and a girl no better than she should be, and the whole affair is not very savoury, when all is said and done. Additionally, I hardly get value from the transaction of late; I seem to be lacking in enthusiasm in a certain area.

We are sat in a cosy, old-fashioned chophouse – the finest of its type, very clean – the sort of place I like best; sadly, they have mostly been displaced by those showy types of restaurants that I find quite vulgar. It is a fitting farewell to Nel; after all, she has served me well, and saved me, mostly, from the worst excesses of Cremorne and Paradise Wharf.

'How are you, Mr Mortimer?' she asks. She does not use my first name; I like to preserve the dignities of rank. Of course, I call her by her Christian name, or rather its abbreviated version.

'Quite well, on the whole, Nel, I thank you. I am very caught up in my work, however, and so a little tired and distracted.'

'You do look a little tired, sir, if you do not mind me saying so. I have been continuing to follow the story of that evil man in the newspapers. It is so shocking, and you must have been very preoccupied with it all. I hope that you will become a little easier now that he is gone from the world?'

Nel can read, speaks very nicely, and is really quite intelligent for one of her sort. I do not mind unburdening my mind to her. It is quite relieving.

'Oh yes, certainly. But, in many ways, I will be busier than ever. There is so much more to write about with regard to this great question of lunacy.'

A sharp-looking waiter appears, a clean white napkin slung over his left arm.

'Good evening, madam, good evening, sir,' he says in a nasal voice that sounds half-cockney, half-Anglo-Italian. He proceeds to rapidly deliver the bill of fare. 'Just ready, we have roast beef, boiled beef, roast haunch of mutton, boiled pork, roast veal, roast ham, salmon and shrimp sauce, pigeon-pie and rump-steak pudding.'

'I think a little salmon, then the roast beef and roast ham would be just the thing,' I say, speaking very slowly and pausing between groups of words. 'With your usual side dishes. Oh, and a bottle of that good Burgundy of yours.'

The waiter gives me a look of painful toleration. 'Very well, sir; coming up, sir.'

He disappears, and I smile at my companion.

'Are you quite well, Mr Mortimer?' asks Nel. 'You seem to be having a little trouble with your mouth. I have noticed it for some time. Perhaps you need to have a tooth extracted?'

'I am quite well, dear girl.' I touch my cheek. 'Perhaps I do have a problem with a tooth. I must get it looked at.'

'Yes, sir; do take care of yourself.'

'I will, Nel, just for you.' I am feeling rather indulgent and a little nostalgic this evening. 'It is partly because I am so preoccupied with my work that I believe that this is the right time for us to end our little arrangement. I must now commit my heart and soul to this thing that has become the business of my life.'

Nel's face droops. 'I am sorry to hear it, sir. But I can understand your reasons; I confess I have been expecting it for a while. I have been very grateful for our time together and all your kindness.' She forces a smile. 'But all good things must come to an end.'

She really is a good girl, is Nel. I smile at her warmly, pleased with her response.

'I thought you might like to have a little treat,' I say, 'a form of fond farewell, as it were. We shall have our good dinner here, then take in a play.'

'That sounds lovely,' Nel says.

The waiter appears to briskly set down the wine and two glasses. I take a sip of the burgundy, nod appreciatively, and he hurries away.

We thoroughly enjoy our repast, which is very good, though my appetite is a little off of late. I am imbibing the burgundy rather swiftly, however, and find that I have called for a third bottle before I know it. I am now feeling a moderate sense of wellbeing, for surely this is the right thing to do, and Titania will love me at last.

'Will you not tell me something about your work, sir?' asks Nel. 'It might relieve your mind and heart a little.'

'Oh, it is far too clever and serious for pretty little Nel.'

'I would not mind hearing it. I have read things in

the newspapers, as you can imagine. I might not fully understand it, but it would be pleasant to hear it from a professional man.'

'Yes, there is much nonsense and sensationalism in the common press.'

'The main thing I cannot comprehend, Mr Mortimer, is why anyone could commit such terrible deeds.'

'You are not alone, Ellen. It is a weighty topic that even our finest minds will struggle with and dispute over. I sometimes think that Jones had a most terrible form of madness, and then I start to wonder if the devil got to him. I never believed in such things before, having kept my God at rather a distance, reserved for church on Sundays, and so on.' I smile to myself, and look at Nel indulgently. What am I doing talking about the mysteries of theology to a girl, and a common girl at that? And I am finding the effort of putting so many sentences together rather tiring. 'Well, in short, I suppose we will never really know.'

'You must be so glad, at least, that you do not have to return to that dreadful asylum place?'

'Well, yes and no. It is not as terrible as one might think. Indeed, I was happily surprised and intend to write many positive pieces about such places.' I pause. 'And then, you know, there is another reason, connected to the asylum, why I must end our liaison,' I announce, feeling very confidential.

'Oh?'

Nel's pretty blue eyes are wide, and her small mouth

forms the shape of the sound. She is not unlike my love, in some ways, when I look at her through half-closed eyes, though, naturally, no one could compare to Titania. I gulp back another glass of the delicious burgundy, then lean across the table, tapping my nose with my right forefinger.

'I am in love,' I whisper, then giggle. Did I just giggle?

Nel looks a little surprised, then smiles. 'But that is delightful news, sir.'

'Is it not? I am in love with an angel sent down from heaven for me alone.'

'How wonderful.'

'Titania; that is her name. Miss Titania Rosetti.'

'Tis a very pretty, poetic name. Like something from a fairy story, almost.'

'Yes, indeed; she is a very pretty, poetic person; she is my Ophelia.'

'I am very glad for you, Mr Mortimer.'

I grin at her, then touch my cheek again. I think it is twitching. I really must see a surgeon. 'I met her at the asylum, you know.' I look round quickly, realising that my voice has become a little loud.

'Oh?'

She looks shocked.

'She is not mad, you understand,' I say, keeping my voice lower this time. 'Or rather, she was mad, but is no longer so.'

'I see. Well, if you are sure, sir. I wish her well; we can all go through queer times; life can be hard.'

'You are so right, Nel; your compassion does you great honour. I fear that I am going a little mad myself with my love for her.'

My right cheek is twitching frantically. At the same time, the whole right side of my head feels like it is frozen.

Nel smiles gently. 'It can sometimes take a person that way, I believe. But it will all settle down.'

I feel a tear roll down my cheek. Nel raises an eyebrow for a moment before putting out her right hand to pat both of mine.

'Don't take on so, Mr Mortimer; don't fret yourself; it will all come right. You're just overtired. Poor dear, poor, old dearie.'

I sniff and reach into my waistcoat for my pocket watch.

'I think that we are too late for the theatre,' I say, 'and, in any case, I fear that I am not quite fit company for it. Shall we adjourn to the lodgings?'

'Of course, Mr Mortimer; right you are.'

The waiter – insolent fellow - gives Nel a sardonic look as I scramble for my pocketbook, drop it, pick it up, and finally pay the reckoning. We bundle up and step out into the night; spring is here but the nights are still chilly, and it is raining. I trip a couple of times. Dear oh dear, I am feeling quite weak; I must be ill. My right leg particularly cannot seem to take my weight. But Nel, dear girl, seems to right me.

We are in our usual lodging room in Covent Garden, very decent and clean – which, indeed, it should be, for the price they charge – as well as pleasantly warm from the dying embers of a fire. Two glasses of wine sit on a slightly blackened, silver tray on the bureau. I quickly drink one of them, but my face is twitching again and the wine drips down my chin. Then the glass seems to slip from my hand and crashes onto the floorboards. I stare at it, then ignore it, and sit down upon the bed. I turn away from Nel as she completes her own ritual. I like to maintain the dignity of both of us; I am a gentleman, after all, and do not hold with deviant or rough behaviour towards the female sex, even those of the lowest sort. I remove the rubber from my pocket and place it on the bed. Tis newly washed, of course; I maintain the strictest cleanliness in these matters. I even do the job myself; I fear poor Mrs Hopkinson, as obliging as she is, might draw the line at such a task.

Now, I must undress but I do not seem to have the will. Nel comes over to me, clad only in her white corset, shift and scarlet stockings.

'Come, Mr Mortimer,' she says, softly, 'let me help you with your clothes.'

She stands right in front of me and takes off my top hat, which I had forgotten I was still wearing, and places it on a nearby chair. Then she helps me out of my great coat, with a struggle, which has now left wet patches on the coverlet from the rain. My dress coat comes off fairly easily. Now Nel attempts to pull off my muddy boots, which appears to be no easy feat. She falls backwards in the attempt and sits on the floor, laughing. She gets up and takes off my shirt but is unable to remove the stiff collar, which is pinned to it at the back. So now I am wearing my vest with a starched collar and my shirt hanging down my back, as if I have attempted to hang myself from a sitting position.

Nel is trying to stop laughing, I can tell, but she cannot help herself. I fear that my dignity is at stake, but her laugh is so infectious – a sort of light, gurgling chuckle – that I allow myself to let go of my pride for a moment, and laugh too. I am so tired, no doubt exacerbated by the warm room, and my head is beginning to ache. I laugh loudly this time; it is quite relieving. I lie back on the bed, my legs still clad in my trousers and one of my boots dangling over the edge.

Nel manages to lift my legs up onto the bed and turns my body slightly so that I am lying in a more comfortable position. She pulls at the coverlet to get it free from the bits of my body that are lying on it, then throws it over me and gently tucks me under it. Sitting on the bed next to me, she pats my heated, damp head with her cold hand, and wipes away some tears that I'm now shedding; she is shivering a little.

'Never mind, Mr Mortimer,' she says. 'Do not fret, dear, do not take on so. You're suffering from exhaustion; that's what it is. You men must needs work so hard at your professions; it really must take its toll on your health. All you need is a good night's sleep and you'll be right as rain. Take your well-earned rest, now, sir. There, there; there, there.'

I smile at Nel weakly, then close my eyes. She really is a good girl. She continues to whisper quietly and to smooth my hair as I drift off to sleep.

CHAPTER 31

I MAKE MY FAREWELL to a fresh and neatly dressed Nel, paying her twice the usual amount. My head is aching, my eyes sore and my mouth dry. I call the young boots to procure me paper, ink and some strong coffee. I must write a response to Titania; I cannot be at my ease until I have done so.

The boots, sulky and servile at the same time, returns with a coffee pot and a chipped cup, and places it onto the small bureau at which I am sat. The smell only enhances my nausea, but I take the pot, hands shaking, and pour myself half a cup full. What should I say to my love? I must be as gentle as I can be. I will simply say that she cannot know her own mind. I will give her all the time she needs, but she must not cut me off, for she would be doing herself, as well as myself, a great disservice. If only I knew where she lived. I do not think it can be that far away if she corresponds via the post office at Charing Cross.

The boots knocks again and delivers my paper, pen and inkpot. His grubby neckerchief is covered with ink. I am not sure what the boy has been doing with it, eating it? I press a few coins into his greasy palm and am glad to get rid of him. I sigh, force down some mouthfuls of gritty coffee, and apply myself to my task.

There, it is done. I am not needed at the office today, Saturday, thankfully, so I think I will take a little wander down to the post office at Charing Cross to post my letter. I get up and catch sight of myself in the glass. Stubbled, dishevelled, red-eyed; not a handsome sight. Never mind; I will put myself right when I get home to Chelsea.

It is a mild, pleasant day. I can even hear a few birds struggling to chirp over the general London din. It is the 15th of April, I note from a newspaper on a nearby stand. The year is running away from me. I do not seem to have fulfilled the promise I felt at its commencement, and have wandered off course.

I walk very slowly down the Strand, my right leg dragging. I must dig out that old cane left to me by my grandfather. I am burning up. Perhaps I have a fever? I stare intently at passing ladies – on foot, in carriages, on buses – with auburn hair, but there are no toffee-coloured eyes. Where are you, Titania? I arrive at Charing Cross and post my letter. Perhaps I will rest here for a short time. I sit myself down on a bit of wall and let my eyes dart over the crowd. Perhaps she will appear with her idiosyncratic companion, Miss Millais. I have been wondering about her. She was really rather queer.

I am now concerned that she may not be who she says she is, and has been imposing on my love in some way.

I am sleepy. I feel dreadful, as if the world is closing in upon me. I want to lie in a cocoon of silk, with Titania pressing a cool compress on my brow. A whinnying horse decides to deposit its mess on the pavement nearby and I vomit onto the street. I am looked at with disgust. I must go; this is very unseemly. I force myself up and flag a hansom.

'Jolly evening, sir?' says the brown-toothed driver, opening the door of his vehicle for me. 'Eaten something that's disagreed with you? Perhaps one oyster too many?'

Really, Londoners are so insolent. I sit in the cab, praying that my stomach will not suddenly deposit more of its contents. The ride is even bumpier than usual; the satirical driver is doing it deliberately, I can tell. We arrive at my home in Chelsea at last. The driver argues with me about the fare. I do not have the energy to fight my case, which he can tell, and I give in.

'Mr Mortimer, sir; I am so glad to see you,' says Mrs Hopkinson, as I hobble through the door to my rooms. 'I just thought I'd call in today, though it's not my day. I hope you don't object. I was a bit fretful about you. And, oh, dear, you look quite the fright, if you don't mind my saying so. You're not looking after yourself properly, sir; I've told you before. Come now.'

She helps me out of my coat, and presses me into my comfortable chair.

'Will you have a peck to eat?'

My nausea rises at the question, but I also feel a sort of hollowness that might benefit from some sustenance. 'Perhaps just a little something, thank you. Nothing too heavy; I am feeling a little unwell.'

Mrs Hopkinson fails to disguise a quick grin, flashing her four front teeth, just two at the top right of her mouth and two at the bottom left of it. 'Right you are, sir; and let me bring you a glass of small beer. That can work wonders in these cases, I've found.'

I sit back and close my eyes, so thankful to be home. Mrs Hopkinson bustles quietly in the small kitchen; her presence is rather soothing than otherwise. I manage to drink some of the small beer and indeed, my stomach settles slightly. Mrs Hopkinson helps me to the small dining table and puts a plate of food down in front of me.

'It's just a simple bit of chicken and some boiled potatoes, but it will do you the world of good.'

Mrs Hopkinson leans on the table for a moment, holding her back and wincing.

'Are you quite well, Mrs Hopkinson?'

'Oh, just a few twinges; it's my age, I'm afraid; can't do nothing about that, sir.'

'Well, do take a seat for a moment.'

Mrs Hopkinson is about to protest but winces again and decides to take up my offer, slowly lowering herself into the chair opposite me. 'I do apologise, Mr Mortimer; I won't be a moment.'

I eat my meal slowly. It's very good, as are all the meals she makes for me. I look across at my housekeeper. She is stout and thick of legs; her face is creased and sagging and she has a thin mustachio. I do not like ugly things generally. Perhaps it is the artist within me; I like to have beauty all around. Still, she has very bright blue eyes, which are rather charming. She has been with me five years. I know nothing about her.

'Do you have a Christian name, Mrs Hopkinson?'

'Bless me, sir, I should hope so; what kind of baggage would I be if I didn't have such a thing?'

I smile. 'May I ask what it is?'

She looks shocked. 'Oh, it's Matilda, but everyone calls me Tilly. We were all Marys in our family and so my old ma went and decided to go in for a change, like.'

'Well, Matilda – Tilly - thank you for your care. I am very grateful.'

Mrs Hopkinson looks astounded, then smiles broadly, her red gums on display. 'Oh, it's nothing, sir; a pleasure. You're no trouble at all.'

'Do you happen to know where my old cane is, Mrs Hopkinson?'

'Oh, yes, it's in the bottom drawer of the press near to your bed. I will get it out for you.'

'Thank you. You are quite the wonder.'

She beams again. I put my hand over my mouth to stifle a yawn.

'Well, I really must get some rest now, Mrs Hopkinson.'

'You must really need it, sir. Look at those dark

circles under your eyes. And you speak so slow. And then there's your leg and the side of your face. I hope there ain't nothing distressing you, Mr Mortimer? I know it's not my place to ask, but you seemed so content when you first returned from Hampshire, and now you seem more like a gent who's got on the wrong side of a prize fighter, and had the stuffing knocked out of him.'

I should be offended at Mrs Hopkinson's impertinence, but I find I am not. Perhaps I am just too exhausted today to preserve a proper barrier with my servant. And now the poor dear is weeping a little.

'I'm just so very fretful about you, sir.'

'Do not distress yourself. I do have a few things on my mind, rather,' I say.

I feel that I am speaking more words, but no sound comes out. My mouth opens and closes; silence.

'I fear,' I manage, at last, 'that I may be unlucky in love.'

'You, Mr Mortimer? No. A handsome, eligible gent like you? The ladies round here have been setting their caps at you for years, I assure you, but I don't think you take no heed of them for most of the time.'

Oh dear, this conversation has become a little vulgar. But it is also rather relieving.

'I am afraid that I already have a specific lady in mind, but the object of my desire is proving somewhat elusive.'

'Lusive? That doesn't sound good. Take no notice, sir, I say. She don't deserve you.'

I cannot help but smile.

'But do forgive me for running on,' Mrs Hopkinson continues. 'I'll leave you in peace now and let you get your rest. Just one more thought. You don't seem to have heard from Mr Rockingham for a while. I know a letter from him always brightens you. Perhaps you could write to him. I'm sure he'll give you better counsel than an old bird like me.'

She gets up slowly, wiping away her tears, and pats me on the shoulder. She disappears briefly into my bed-chamber and returns with the old oak cane.

'Here you are, sir. This will help. I'll take my leave now.'

She looks at me for a few moments, trying not to cry again, I am sure, then makes her way to the door. I get up wearily and go to my bed with the help of the stick. It is a relief to lie down.

Mrs Hopkinson is right about Mr Rockingham. Is he not my father figure? I must be honest with him and tell him about Miss Rosetti. And now I think upon it, perhaps I should write to Mr Friend also. He will have access to the records. He might even give me Titania's address. Yes, that is it. And does he not have a sister in London, if I remember rightly? Perhaps we could meet when he is next visiting her; I could get much more information in person. Oh dear, my brain is fevered again; I must write my letters before I can cool it down. I force myself out of bed and make my way to my bureau.

CHAPTER 32

I WAKE UP IN the night, sick with fear. An old hag dressed in black is approaching me. Wild, withered, bearded. Thin lips stretch across rotten teeth. She is a witch, a weird sister. Her yellow eyes and rotten breath are upon me, as she raises her talons to strike.

I am stood in St Luke's church in Chelsea looking across at the painting behind the altar, which depicts the deposition of Christ from the cross. I feel as if I could reach out, take the forward foot of Christ in my hands, and bathe it. I am sore in need of comfort. It was just a dream, but when I woke, my mouth was twitching uncontrollably and I find that my right leg is worse, and I cannot move it forward without great deliberation.

I have started coming to weekly church services again, and sometimes call into the church at other times when it is quiet to sit for a while and refresh my spirit. I remembered the peace I felt, briefly, in the chapel at Allingsford asylum, and that prompted me to come here.

The Sunday morning service has just finished. Now we are exchanging blessings and taking our leave. I nod at the other congregants as I walk slowly down the aisle to the door. After saying goodbye to the rector, I am accosted by the usual selection of mother hens with their chicks, all smiling, fawning and proffering invitations to tea. I think of Mrs Hopkinson. What a wise woman she is. I force myself to be polite, to keep up appearances. I must try not to judge so harshly. My heart is a little softer now and I must be more open. There is only one woman for me – Miss Titania Rosetti – but I must not be disdainful of others. I talk and smile as best I can, and even accept some invitations. Some of them look at me strangely.

Now I am free, and I can go home. I wait only for advice from Mr Rockingham and Mr Friend. It has been a week since I wrote to them. I am elated and anxious to find letters from both when I arrive home. They were mistakenly given to the kindly engraver who resides in rooms in the house next door; one of his boisterous children delivers them.

I sit down in my comfortable chair to read my letters. Mr Friend's is disappointing. He is unable to disclose confidential information. I am embarrassed, and feel very foolish, for having asked. Of course, I could not have expected anything else. However, his tone is amiable, and he says that he would be happy to meet me if I still wish it; he will be in London soon. I will do so. He may be more forthcoming in person, or even let slip something he should not.

Mr Rockingham's letter is tender and heartbreaking. He is very sorry for me but can only counsel me to try and forget Miss Rosetti, however hard that will be. He reminds me, in the first instance, that I barely know her, that it takes time to get to know someone, and that love must be sustained by a rational and sustainable affection and commitment. It is folly, as well as self-destructive, to invest so much in a phantom. But I do know her, Mr Rockingham. I know her in my heart. That is all that matters. I have wasted so much time in my life trying to be sensible.

In the second instance, and more importantly, in his opinion, he points out that Miss Rosetti suffered a bout of madness, and though it was mild, and she is cured, there is always a danger that it will reoccur. He mentions, with great delicacy, my poor mother, saying that even if Miss Rosetti and I met as equals in a society drawing room, there could still be danger in such an alliance. There is still much for us to learn about the inheritance of madness, but there is a risk of taint in future generations. I do not think that this is just. Mr Rockingham, who is all compassion, to be so hard. Would he have said the same of my mother?

Finally, he counsels me to make sure I balance my hard work with enough rest and recreation, pointing out the increasing prevalence of professional men in private lunatic asylums suffering from a form of insanity caused by overwork in this ever-rushing, ever-competitive world of ours. He encloses details of a highly respected alienist. An alienist? Good gracious; does he think I am mad?

I get up and walk over to a corner on the south side of my parlour. There is a gown hanging on the outside of a wardrobe. The gown is made of a claret-coloured plush velvet. I stroke it tenderly. I confess it is for her, Titania. An artistic lady at a dinner party was wearing something similar and I saw at once that it was just the style to suit my love. I asked the lady how to get such a dress made up for a friend of mine, and she arranged it all for me. I hope the size is correct, but we can easily have it altered if necessary.

Am I going mad? No, surely not. It is just that I do not know what to do.

I am interrupted by a visitor, Dickie Dodds, the sporting writer from the *Times*. He rushes in like a locomotive engine, his bald head shining, his cheeks ruddy, his legs muscular. He has just returned from the country, where he has been hunting, shooting, fishing, or whatever sporting gents do at this time of year. I feel like a sickly child in comparison. We sit down in opposite chairs, and he runs on pleasantly for some time. Then he stops, looks at me intently, and reaches over to press my hand.

'Now, old boy, what's all this then?'

I must look bewildered.

'Come, Mortimer. You have not been right for some time. You are neglecting your attendance at the office and are behind with your copy. Better me telling you, old boy, than the governor.'

I am about to protest but notice his kind grey eyes and softened voice.

'I am a little unwell, I think,' I say.

'I can see that. Have you seen a physician?'

I shake my head.

'You really must. Promise me.'

I smile weakly and nod my head.

'Good man. Now, Mortimer; I also suspect that you have had some great disappointment in your life. I will not pry into what it is, unless you want to tell me. But you must not throw away all you have achieved in your work on account of it. We are all very proud of you at the paper. Do not let whatever it is ruin all that. There are enough pimply upstarts desperate to sit in our chairs, you know. Do not let one of them steal yours. Especially now that Jones has just been executed and he is more famous than ever. That fame will not last, so you must capitalise on it now.'

Dodds mimes the rope being tightened around someone's neck and waggles his thick arms like a man twitching at the end of it.

I give an involuntary chuckle.

'There. And do not be shutting yourself up either. My little woman, Gusta, now, is not what you would call artistic; she wouldn't know a Turner from a tablecloth. Much like myself, in truth. But she's got the best heart in the world and a talent for roasting a fowl that you will not see for many a mile. You are welcome to dine with us any day of the week and we will do our best to fend off those legions of female admirers of yours. My own daughters are pleasant enough company and will not bother you. Adelaide can be a little much, 'tis true, but she is softer at home, and we are hoping that this bluestocking nonsense is just a phase.'

I am crying again. So much kindness. The poor man looks a little embarrassed but bravely ploughs on.

'We all have hard times, but there is always hope, old fellow. Now, I must be getting on. Oh, before I forget. Here are a few little things for you.' He reaches into his deep waistcoat pocket, pulls out a bottle of finest cognac, and presses it into my hands. 'Just a little tonic, something to keep the cold out. Now, where did I put the other thing? Ah, yes, in the same place. I am a bit hapless without Gusta to take charge of me.'

He pulls out a small parcel wrapped in red paper and gives it to me. My hands shake and I fumble with the string and paper, but Dodds comes to my aid. Out comes a charming walnut box decorated in a gold mosaic pattern.

Dodds grins. 'Turn the key on the side there.'

I do so, and am startled to hear the rickety tune of a popular street ballad about Cedric Jones.

I laugh. I have just got used to the tune when the lid of the box bursts open and a puppet figure jumps out. It is Jones. I jump. As with the ceramic figure, the facial likeness is very good, particularly the evil grin. As the body is depicted simply by the spring mechanism covered in white cloth, apparently an apron, his top hat is decorated with poison bottles.

The shock sets off my facial twitching, but I am also laughing.

'It is very clever, is it not?' asks Dodds, chuckling. 'It is the very latest thing in Jones madness. I bought one for my youngest girl and we get no music at home now but this.'

I cannot stop laughing. I fear that I am a little hysterical. Dodds gets up.

'Right, Mortimer. I must be going. And you will remember what I said? Promise me.'

I nod.

'Do not get up,' he says. 'I can find my own way out. Do just get well.'

He shakes my hand heartily, pats my arm and takes his leave.

Dear man; I had always thought him rather crass. I sit, weeping. My heart is so open, now, that I fear I can never close it up again.

CHAPTER 33

Nan Carter

I'M SAT WITH Mr Friend in the tearoom at Euston station. I thought a short meeting in a busy place like this would be the best thing. But the best thing for what? Why am I doing this? I should have just told him that I had changed my mind since leaving the asylum. But no, what do I do? Write straight back to him and suggest this. Well, I must put an end to it here, even though it hasn't really begun. I am nervous and excited.

'I am so glad to see you, Miss Rosetti, and that you are looking so well. I hope you are feeling it?'

'Thank you, Mr Friend. I am.'

'And thank you for meeting me. I was hoping to impress you with somewhere a little more luxurious than this for our first encounter in London, but I am happy with whatever suits you.'

Friend grins, then grimaces as a grimy waiter slaps down two teas and fruit buns on the table.

'Next time, we shall progress to some fried fish on a street corner,' I say, smiling. Little does he know.

'Next time, indeed. I shall hold you to that.'

I can't help but smile, and he smiles back, holding eye contact. Oh, stop this, you foolish girl.

'Are you planning to return to your profession?' he asks.

My profession? Oh, he means the governess trade. 'Yes; no. Well, things are little uncertain just now.'

'It might be advisable to take a little time after your,' – he pauses – 'ordeal, before returning to work; if circumstances allow, that is.'

I think of Jones wriggling his head in his tasselled nightcap, and his threats to cut away my womanhood. I think of the dead room, and shiver, though it's a lovely day. I think of running from him to Mortimer, out of the frying pan and into the fire.

'Yes,' is all I can manage.

'I am only sorry that I did not realise sooner, that I did not do more. I cannot tell you how much it pains me to think on it.'

I feel close to tears. 'It is done, and I am safe and well. How are you, Mr Friend?'

He looks at me tenderly, aware that I want to turn the subject.

'Oh, well enough, I thank you. Life at Allingsford is settling down somewhat though we are still over-run with journalists, as well as curious members of the public.'

I take a bite of the slightly stale bun, and a sip of tea. 'How did you get into your profession? You seem a strange fit for it, if you do not mind me saying.'

Friend smiles. 'You are not the first to point that out. It is rather a long story.'

He is just about to continue, when we are interrupted by the approach to our table of a young man and an older woman. The man looks like one of those young toffs who frequent The Parrot, and the older woman on his arm, no better than she should be – though I can talk – is clad in a frowsy red gown and too much rouge.

'Why, it's Nancy Carter, star of The Parrot and Bottle, ain't it?' says the toff, doffing his topper superciliously. 'What an honour to bump into you. The chaps will be green-eyed with envy. They're all going mad over you, Miss Carter.'

The frowsy woman exclaims loudly. 'Oh, and ain't you a beauty? Make the most of it, my girl; it don't last forever.'

Oh no; this is bad luck. What do I do? What do I say? I can't look at Friend. 'Oh, I think you may have mistaken me for someone else, sir. My name is Miss Rosetti.'

The toff bends forward to leer at me. I try not to recoil from the odour of stale champagne and strong coffee on his breath.

'No mistaking that pretty face and those legs, too, no doubt, if you want to give us a flash of them.'

'Sir,' says Friend, 'you heard the lady. You are insulting her. Please take your leave.'

'Yes, leave the poor girl alone,' says the frowsy

woman, winking at me. 'She just wants a bit of peace and quiet while she ain't working.'

'I do not like your words or your tone, sir,' says the toff, addressing Friend.

Mr Friend stands up, looking angry. The toff, a good foot shorter and a great deal younger and slighter than Friend, softens his stance. Friend sits back down.

'But I am not the chap to bear a grudge. And now I understand.' He turns to me. 'You are going incognito, aren't you, Miss Carter, eh? Nudge, nudge, wink, wink. Message received and understood. We shall leave you in peace, and may I thank you for the pleasure you give, Miss Carter. Farewell.'

He nods at Friend, doffs his hat again and leers at me, and the pair clatter away.

I raise my head and risk a look at Friend. My face is burning. 'This has happened a few times lately,' I say. 'Apparently, I look very like an East End, music hall performer.'

Friend stares at me, concerned. Then his facial expression starts to change, as if he's making a discovery.

'Indeed? How strange. I do love a good music hall performance. It would be so interesting to see this Miss Carter given the likeness. Would you like to join me one evening?'

'Oh, no, mama does not like me to frequent such places. And it would not be good for my reputation, as a respectable governess, you know.'

'Oh, that is a shame. I do so appreciate good music

in all its forms, and can see no harm in a respectable music hall turn. I would certainly love to see this Nancy Carter. I shall go along this evening.'

He looks at me, challenge in his eyes. Oh Lord. How can I get out of this? Perhaps if I tell Sailor Bill that I'm not very well this week, then Friend will have returned to Hampshire and be none the wiser. But I can't do that. I wouldn't want to let Bill down; he's been good to me. And I need the money. And I'm building up an audience.

Oh, stuff it. Could I just come clean to Friend? Or at least tell him a version of the truth? But he's a part of those in charge at Allingsford. He's got my false records. I could end up in prison. I can't risk that. I've got to keep my word to Nel, and work the best I can to help her and ma.

The next step is decided for me.

'Your name is not really Titania Rosetti, is it?' Friend asks, smiling.

I open my mouth as if to protest, but nothing comes out. I slowly shake my head. Oh, Lord, what have I done? Friend laughs, and so do I, and then we find we cannot stop. He takes my hand and we both sit there, spluttering, shaking, clutching our stomachs, like two lunatics back at the asylum.

I arrive home, thrilled and terrified about what's just happened. And what will I tell Connie? And how could I ever explain it to Nel?

Ma's having a lie down and Nel's sat reading a

Dickens serial that ma borrowed from Herr Konig and that I finished recently. I go to her, kiss her on the head and present her with the posy of primroses and violets that Friend gave to me.

'Flowers for a flower. How are you today, Ellen Carter? I've just been for a dish of tea with a friend.'

Nel looks up at me, her eyes cold, her face pale, the lines on it more prominent. Oh no, what have I done? What does she know?

'I know I didn't buy them myself, Nel, but you should have them. You should have everything lovely. It's spring, and it's a beautiful day out there.'

Nel is still, but shaking very slightly, her fingers tapping the red spine of the bound novel. This is bad, very bad.

'What's the matter, Nelly? Please tell me.'

Nel takes something out of the pages of the book. It's a letter. In fact, it's Mr Mortimer's last letter to me, or rather to Miss Rosetti.

'What are you doing reading my letter?' I ask, snapping, hoping to get her on the defensive whilst I think of something to say, some excuse.

'*Your* letter? Oh, but it seems to be addressed to a Miss Titania Rosetti. Very curious. I was quite intrigued to find such a strange thing in the pages of this book – especially as that's the name of the woman who Mr Mortimer told me he's in love with – and so, naturally, I read it.'

'Nelly, I...'

'I'm just so bewildered. My mind's upon the stretch so much that I think I'm going mad. I can't even begin to think of a rational explanation for this. Why is there a letter to this Miss Rosetti in our house? And then, I think, maybe it has something to do with my sister's mysterious time in Birmingham. Or maybe that was a lie and she was really in Hampshire. But then, Mortimer said that he met this woman in a lunatic asylum, of all places. So that can't be connected to you. Or can it? My poor brain just goes round and round.

'Oh, Nan. Who are you? I barely seem to know you anymore. What the hell is all this? I think I'm going to end up in an asylum soon myself.'

I've no idea what to say. Could I try the truth again? Surely, it's too dark, too awful for Nel to hear. What would she think of me? She might never be able to love me again. She might never be able to love me again as it is.

'Oh,' she continues, 'and if, for some lunatic reason, you are this Miss ridiculous name Rosetti, thank you for ruining the one good thing in my life – no, *our* lives, actually – the arrangement with Mr Mortimer. Now, I might end up with some evil wretch who…, and I've got to find someone else soon. And what about poor ma? And it's all down to you.'

Nel is sobbing, and keeps shrugging her shoulders. 'I just don't know what to think. I really do not. I am truly mad. Oh, Nan, why do you hate me so? You must do, to put me through these things again and again. That's all I know for certain. That's all I know…'

Right, that's it, there's only one thing for it. I pull a wobbly chair from the table, position it opposite Nel in the comfortable chair, and sit down. My voice is firm, clear.

'Listen to me now, Nel. Don't run away from me. Hear me out and then you can do whatever you want.'

Nel, her sore eyes wide, looks as if she's about to protest, then nods.

'You won't like this, Nel. You won't like it one bit. I'm going to tell you every single thing that happened while I was away, and what has happened since. You can hate me for the rest of your life, if you like, but you must please promise not to tell ma. However selfish you think me, it's for her sake.

'And Nel, before I begin, you can't ever believe that I hate you. I despise myself for what I've put you and ma through, but you know that I love you both more than anything in the world. And you need to know that as long as I'm around, I will try, try so very hard to make sure that you never need to slave with a needle again, or do anything with any man who hurts you. You won't believe that at the moment, I know, and I cannot blame you, but I've said it.'

Nel nods again, more in defeat than belief. But I take a deep breath, and begin.

CHAPTER 34

CON AND I are in the bar again at the Shakespeare. I've got a night off while Bill gives a new turn a try. It's some kind of female contortionist involving a snake; they sing and dance together. Well, it takes all sorts. It's just so lovely to be in this pretty bar with mostly civilized people drinking a glass of champagne. And I feel so clean and fragrant.

'I've got a surprise for you, Nan,' says Con, her eyes bright.

'What is it, my dear? Are you trying out for Juliet? "Romeo, Romeo, ain't it hot in here?"'

Con giggles. 'Oh no, you've got it all wrong. It will be "Romeo, Romeo, pass me the pisspot, you rum old cove, I'm feeling rather bilious".'

I nearly spit out my champagne from laughing. 'Oh, Connie; I love you so much.'

'So you should, my dear. Now, here comes your surprise.'

I look round and spot Harry Visconti coming towards us. He bounces over, all life and energy – a marked contrast to his former melancholic state – and sits down in between Con and me.

'How do ye do, Miss Carter?' he asks, then grins broadly. His eyes are bright and the tips of his large ears seem to be glowing pink. He's even flasher than usual tonight, wearing a silk red waistcoat – to match his hair – embroidered with what look like black racing horses.

'I'm well, Mr Visconti, thank you. So happy to be spending some time here with Connie.'

'Oh, and ain't she glorious?' he says, leaning over to kiss Con on the cheek.

'She certainly is, sir,' I say. 'No-one more so.'

'Well said, Nan.' He plants another kiss on Connie. 'I hear you've been working very hard at the Parrot?'

'I'm trying,' I say.

'You're doing better than that, by all accounts. Sailor Bill couldn't be happier.'

I smile with pride.

'Though he won't be smiling much longer,' Harry continues.

He assumes a sombre look. My heart sinks. Oh no, please don't let me lose that job yet. It's not much, but I need it.

'Because you'll be coming over to the Shakespeare,' Harry almost shouts. He lets out a loud guffaw.

I stare at him. 'You mean with my act? I'll be performing here?'

'Yes,' says Con, practically bouncing in her seat.

'Are you sure?' I ask, looking at Harry.

'I should hope so, dear,' he says. 'Well, I've been to see you a few times, though you won't have noticed me, and your act has come on a treat. The audience just love you, and that's the trick. I think we'll have to make a few small changes to accommodate the slightly more refined clientele here at the Shakespeare. I've been thinking how best to do that. But, overall, we'll keep the act pretty much as it is. Well done, Miss Carter.'

'Thank you,' is all I can manage to say, so I get up and kiss Harry on the cheek.

'Dear oh dear, Connie will have your eye out,' says Harry, smiling. 'Right, I must be getting on. Come here on Monday afternoon and we can run through the act. Then I'll start you on a couple of nights a week to begin with.'

He springs up, kisses Connie on the head, then canters off. Con and I polish off some more champagne, laughing and making starry plans. I tell her about my confession to Nel.

'Oh, Nan, I wasn't expecting that.'

'Nor me.' I sigh. 'But it had to be done. It was the only way.'

'And how did she take it?'

'Very quiet. Too quiet. I think she's still in a state of shock.'

'Give her time. She'll understand it all, and come round.'

'I do hope so. Whatever happens, I must look after her and ma.'

'Hopefully, the work here will help. It should be better paid than the Parrot, at least?'

I smile. 'Yes, that's a good thought. She hasn't found a new gentleman friend, as yet, and maybe now she won't have to. She hates the whole thing, the finding of someone. The arrangement with Mortimer was so steady, but, of course, I ruined that.'

'Not deliberately. At least now she knows why.'

I nod, feeling a bit weepy, now, at what should be one of the happiest moments of my life.

'Come on Miss Nancy, let's not waste the rest of this champagne.'

Connie pours out the last of the bottle into our two glasses, and holds her glass with her little finger turned out in her fine-lady-drinking-tea fashion. I laugh, then continue to smile at my friend through my tears.

CHAPTER 35

Harris Mortimer

I AM SAT IN a comfortable velvet-covered chair in a handsome drawing room overlooking Regent's Park. The clock ticks softly and, outside the window, birds twitter in response. The room smells of fresh flowers and beeswax. I am suddenly aware of my own smell in contrast, which is not very sweet. I feel a flush of shame. Was this a bad idea? I decided to take Mr Rockingham's advice, and try the alienist. I think that the kindness of Dodds undid me in some way. I realised that I had real friends, and that Mr Rockingham was my dearest, and I should not eschew his wise counsel, meant always for my good.

It is rather soothing than otherwise being here. The renowned alienist, Dr John Goodenough, is sat in a chair opposite me, and is a very comfortable, reassuring presence. He is tall and bearded, with kind hazel eyes and thick white hair that sticks straight up in clumps, as if he has had a shock.

'Welcome, Mr Mortimer, sir,' he says, in his smooth Edinburgh brogue. 'I know that Roderick Rockingham brought us together. What a good chap he is. We studied together, you know, and have been friends ever since. He could have his own practice now, but he is committed to the public good, and has devoted his life to it.'

I nod and smile. It is gratifying to hear Rockingham spoken of so fondly.

'Now, do try to be at your ease, Mr Mortimer. I know that this sort of thing can be daunting the first time. But we are here to get you well. And we will. You are quite in the best company, you know. Some of the highest and most eminent members of our society seek the help of my profession, and, indeed, have sat where you sit now. Rather than being a cause for shame, it is quite the opposite; it is a badge of honour.'

I am a little surprised, but pleasantly so.

'Indeed, sir,' continues Goodenough. 'In our highly competitive society, it is only natural that creative, ambitious temperaments like yours should be subject to the occasional neurosis.'

I nod. He is right.

'Now, sir, before we begin, I must entreat you to be as honest as you possibly can with me. It is the only way to effect a cure. We need have no qualms about delicacy. We are both men of the world together, and I have heard everything under the sun. I assure you that I am unshockable.'

I manage a smile, though am nervous about what I may need to confess.

First, he examines me, looking over my head and body, and is pleased to note that my head is symmetrical, my features regular, and my ears formed correctly. He makes a few notes.

Now, he asks me to tell him about my life from childhood, and whether either of my parents suffered from nervous conditions or insanity. I tell him about my mother.

'Oh, that is very sad, very sad indeed. My heart goes out to you, sir. In terms of hereditary transmission, daughters are far more likely than sons to inherit these conditions from their mothers. So we can be optimistic on that point, but should still remain cautious. Have you suffered from any incidents of mental incapacity in your own life before? Think of any occasions when you have been melancholy or nervous, or other times when you have acted strangely, or outside the bounds of your normal temperament.'

'I did display some unusual behaviour at school, for a period. I found that I could not resist taking items from the other boys, and around the school. I am so ashamed to talk of it now. The word kleptomania was used, I believe. It passed almost as soon as it had begun, and things were smoothed over. I was very fortunate.'

'You are doing very well, sir; do go on.'

'And then, about a decade ago, now, I was forced to take some time resting in the home of a doctor friend. I was training to be a lawyer and found that it did not suit me. I seemed to have some sort of crisis.'

'A not uncommon reaction to such a life stage, you know. And what behaviours did you exhibit at that time? How were you feeling?'

'I was very melancholy and wept a lot. I could not focus on anything. I did not sleep and sometimes had nightmares. I drank a lot, and, I…, indulged in other immoral behaviours.'

'Did you have relations with prostitutes?'

I nod.

'And are you doing so, now? Remember I pass no judgement, Mr Mortimer.'

I nod again.

'And do you indulge in onanism? Self-pollution?'

I hesitate, then nod again.

'You are doing very well indeed, Mr Mortimer. We are making progress already. Onanism is a common weakness. But you must know that both these behaviours – self-pollution and the use of prostitutes – use up vital lifeforce and sap the will. And they have been linked to certain forms of insanity, including idiocy.'

He looks at me sternly for a moment, then smiles. 'However, there is no need to despair. My cure is simple and old-fashioned, but highly effective: marriage. It is always the safest and best way to preserve our bodily and mental health.'

We talk about my experience, hopes and fears with regard to the fair sex and I manage to tell him about Miss

Rosetti. He is kind but stern, and agrees with Rockingham's judgement. She has become almost a monomania on my part. Even if she reciprocated my feelings, our union could be unsafe given her own mental sufferings. I must exert myself and put her out of my mind. Once I achieve this, I will soon meet a woman worthy of me and will find my happiness.

We discuss my profession, and the grave dangers of overwork.

'I advise all my patients in your position to take a rest from their profession if they can. The seaside, the countryside, or mountain air. However, where this is not possible, you must take some immediate steps to manage your professional life. Never return to your work after your evening meal. Rest is vital. Have a warm bath daily. Take regular exercise in the fresh air, but never to the point of exhausting yourself. Walking, fishing and riding are the sort of thing. If you are short on time or stuck indoors, some people find the use of dumbbells very effective at casting out any demon within. How is your appetite?'

'Not very good.'

'I will give you a list of beneficial foods to help build you up and aid your digestion. That good housekeeper of yours can take charge of your diet. The stomach is intimately linked with our nervous system.'

I nod. It is quite relieving to receive forthright advice.

'Are you aware that you twitch on one side of your face, that your speech is sometimes slow and deliberate, and that you drag your right leg? You use a stick, so you must be aware of the leg.'

I am a little shocked to hear these things put to me so clearly and candidly, even though others have mentioned them, and I am mostly aware of them myself.

'Yes, to a degree.'

'Our bodies adapt to these things so that we become less aware of them ourselves. They are quite typical symptoms of a man experiencing this kind of neurosis. Have you noticed anything that happens before these symptoms get worse? Do you have any delusions, or nightmares, for example?'

'Well, I have been having a strange dream of a woman, a dreadful old hag, who is coming to attack me. I will admit it is terrifying.'

'I once had a patient who experienced something similar, and it always prefigured a brain seizure. Happily, your case is not so serious. The witch will disappear, I assure you, as you recover. I will prescribe you a nerve tonic, something simple containing iron, quinine and strychnine. There are other things available such as mercury and opium. But let us not overdo the pills at this stage.

'I firmly believe, Mr Mortimer, that your cure is in your own hands. I am very confident that you will soon recover. But you must take my advice. Above all, you must work on your sexual continence, cast away from you the idea of Miss Rosetti, and find yourself a sensible woman to marry.'

I agree to consult Dr Goodenough again in one month's time, and leave his house clutching my prescriptions. As I go, I notice a familiar-looking man coming in; it is a member of Her Majesty's government, I am sure, Lord something or other. I feel almost proud.

I am exhausted, light-headed and strangely calm. I must sleep. I flag a hackney cab, and sit very still and peaceful on my journey home.

CHAPTER 36

I WAKE UP. IT is light, but must be early. I seem to have slept for a long time, and well. I woke up in the night, but only to relieve myself. I am not sure if the weird sister visited; perhaps she did, but did not stay long.

I feel a small sense of hope. Today, I must try. I must try to follow the advice of Mr Rockingham – dear man – and now good Dr Goodenough, alienist to the aristocracy and all the best of society. I could never have imagined how relieved I feel to have unburdened all the guilt, pain and suffering of my life to such a sympathetic ear, to one who knows the world, and knows that I am not alone in all this; quite the opposite.

I would love to take a change of air and scene. I dream of Italy. But that must wait. Now, I must commit myself to my work, without harming myself. Dear Dodds was right. I have worked so hard to get to an exalted status in my profession, and yet I have been letting it slip through my fingers like sand. Besides, I need the income. I do have some property from my parents. I will never starve. But life is so expensive; I have standards to maintain; indeed, I would like to further rise in the world. Now that I am connected to aristocracy, who knows what opportunities might come my way?

I realise that I am in my vest and drawers again, rather than my usual pristine nightshirt, and I know that I smell badly. I am so ashamed. To think of my visiting Dr Goodenough in such a degraded state, and passing Lord whatever-his-name-was at the door. And poor Mrs Hopkinson would be horrified. She is away for a week visiting some of her endless relations in Sussex. Today is the day I will cleanse myself; I will become pure again.

I get up and relieve myself in the chamber pot. I am disgusted by the mess inside, not least the foul smell of it, and press the lid on tight and push it away under the bed. But this is good, I think; disgust is good – it will set me aright. I have a bathtub in my bedchamber but cannot think how to get hot water and fill it. And I have forgotten how to light the fire. Have I ever known? Well, well, I will have to shiver. At least it is not winter. Mrs Hopkinson – God bless her – has left a pitcher of water on my dressing table. I pour some into the ceramic basin, then scrub myself from head to foot with the icy water and carbolic soap, giggling, shivering and hopping from foot to foot like a schoolgirl, then wrap myself up in my beautiful green and blue smoking jacket. I rarely smoke, but it is such a delightful item to wear around the house. I twirl a little and shake my head.

Now I must get rid of my excess of hair. I usually go to a local barber, where I am shaved, trimmed and oiled to perfection; it is a very pleasant experience. I am not quite ready to face the world as I am, however. I will do it myself; how difficult can it be? Now, where is that old shaving set gifted to me by my father when my voice broke? I have never used it; I suppose it was more symbolic than anything. I hunt around in the two chests of drawers in my bedchamber and find it in the bottom draw of the second one. Ha – here it is. I open the silver case and take out a strange-looking knife. Hmm. I will need soap. I go back to my washbasin, still full of soap and water, and attempt to create more of a lather. Unfortunately, the cold water is not very effective with this soap. Never mind. I cover my beard, face and head in the poor lather, take the blade and begin. I am interested to watch myself in the looking glass, bits of hair falling to the floor.

This has indeed been a fascinating process; I must talk to the barber next time I visit about his profession. I have not been very successful. My skin is now covered in cuts and dried blood, and I have tufts of beard, moustache and hair sprouting at curious angles from my neck upwards. I run some bear's grease through the remaining bits of hair and skin, which is rather soothing. I giggle again. I am really quite enjoying myself; perhaps I have turned a corner at last. I pull on some trousers and a shirt. That will do for today.

Now, can I make some tea? I am thirsty, and I

recognise a feeling of mild hunger; more good news. I go down into the basement kitchen and look around me. I scratch my head, wincing when I encounter a cut. I wander into the small pantry and see a jug of cold milk, some bread and butter and some kind of pie on a shelf closest to the door. God bless Mrs Hopkinson again. Never mind the tea; this will do. I take these things through to the kitchen table, find a knife, and sit down. I drink some milk straight from the jug, manage to cut a bit of bread and some pie, and eat them slowly. Delicious. I feel like a boy again. The pleasures of small things; I must do this more often.

I make my way back upstairs and to my living area, sit down at my bureau and write a short note to the guvnor at the *Times*, expressing my regret for my recent behaviour, vowing to reform myself and saying that I will be at the office tomorrow. I hope he knows how sincere I am. Well, I must prove my sincerity with action. I will give the letter to one of the street boys to deliver direct and see if he can bring me some strong hot coffee while he is about it. I do this.

I return to my sitting room, the south side of which is divided into two parts, one devoted to my professional life and one to Titania Rosetti.

This is the terrible part. I do not know if I can do it, but I must have courage. I must try. I stare at the sketches I have made of her; there are hundreds of them. There she is, her face pale and panicked at my carriage window, or angelic, singing at the piano in Allingsford

Hall, or sat peacefully at the large window in the day room, waiting to turn around to greet me. Now she is sat at the head of my table, or nursing one of our children, or singing at our own piano. I am rather a talented artist, and the sketches are beautiful. There is a small wardrobe in this side of the room, where I have placed a selection of velvet dresses in blue, green, red and gold, some of the colours I feel will most become her. I had been meaning to add many more items to the collection, so that she is wanting for nothing when she comes.

I look at all this, touch it, stroke it. I take a deep breath and rip the pictures from the wall, screw them up and throw them on the floor. I take the dresses, all except one, slice them up with my shaving knife, and drop them on the floor too. Now I am stamping furiously on them, and dancing, and laughing; I am hysterical.

I am calm again. I take the remaining dress, an exquisite thing in sapphire blue, kiss it and hold it to my head, then put it away in the press.

Now I must work; I must be prepared and knowledgeable for my return to the office tomorrow. I will also accept dear Dodds's hospitality. I must leave some money and a note for Mrs Hopkinson, who returns tomorrow, asking her to purchase my tonics and the requisite food to aid my recovery. I will purchase some dumbbells as soon I can. I will write to Mr Rockingham, telling him about my consultation with Dr Goodenough, and thanking him, as always, for his tender care and wise counsel.

I sigh. It is overwhelming. But I can try. I must try.

CHAPTER 37

Nan Carter

I'VE NEARLY ARRIVED at the Albion restaurant on Drury Lane, where I'm meeting Mr Friend. He's looking forward to hearing my whole true story, he says. Well, he won't be getting that. Friend insisted on meeting me just outside the restaurant so that he could escort me inside. I don't worry about such matters, but I suppose it's the gentlemanly thing. I march in anywhere, bold as you like, and if people think that I'm a whore, let 'em. Besides, I've heard that respectable ladies even dine alone in restaurants now, though I think that's generally for luncheon, as they call it, rather than at night. I'd like to do that one day. Anyway, the Albion is a very fine, respectable place, where gentlemen take their wives and daughters.

There he is, the tall, angular figure approaching, and I'm smiling away like an idiot, drunk on his way to the gallows. Friend's smiling too, grinning from ear to ear, you might say. He doffs his hat in greeting and then takes my hand to shake it, rather than to kiss it.

'Miss Nancy Carter, I believe?' he says. 'A friend of Miss Titania Rosetti?'

I smile and give a satirical bow. I'm feeling quite lightheaded.

I take Friend's proffered arm, and we enter the restaurant. I'm dazzled. It's beautiful, the lights from the lamps dancing over the red, green and gold and the glittering chandeliers. I want to dance myself, to twirl round the tables, then jump on top of one and deliver my turn, flashing my violet-coloured stockings at the horrified, respectable folk. A bowing waiter with heavily oiled hair seats us at a table next to a wall, with a good view of the whole place. The linen tablecloths and napkins are quite the whitest I have ever seen, and I sit back in my very comfortable chair admiring the view.

'Thank you for this,' I say.

'It is very much my pleasure. I ordered the venison for us today, in advance – I hope you will not object – they need time to prepare it, so I went ahead. You can only get it in season, and it is so delicious.'

'I've never eaten it before; I'm looking forward to it. I have to confess, too, that I've never been anywhere this splendid, though undoubtedly Miss Rosetti has been many times before.'

'Then I'm happy to be able to introduce you, both

to the venison and the splendour. You deserve to be swaddled in splendour, I am sure.'

'I quite agree with you, sir,' I say, laughing.

The waiter appears to pour the claret, and remark that the venison is very good today, and our first dishes will be soon on the table.

Friend raises his glass to me, and I return the gesture, sipping at the beautiful deep red liquid with great satisfaction.

'Your beard is even wilder than before,' I say, gazing at it over the rim of my glass. That was a somewhat direct and unladylike thing to say. I can't help but examine every bit of him and then a resulting thought just pops out.

He grimaces. 'Yes; I fear that I am getting too old for this fashionable beard nonsense and am beginning to look quite ridiculous.'

'Not ridiculous, sir, but it makes your face a bit too hidden.'

'I shall take that as a compliment, and shall trim it down at the very least, on your advice.' He pauses. 'And speaking of hidden, Miss Titania, Ophelia, Desdemona, Viola or my favourite, Nan, thank you for telling me your real name.'

'You know your Shakespeare, sir; I'm impressed.'

'Not as well as you, it would seem.'

I wasn't quite sure what voice to use this evening, but I find that I can't sustain much of a pretence anyway and gradually settle into my usual London twang, with a bit of fine lady thrown in for the benefit of the waiter. I must sound more comical than Connie at the tea with Mortimer.

'I would be honoured if you would tell me a bit more about Nancy Carter,' continues Friend.

'I think I'd like to hear a bit more about you, first, Mr Friend.'

Can I trust him? I'm not sure. And after Connie made that joke about him being another murderer, I started to think, not that he's a murderer, but that he could be any other number of things. I do usually have quite a good instinct. You have to when you're a young woman living the life I do. Still, you never know. The problem is that I find myself so relaxed in his company, I could be tempted to confide anything. I must stay alert.

'You can ask me anything you like,' he says, 'I have nothing to hide, apart from my face, that is, with this great shaggy beard.'

Some soup arrives, which is vaguely brownish in colour but very tasty. I'm quite au fait with the use of cutlery, pick up the correct spoon and begin to eat my soup in a very ladylike fashion. Ma taught us girls all this, even though we barely have a few forks and pots at home, in the hope it would be useful, and here I am, displaying my skills. Good old ma.

'Why are you doing the job you do?' I ask. 'We did not get chance to talk about this last time. How did you end up at Allingsford asylum?'

'Tis a fair question. It is not where I imagined I would end up in life, but I suppose that is the same for many people. I grew up in Herefordshire, from a long line of farmers. I was always restless, and could not settle to anything, least of all farming. I always loved music; I wrote scores and songs for all sorts of things, with only a bit of success. I went to France, but it did not go well, and I returned home in defeat. Through his connections, my father secured me the opening at Allingsford. I was completely unsuitable and unqualified for the role, and they should not have accepted me, I suppose, but connections do much, and I think they liked that fact that I was musical. My father presented the opportunity as a punishment, I am sure, and I felt it as such. But I needed to do something, and to earn my bread, and so it began.'

'And how long have you been there?'

'Three years. Even my father is impressed. I would like to return to music at some time in the future, but I have not been unhappy in my current life.'

Now there are dishes of fish before us – sole and cod, I think I can identify – they smell delicious – and some potatoes with melted butter. I'm salivating. Friend helps me to a good portion. He obviously credits me with a good appetite and I'm glad of it.

'Do you have any brothers or sisters?' I ask.

'There was an older brother, who sadly died when I was a child. He would have been the ideal son, my father seems to feel, which only exacerbates his disappointment in me. I have a younger sister, Violet, who is thriving, and living here in London with her attorney husband. You would like her.'

How do I now share information about my own family? This man has my records at Allingsford. They won't say much, as I was taken in as a wanderer in Allingsford itself, and gave Connie's London address as the address of my family. But he knows they are mostly a lie.

'I am sorry to hear about your brother,' I say.

'Thank you.' He looks at me kindly. 'You do not have to tell me much about your life if you are worrying about that, you know. As far as I am concerned, you are a discharged patient, and your case is done with. There would be no need to revisit it. To be candid, I did wonder a bit about you; it never seemed quite right. But I did not over-think it. I would only like to know a little more about you as a person because I am interested in you.'

I smile at him. He does seem to have a knack of saying the right thing.

'Thank you,' I say. 'I can only say that I went through a very difficult time in my life, which led me to Allingsford, and I took another name.'

Friend nods. 'One thing I have learned from Allingsford is that so many people struggle with the battle of life. I do not think that I was myself for a time when I returned from France. In other circumstances, who knows what would have happened to me?'

He reaches out to press my hand. 'Well, I am only glad that you are well again.'

'Thank you,' I say. 'And I live with my mother and sister, Nel. That is the only family I have.'

I'm not ready to mention Penny; that would be too much, would open up so much.

'And,' he says, smiling, 'you are a music hall sensation. I'm the envy of London for being in your presence.'

'Not quite, sir. I've been performing at the Parrot and Bottle, as you know,' – I grin – 'which is not exactly the most genteel establishment in London. But it's gone quite well, and Harry Visconti, at the Shakespeare, is now going to give me a chance there. I'm on next Tuesday evening. I'm rattled with nerves, but so thrilled. I mustn't get too carried away, though; I have a habit of doing that.'

Friend laughs. 'There's nothing wrong with getting excited. I would love to see you perform, if that does not make you feel too uncomfortable. I am hoping to be back in London in a month or so.'

I suppose it would be a bit queer really, but here I am as partly myself anyway. And if my act doesn't put him off me, nothing will.

'You are as free to be a customer of the Shakespeare as anyone else, sir,' I say, but smiling. 'I would be glad to see you.'

'That is very good news, as I have already invited Mr Rockingham and the Committee of Visitors. I thought we could make a night of it.'

I laugh. 'I look forward to meeting them in the bar after the performance.'

Now the waiter appears again wheeling the meat, vegetables and clean plates, and I stare in awe as he slices great slabs of the venison, brown and pink, onto our plates, and then Friend heaps on more vegetables.

'I've never seen so much food in front of me,' I say, aware that I'm giving away my background and state of relative poverty, but not minding. 'Do people eat like this every day? Nobody would be able to fit onto the omnibuses, if so, and the poor horses would collapse from tugging the weight. I suppose large, and rich, ladies and gentlemen, are in their own carriages and pay for their own poor horses.'

'Quite. Do make the most of it, though. It is a special occasion for me being in the presence of the one and only Miss Nancy Carter. There will be cheese afterwards, too, should you be able to manage some.'

My eyes widen, but I tuck into the venison nonetheless and resist the urge to sigh with happiness. I really could become quite fat if I was rich; I don't know how fine ladies stay slender.

As we eat, we talk a little about Cedric Jones.

'I still do not know what to make of it all,' he says. 'And I am truly horrified by what he put you through. I am not sure that I can be a good judge of character. I never really took to him – he was certainly an odd fish – but I never particularly disliked him, either. He did have the strangest, darkest sense of humour, but I thought that was a way of dealing with his line of work, like soldiers about to go into battle. I never dreamed that he actually meant some of the things he said, let alone that he would carry those views to such unthinkable, evil ends.'

'I disliked him from the start. He gave me the creeps.' I wriggle my shoulders and shudder. 'And there's still no escape from him, even though he's gone. You can see his image all round London. He's been quite the sensation since last November and will be for some time, I should think.'

'Yes, I have seen some of it – it is quite disconcerting to see the 'asylum monster' – plain old Cedric Jones to us – everywhere.'

'Do you think he was mad or evil, or both?'

Friend sighs. 'There's a question. I suppose if there is evil in the world, then he is evil, but such evil is surely madness too. I do not have a simple answer. I tend to overthink these big questions, which only makes me more confused and doubtful.'

'Perhaps too much certainty is not good either. I'm probably guilty of that. To me, there's evil everywhere in this world, in all shapes and forms, and I do my best to fight it, and protect the good.'

'Gracious, what a warrior you are. I shall have to watch myself.'

'Indeed, you shall, Mr Friend,' I say, and laugh.

'Will you not call me Matthew? It does feel more appropriate to this new situation.'

'Yes; you are right, Matthew.'

We finish our meal, including the cheese, smiling at each other and talking about happier subjects, music and theatre. I'm horrified when we leave the restaurant at the potential food waste, thinking of all the poor coves out there starving for a crust, or even that I couldn't share all that delicious food with ma and Nel. I think about having a quiet word with the waiter, and trying to take home the leftovers, but that would be very embarrassing and would spoil the whole atmosphere of the evening, including the waiter's respect. I dismiss the anxious thoughts. Just for tonight, I really am Miss Titania Rosetti, and ordinary life doesn't count.

Friend insists on escorting me to a cab rank on the Strand. I whisper the direction to the sleepy, liquorish driver, and Friend argues with him to agree the fare in advance. He hands it to him and instructs him not to drive recklessly. Then he quickly lifts me up so as to avoid the churn of horseshit, oats and hay and deposits me into the carriage. It's delightful; I want to get back down so he can do it again. He doesn't try to kiss me, just shakes my hand again, beams, then waves until my cab is out of sight.

I can't stop smiling as I journey home, even when I'm forced to grip tightly onto my seat in response to the wild jolts of the carriage. I could be on a magic carpet. I'm high on venison and claret, on white tablecloths and chandeliers, and, above all, on Friend, on his cocoa brown eyes, thick wavy hair and overgrown beard, on his frankness, humour and gentlemanliness. So much for being cautious. Foolish Nan.

I arrive home to Nel waiting up for me, as she often does. She smiles at me gently, gives me a cup of cocoa and goes off to bed. I don't know what's going to happen between us. The anger's gone out of her, I can tell that, but so's the stuffing. She's very still, calm and quiet. Sometimes I catch her looking at me with great pity, sometimes even, I think, with admiration. Other times there's confusion, other times – please, no – flashes of fear. She relents, then she retreats, relents, retreats. I accept the love and the coldness without complaint. She wants to love me wholly again, I can tell, but it's a constant battle for her. She can but try and I can but wait and hope.

CHAPTER 38

I'M ON STAGE, stood very still. I'm wearing a plush velvet gown in a vivid green colour, and no stays. The gown is bunched up under a large pair of trousers, held up by the rope belt of my dress. My hair is tucked up into a battered old top hat, and I'm leaning on a black and white cane. I look like a duck out for a jaunt, and I can already hear some laughter in the audience. My eyes are closed. I am ready.

'Come on then, darlin', show us your legs,' some drunken cove shouts, but he is shushed by the crowd.

I'm pleased. A most polite heckle – it's often what's between the legs that they shout about – and a respectful audience. This is a classy establishment, after all.

The piano starts up, and the lights are upon me.

I lift up my chin and waddle round in a circle, then take a few steps towards the audience, stop and lean on my cane. I'm a gent, I'm a swell, I'm a Champagne Charlie. I stare out into the crowd.

'I've got a secret to share,' I say, my voice deep, strong, the accent London-on-the-make (I've copied Mr Visconti's voice but I don't think he's noticed).

'Spit it out then, darlin',' shouts the same drunken cove.

I shoot a withering look in the direction of the voice, and he is shushed again by his neighbours.

I begin to part-speak, part-sing, nice and slow.

'Men like nothin' more than a woman who is bad.'

I give a slow wink and wiggle my behind.

Laughter.

'Though they say they want 'em pure,

They'd rather have a...'

Laughter, a few gasps. I wink twice. 'Woman of allure.'

More laughter.

I take off my topper and place it on the floor along with my cane. My hair, topped by a small crown of flowers, tumbles down to my waist.

Shouts, whistles.

I slowly untie the belt from the trousers and let them drop, jumping from the heap to the side so that the folds of my gown fall into place.

Even louder shouts, whistles.

Now I begin to move, twirling and leaping around the stage using a slack form of some of the ballet moves I learned as a child. I stretch out my arms and sway, then I tip my head forward, letting my hair drop and start to gyrate my head round and round so that my hair swings with it. Now I run and twirl and leap again, sometimes including the head movements as I go so that my hair flies round me as I move. I come to a stop and face the audience.

A few jeers, a few cheers. A 'diabolical'. A hush.

I pick up the top hat, put it back on my head, tucking my hair into it, and wink at the audience. I jump to the right, into the bundle of trousers, lift them up, and attempt, rather clumsily, to tuck my gown into them, but drop the trousers. I hadn't intended this, but I hear laughter, so I do it again purposely and the laughter increases. I finally get the trousers secured with the belt, and sigh dramatically. More laughter.

I bend to pick up the cane, waggling my behind as I do so. Now I waddle round in a circle, stop to face the audience, and put my left hand on my chin, all thoughtful, tapping the cane slightly with my right hand.

'Then again,' I say, 'I take that back.'

'Don't do that, darlin',' shouts another wag in the audience.

'Oh yes,' I say. 'I take that back.

'Though gents say they like their women bad,

'They really want 'em mad.'

Laughter.

'Though they say they want 'em sane,

They love an addled brain.'

Lots of laughter.

I wink. 'Just ask Hamlet.'

I repeat the exercise of removing my hat and trousers,

and the crowd cheers loudly. I repeat my dance, this time pressing my heart with my hands, or mopping my forehead, and wailing, 'Hamlet, Hamlet'. My crown of flowers falls off. I'm surprised it's lasted this long.

I return to the front of the stage and wink. Now I put the hat and trousers back on, this time deliberately even more clumsily than before, letting the hat, as well as the trousers, fall several times before righting myself.

Lots more laughter.

I repeat my circle of waddling, hand on chin, tapping of cane.

'Then again,' I say to the audience, 'I take that back.'

'Don't do that again, darlin',' shouts the same wag, clearly enjoying his self-appointed role.

Laughter; cheers.

'Though men say they want their women mad,

'I've actually heard it said,

'That there's something even better than when they're not right in the 'ead.'

I pause, look round at the audience, and wink. 'It's simply when their dead.'

Bursts of laughter, some nervous titters.

I discard my trousers and hat, repeat my dance, and complete it by falling down in a heap, as if dead.

Cheers, and more cheers.

I am lying dead, never more alive. How long should I wait? I count to five, the tension rising. Now I scramble to my feet, tumbling several times and tripping over myself to reach the hat, trousers and cane. I pick up the trousers, and try to put them on my head. Roars of laughter. I scratch my head and look bewildered. I try to step into the topper, getting it stuck on one foot and hopping round to get it off. More laughter. Finally, I set myself right, stand up straight, salute, and hold out the cane to direct the audience.

'All together now,' I sing.

'For there's nothin' like a woman when she's dead,

'Even better than when she's bad, or not right in the 'ead.

'She's so pretty, she's so quiet, so delightfully compliant,

'Oh, there's nothin' like a woman when she's dead.'

Cheers and roars of approval from the crowd.

I repeat the chorus and the audience sings along with great energy.

The music stops. The audience continues to sing, and takes a while to quieten. I repeat my circular waddle, touching of chin, tapping of cane.

'Then again,' I say to the audience conspiratorially, 'I'm not so sure.'

'Don't be doubtful, darlin',' shouts the wag.

Laughter.

'Oh yes,' I say. 'For now I've thought of one small flaw.'

I wait a few moments, building the audience's curiosity.

'I thought I'd be a winner.

'But who's to cook my dinner?'

Roars of laughter.

Waddle, touch chin, tap cane.

'Then again,' I say.

The audience quietens, all curious again.

I let my trousers drop, remove the hat and place it on the floor with my cane. I jump away from the trouser heap. Instead of leaving my hair loose, this time I twist it neatly behind my head, sighing loudly as I do so. I straighten up, put my hands on my hips, and frown. I look at the top hat on the floor and create a look of malice. I pick it up with my left hand and the cane with my right. I hold the hat at arm's length, and address it as if it's a man. My voice has changed; now I'm a cockney Missus.

'You won't be needin' any dinner, Tommy, my dear,' I say.

I turn, briefly, to grin at the audience.

'When I've finished with you, you'll feel quite queer.'

Laughter.

'We all find our level,

'And yours is straight to the devil.'

I raise the cane with my right hand as if it's a knife, and make deep, stabbing motions to the side of the hat. The hat falls to the floor. I smile with triumph, and raise the cane in the air.

Some nervous laughter.

'All together now,' I shout, as the cockney wife, holding out my cane like a conductor's baton to direct the audience.

'For there's nothin' like a woman when she's dead,

'Even better than when she's bad, or not right in the 'ead,

'She's so pretty, she's so quiet, so delightfully compliant,
'Oh, there's nothin' like a woman when she's dead.'

The crowd are singing, roaring, clapping, whistling. I'm waving the cane and floating on the sea of noise. I've done it.

I don't think I could have got to this place without my suffering. Before that I was too vain, too conscious of my beauty, a bit too aloof, I suppose. But after having felt truly ugly with my illness, I now feel brave enough to inhabit any face, any posture, as ugly as you like, because what does it matter? I've practiced every kind of contorted expression in the mirror, for my facial features, though refined, are mobile, malleable, and I give them all freely to my audience, to you. I give you my pain and grief and rage and madness. I give you my joy, my lightness, my wit and my love.

Harry says that entertaining is half hocus pocus, half reality, giving over the real you to the audience because people aren't stupid, and will sniff out a fake. You should never think that you're better than them or above them, or worse, despise them. I am giving them the real me, in all its ugliness and beauty, wrapped up in tinsel and lights. But I can't help but despise a part of my audience, the ones who really do think there's nothin' like a woman when she's dead. I'm giving them what they want, though. Why else is Cedric Jones so popular?

CHAPTER 39

Harris Mortimer

THERE IS A music hall act in town, at the Shakespeare, that I have not yet seen. The city has been going, as it were, mad, about her, over the last few months and she is now competing with Cedric Jones, it seems, in terms of notoriety and presence on buses, walls and the like. It is as if they have become some kind of strange entertainment duo, and I would not be surprised to see them featuring on a billboard together, advertising a double act. Perhaps Nancy Carter, or 'Mr Carter', her male persona, will dance and sing with the ghost of Mr Jones, canes, saws and poison bottles in hands.

Well, I am going along this evening, finally, and taking a well-earned break from my work, which is jogging along much better than it had been. I am doing quite well overall. I have seen Dr Goodenough two more times. On the last occasion, he noted an improvement in my speech and that my involuntary movements and paralysis had lessened. I take my pills, rest and recreation. I eat my chicken, fish, eggs, milk and cream, and try to take only in moderation my tea, coffee, wine and spirits. I try very hard to avoid onanism and the use of prostitutes, though I do not always succeed. I meet young ladies in social life and try to be less critical of them. I really do want to marry, and then I can finally be cured of my besetting sin. In fact, I encountered recently a very handsome, young lady of genteel birth, and hope to meet her again. I still have moments of despair, but I also have bouts of optimism.

I spruce myself up in readiness for my outing, and look at myself approvingly in the mirror above the fireplace. My dress coat is brushed to perfection, my collar is as white as snowdrops, and my beard and hair are neatly trimmed and oiled. My ghastly paleness has been replaced by a moderately healthy colour in my face, in which my brown eyes look bright and handsome, if I do say so myself. I am holding my collapsible top-hat, which I have not worn for years, in my hands.

'Do you think I should purchase a bowler hat?' I ask the reflection of Mrs Hopkinson, who is stood behind me smiling. 'I fear I am becoming a little stiff and old fashioned with this old chimney pot.'

'Oh no, sir,' she says. 'You are such a gentleman with your silk topper; these bowlers aren't half so refined. I like the old way. And may I say, Mr Mortimer, how well you are looking today, and how much it gladdens my heart to see it.'

'Thank you, Mrs Hopkinson,' I say, turning round to smile at her. 'It is partly thanks to you for looking after me so wonderfully.'

'Oh, it's nothing,' she says, clearly delighted.

'How is that family of yours, Mrs Hopkinson? Your sons and your grandchildren?'

'Oh, all fine and dandy, thanking you kindly, sir. My sons are up to their elbows in grease and steam on those railways, and my grandsons are all for going the same way. Railway fever, I call it, and they're always pulling things apart and putting them back together again. I don't take in a word they're all saying most of the time, but I'm so proud.'

'You are very fortunate in your relations, Mrs Hopkinson.'

'Oh, I am, sir. And they'll look after me when I finish working. When I've seen you settled, that is.'

She smiles her gummy grin, and I smile back.

I wonder what happens to other old servants who are not so fortunate? The subject has not crossed my mind before. Do they end in the dreaded workhouse, or even on the streets? Perhaps one day I will look into the subject, when I am not so taken up with my work on lunatic asylums.

I take a hackney into the city. We are in the latter half of June now, and the weather is perfect, warm enough to soften the tempers of irritable Londoners, rather than hot enough to inflame them further. Even the cab driver is charming today and I look on the usual quotidian sights, somehow made dazzling by the blue sky and glint of the Thames, with heightened awareness and pleasure. Three grubby children are playing in the filth; a rainbow of ladies' hats bob along as a group of women walk together; two old men are shouting at each other across a loaded dog cart; a laughing female costermonger in a straw hat trimmed with flowers proudly shows off her boots from beneath her short cotton gown.

A cacophony of church bells suddenly applauds, and I am strangely tempted to salute them all. I decide to dine at Romano's, for old times' sake, and now it feels full of mildly pleasant, rather than unhappy, memories. I eat my fish and meat with gusto, and delight in the taste of the champagne, which makes my lightness even lighter. I am accosted by some reasonably handsome, bold young ladies, whom I ward off with good humour and a bottle of champagne. I must try not to be tempted in that direction after the theatre. I arrive at the Shakespeare, which is very lively and full, and take my seat, feeling not alone in the crowd but part of it. I am glad to be here, to be alive and well at least.

The show begins with some kind of second-rate, male entertainer. I do not pay him much attention – I am simply enjoying the atmosphere – but the audience applaud him politely enough. Now it is time for the main act, and I exchange friendly looks and smiles with some of my fellow audience members, brought together in a communion of excitement over Miss Nancy Carter. Now she appears, to much cheering, and begins.

She is very comical indeed with her hat, cane and waddle; I can see why she is so popular. Her face looks a little familiar to me under the top hat, but I suppose these women wear a similar sort of stage makeup to each other, and so have a certain look. Now she is taking off the hat and letting down her beautiful auburn hair, which is crowned with flowers. Good gracious, she is rather like Miss Titania Rosetti. I must not alarm myself, however. Many young handsome women can also look rather alike, I know, and I must not start seeing that woman everywhere again. Some vulgar oafs next to me are shouting and whistling.

Now she unties a rope from around her waist and lets drop the gentleman's trousers to reveal in full an emerald green gown, exactly one of the colours I once imagined Miss Rosetti wearing. How strange. The audience around me grows louder and somehow more lustful. She jumps away from the trousers and begins to dance around the stage. I am entranced. My heart and body seem to move with her; I feel as if we are leaping and swaying as one; her hair wraps itself around me. This act is shocking, I know, but my senses are overcome with heat and desire; I am in a beautiful dream. She stops suddenly, moves to the edge of the stage, and stares out at us, the audience. She stares at me in particular, I am sure.

It is She. Surely it is. There is no mistaking that face: its oval shape, the wide-set toffee-brown eyes, the slight snub nose, the small mouth. No, no, Mortimer, you are being quite ridiculous. This cannot be my Titania. What would She be doing performing in a vulgar music hall? This is one Nancy Carter. A commonplace name for a commonplace, vulgar girl. She is beautiful, yes; she is talented, yes, but she is clearly in her right sphere. My Titania could never speak with such an ugly voice, or disgrace herself with such language, or flaunt herself in such a state of undress in front of crowds of men. No, absolutely not. My Titania is a lady. A lady pure and noble, who is only waiting for me to find her so that we can begin our beautiful lives together. Oh, my angel, where are you?

Now, Mortimer, stop this. You will not return to that state of despair, that madness – and yes, it was madness – into which you fell, not when you have come so far. This is simply a small setback based on the coincidence of a female music hall act that happens to resemble Miss Titania Rosetti, a woman you have in any case put from your mind as an impossible, beautiful phantom conjured up by a fevered brain.

But now a thought occurs to me. Perhaps this woman and Miss Rosetti are related in some distant way. Perhaps Titania Rosetti is unaware of this distant relative. I know that my Miss Rosetti must have fallen upon hard times. She was a governess, something most women do only through necessity, and then endured some kind of personal tragedy over a lover, so finding herself spending a period of time in a public lunatic asylum. Perhaps there have been other poor members of the family, like this girl, this girl whom nature has made an almost replica of her superior, who has resorted to shaming herself on a public stage, and no doubt degrading herself in more dreadful ways also. These women are notorious, after all. Do I not know this from my own experience? Did I not dally with these painted theatrical women, who sell their bodies to men as readily as they sell tickets for their shows? Did I not tire of them, and so settle with a regular woman, Nel, to keep me away from that dazzling dirt? As if Miss Titania Rosetti could ever be such a one.

But I must speak to this Nancy Carter, and find out about her relation. Yes, that is the answer. That will settle me, and set me back on the rational and contented path I have been working so hard to tread.

The rest of the performance is passing in a blur. I see this woman's beautiful face, hair and form, but the rest is pure vulgarity. No, it is worse than vulgarity, it is whoredom. I do not believe in the original sin of women, as many men do. I even think that Adam was as guilty as Eve, but that is one of my little heresies. Only look at my mother as a righteous example of pure, untainted womanhood. They are corrupted by this terrible world we are in. This is a world where this Miss Carter, once an innocent girl, born to be the helpmeet and comfort of man, can create this shameless and shameful mockery of the pure Miss Rossetti, a wanton devil sent to taunt and writhe, and seduce innocent men to their doom.

And now this Nancy Carter is speaking in the voice

of a cockney Mrs, hard, grating, vile, and she is actually murdering her husband. And the audience is laughing and cheering. This is really too much. I shall have to write a piece for the *Times* on the degeneration of public entertainment. How can these people laugh and cheer over such melancholy subjects as madness and murder? It is obscene. What does it say about them? What kind of world are we creating? This is as bad as the mania for, nay, the worship of, Cedric Jones, a vile murderer. We are gone mad, quite, quite mad.

CHAPTER 40

I AM STRUGGLING TO wake up, to fight myself out of my nightmare. I can feel claws gripping my throat, bristles upon my cheek and hot, foul breath upon my face. I am writhing and my legs are kicking. I am choking.

I wake up clutching my throat. She seems to be gone. I cry with relief. Several weeks have passed since I saw Nancy Carter at the Shakespeare, and the hag has been visiting me again. I get up, afraid that the witch might still be hovering in the room somewhere. I walk slowly to my sitting room, pull out the chair from behind my desk, sit down upon it and take up my dumbbells. They are cast in bronze and very heavy. I lift my arms up and down, up and down, driving the demon away.

Mr Friend is sitting opposite me. He has a sister who lives in the area, so it was convenient for him to call here to my Chelsea home. I thought that I no longer needed to see him, indeed that it would be wiser if I did not given the need for me to free my mind of all associations with Miss Rosetti. However, now I am glad that he has written and offered to call. I can ask him some questions, but I must remain calm and rational.

'Thank you for calling, Mr Friend,' I say. 'It is very good of you.'

He is looking very well.

'Not at all, Mr Mortimer,' he says, and takes a sip of his brandy. 'I am only sorry that I was unable to be more forthcoming in response to your letter.'

'Not at all, sir. Indeed, I confess that I feel rather ashamed of that now. I do get very involved in my work, you know, and I fear that I became a little fixated on getting hold of every bit of information I could.'

'It is only natural, and part of the reason why you are so impressive at what you do, I am sure.'

'Thank you. You are very good.'

Friend agrees to talk a bit more about life at the asylum for my research purposes, as we did not have that much time when I was visiting Allingsford. We have a very pleasant, informative conversation over our drinks. He really is a most amiable fellow.

'Do you know,' I say, as we are finishing our brandies, 'that I had the most unusual experience a few weeks ago at the Shakespeare music hall, of all places. There is an act there called Nancy Carter, and she could be the twin of Miss Titania Rosetti from the asylum. It was quite uncanny, and my wits were somewhat bewildered for a few moments.'

Friend seems to look a little embarrassed. I hope he does not think music hall too vulgar.

'Oh, yes, I have seen Miss Carter too,' he says. 'It is a very good act. Rather risqué, I know, but rather brilliant too. I agree, there is a strong likeness. It is just one of those odd coincidences that will sometimes happen in life.'

'You do not think that Miss Carter and Miss Rosetti could be related, do you? They are so very alike; it seems more than coincidental.'

I fear that the side of my mouth is twitching again.

'I cannot imagine it,' says Friend. 'They must be very different women, from very different backgrounds, leading very different lives.'

'Still, that does not necessarily preclude a connection. Have you heard from Miss Rosetti since her departure from Allingsford?'

'No. It is not something that would generally happen. Once a patient is cured and discharged, their connection with the asylum is, happily for them, severed.'

Friend shifts a little in his chair, crosses and uncrosses his long legs.

'Yes, I see. I do wonder, though, if in this instance it might be worth making contact with Miss Rosetti about this Nancy Carter? Perhaps they are related and have lost contact, or are even unaware of each other's existence?

If that is the case, surely it would be a kindness to bring them together.'

I am vaguely aware that I am sounding like a bad novel.

'I am not sure that that would be the right thing to do.' Friend pauses. 'Are you quite well, Mr Mortimer? Your speech sounds a little tired. Can I get you a glass of water?'

'Oh, no, I am quite well.'

'Are you sure? Perhaps you should see a physician?'

'That is none of your business, sir.'

'Yes, you are right; I do apologise.'

'I am so sorry, Mr Friend. Please do forgive my irritability. I am not sleeping very well at the moment and have become a little overtired, I fear.'

'I am sorry to hear that. Do you take anything to help? I do occasionally. Being awake in the night tends only to exaggerate one's fears, I find.'

I nod. He is a thoughtful man. 'Yes, and I have been having some rather bad dreams. I am sometimes visited by a terrible woman, a cross between one of the witches from *Macbeth* and one of those devil spinsters that Cedric Jones was so fond of.'

He does not laugh at me, but looks at me with great compassion. 'That sounds truly terrible. It is not surprising, perhaps. You have spent so much time in his company, alive and deceased. It must have been very distressing at times.'

'Yes, that is true. And our minds can work in strange ways, as we are all aware.'

'Well, I must take my leave now,' says Friend, 'my sister is expecting me for dinner. I hope you are able to get some good rest, and will soon feel more like your old self.'

'Thank you. And thank you again for taking the time to see me, and to talk about your work.'

We get up and shake hands. A tear rolls down my cheek. Friend looks at me pityingly as he makes his departure.

I go to the clothes press, dragging my right leg slightly, and take out Titania's gown from a drawer. I sit down, and hold it to my cheek, luxuriating in the feel of the soft velvet.

I like Friend a good deal. But then, I did not quite like that look of pity he gave me. Who is he to pity me? He is only a glorified clerk, after all. Oh, I am being unkind. But why did he look so embarrassed, guilty, even, one might say? What if, after all, he is, himself, interested in Miss Rosetti? Perhaps he is even courting her already, and that is why she is resisting my love. He has stolen her from me. I remember again that sly smile he gave when we first discussed my Titania at Allingsford. He is a grinning serpent. I do not know how dear Mr Rockingham has been deceived by him.

What should I do? Oh, what should I do?

CHAPTER 41

Nan Carter

MATTHEW HAS TOLD me about his meeting with Harris Mortimer. And since then, Mortimer has not only been attending my performance every night but hanging round the music hall stage door, trying to get to me. I have managed to sneak away from him so far, but I will not be able to do so forever. I must see him and try to end this thing once and for all.

I take a deep breath and walk out of the door, arm-in-arm with Connie.

A man steps forward. His hair and beard are unkempt, his clothing dishevelled; there is a wild look in his eyes. It is Mr Mortimer.

'Miss Nan Carter?' he asks.

'Yes, sir.' I squeeze Connie's arm.

'And…, why, it is Miss Millais. How strange.'

'Yes, it's me, sir,' says Connie.

There is little use in any pretence, now. It would only muddle poor Mortimer's head even more.

'But how is Miss Rosetti?' He addresses Con, and turns his head back and two between the two of us, quite bewildered.

'Come back inside with us, sir,' I say, 'and we can have a little conversation.'

My voice is my usual one. I gesture to Mortimer to follow Connie and I back inside the hall and up the stairs to the more genteel bar. Connie and I sit close together and Mortimer sits down opposite us.

'Would you like any refreshment, sir?' Con asks. 'Perhaps a nip of brandy?'

Mortimer is sweating heavily. It is a hot night and the bar is stuffy.

'Well, perhaps a small one; that would be most kind,' says Mortimer.

His hands shake a little; I hope that the poor chap hasn't developed a thirst. Connie turns round to the barman, who brings all three of us a glass of cognac plus some soda water for Mortimer. We sip at them, Mortimer staring and staring at me, then turning to Connie in disbelief.

'Miss Carter,' he says. 'Perhaps you know who I am from your friend here? Indeed, I am not surprised that you and Miss Millais are friends because I am sure that you are also connected to Miss Rosetti, that, in fact, you are closely related. I just cannot quite fit it all together. I am rather confused and fatigued.'

Mortimer wipes his brow with a rather grubby handkerchief. As Matthew told me, the right side of Mortimer's face is twitching slightly and some of his words are pronounced very slowly and deliberately. He lifts his right hand now and then as if he wants to reach out and touch my face. Oh, this is dreadful.

'Seeing you close up now, without your stage paint, you are more like Miss Rossetti than ever,' says Mortimer. 'Are you twin sisters?'

'No, Mr Mortimer,' I say. 'And, yes, I know who you are. Now, I've something very important to tell you. You won't like it, but you must believe that I'm in earnest.' I take a deep breath. 'There's no such person as Miss Titania Rosetti. Or rather, I am she. Me, Nancy Carter. I had a sad time in my life and spent my time at Allingsford asylum under an assumed name. That's over now, and I'm back to my old life. So you're chasing something that doesn't exist, that never really existed.'

Mortimer stares at me, then laughs.

'That cannot be true,' he says. 'I held Titania Rosetti in my arms. She is a true lady; she is flesh and blood.'

'As I said, that was me, sir. Me, Nancy Carter. I'm truly sorry for the hurt I caused you. But it was done unwillingly. And then when I was discharged from the asylum, and you were writing to me, I was afraid to write and tell you the truth. I hoped that you would forget about Miss Rosetti eventually. But you have not. And this has gone on long enough. I am meeting you again – here, now – so that I can tell you the truth. Titania

Rosetti does not exist. You must accept this truth, get on with your life, and be happy again.'

Mortimer takes a sip of soda water, but it dribbles from the side of his mouth. He wipes it with his dirty handkerchief.

'But,' he says, 'I met Miss Rosetti for tea – it was delightful – with Miss Millais here.' He turns to Connie and examines her intently. 'You can surely attest to the occasion.'

'Yes, sir,' says Con. 'But, like Nan here, I was playing a part so that I could accompany my pal. My name is Contance Roberts, not Miss Millais. I am not a lady's maid, but a barmaid here at the Shakespeare.'

Poor Mr Mortimer. All of this sounds more and more nonsensical and queer to him, I can tell. I can sympathise with his reaction, but it's like he's deliberately refusing to understand. He opens his mouth, as if to speak, several times, his top and bottom lip coming together in the movement of a fish.

'And, Mr Mortimer,' says Connie, 'my act wasn't very good; you must have noticed.'

Mortimer frowns, then nods. 'It was a little strange; this whole thing is most strange.'

Con orders another brandy for him. It is placed on the table in front of him and she gets up and squeezes the glass into his right hand, which is stiff, claw-like.

'Come now, sir,' she says, 'take another drink if you can; it will do you good.'

He stares up at her lovely kind face and manages to take a few sips without spilling them.

'But I love her,' he says. 'I love Miss Titania Rosetti, and I know that she loves me. Surely, your soft womanly hearts can appreciate that. It has all been a terrible misunderstanding. You can give her my details; here,' – he takes a visiting card from his waistcoat pocket and places it on the table – 'or she can contact me by way of the *Times*, you know. That is all I ask. Please. I beg you.'

Con, who is patting Mortimer on the shoulder, looks at me in despair, and sits back down.

'Mr Harris Mortimer, sir,' I say, trying to be as firm and clear as I can. 'I'll tell you the truth one more time, but not again. There is no such person as Titania Rosetti. I was that woman, Titania Rosetti, me, plain old Nancy Carter, who you see before you. I was in Allingsford public lunatic asylum in Hampshire for a while, where you came across me. I had taken a different name, you see, as part of my temporary insanity, I suppose. I had been suffering from a great sorrow and a mental malady. From what you have seen and discovered through your work, you, of all people, must know what strange things the mind can do. You helped me get away from Cedric Jones. You were kind, and I'm truly grateful. But now I'm better, free again, and back to my real life. I'm a plain London girl, who now performs on the stage, and I've never in my life been a governess, or indeed been jilted by a lover.'

'You must believe her,' says Connie, her green eyes very earnest. 'You must indeed, Mr Mortimer, for your own sake.'

She puts out one of her small plump hands and presses one of his.

'I'm grieved for you,' I say, 'truly, but it can't be helped. You must find yourself a real lady, and not a dream; a woman of your own rank, who can make you happy. I'm sure that there are many such women out there, if you'd only open your eyes to the real world. It cannot be such a difficult task.

'And if you would please stop coming to the stage door at night. It is a little frightening for a woman, though I know that you mean me no real harm.'

He's just staring at us both, his mouth making the same fish-like movements.

'I know what it is, sir,' I say, 'to suffer so terribly in mind and heart, but things will change. You must believe what we have told you. Then you will get better, and be happy again. We must go now.'

Connie and I get up, say 'goodbye', and Con looks at the bar man and nods as if to say, please look out for him. For a few moments, it seems as if Mortimer is going to get up and follow us, but he changes his mind, and shrinks back into his chair.

I'm near to tears. But I've done all I can now. I just hope that he can realise the truth, and be well again.

CHAPTER 42

MATTHEW AND I are sat in Café Monico on Tichbourne Street, taking a pastis and a cigar. It's the end of the first week of July and a storm is brewing; we've managed to find a cool spot inside. Matthew laughs at my knowledge of the continental city, as he calls it, and says that it's like being back in Paris for him. Well, I am a Soho girl, and, within our little enclave, we are continental, even international, considered a bit foreign and suspicious by some.

'It was terrible,' I say. 'I really think he is mad.'

'I believe so too,' says Matthew. 'Poor, poor fellow. I suspected that he was becoming a little strange when he moved into the asylum, and especially that he had become fixated upon you. One doesn't like to speculate too much in that direction, however; we can all be strange at times, and it can be too easy, when you work in an asylum, to look out for signs of madness everywhere. But when I called upon him, I was very concerned.'

'You don't blame me in any way, do you?'

'No, you foolish girl. If it had not been you, it would have been some other person or thing.'

'You will speak to Mr Rockingham about him, won't you?'

'Assuredly. As soon as I get back tomorrow, I will go straight to him. Rockingham is very good, very compassionate, and will know what to do for the best. He was friends with Mortimer's parents, it seems, and has even been a sort of father figure to him over the years.'

'That makes me feel better. I am a little anxious about Mr Rockingham finding out about me, though. It would be awful for him to know I'd deceived him. And then do you think he would do anything against me?'

'No, I am sure he would not. I will say as little as possible, but I can be candid on some points, saying that you took an assumed name, for example. Indeed, I do not know much more, so there is little for me to tell. Even if he were very vexed, which I doubt, he would not spend time chasing you when there is so much work for him to do.'

'Thank you, Matthew.' I press my right hand on his across the small iron table. 'And thanks for not pressing me about my Allingsford story. I think you know from my records that I lost a younger sister, Penelope. It nearly killed all of us, I think; ma, Nel and me. I truly believe that I was mad for a time, mad with grief, at least. And I think that's all I can say on the matter right now. I don't know if I'll ever be able to say more.'

He squeezes my hand. 'You need say no more. I, too, lost someone very dear to me. Not my older brother, whom I mentioned, as that was so long ago. When I went to France, I eloped with my childhood sweetheart. It was a foolish, impetuous thing to do, but we were so young and had read too much romantic poetry.' He laughs dryly. 'She died of consumption. I have felt the weight of guilt ever since, as if I somehow took a knife and stabbed her.'

My heart beats fast. I lean over and kiss him gently on the forehead. 'I am so very sorry.'

'It is not that I miss the love that we might have had, for I think the union would have turned sour soon enough. It is that I am the villain who took a silly young girl away from her family, forever.'

'She chose to go too.' I cannot say anything of greater comfort, and simply hold his hand.

'Well, well, this is cheerful talk for our last afternoon together before I return to Hampshire.'

I smile. 'Let's have another pastis, and I'll have another go with this cigar. I haven't smoked one for years; I'm not sure it's doing my throat much good.'

'As charming as you look with that cigar, I would rather you were still breathing.'

'Garcon?' I look up and nod at the round, elderly waiter, whose fat chin appears to extend from below his lip to the top of his chest, obscuring any neck he may once have had. He soon delivers two more glasses of pastis.

'It is the famous Miss Nancy Carter, no?' he asks, his small, brown eyes bright.

'Oui.' I nod, smiling widely. I must admit that I'm still enjoying the attention I've been receiving, which has only grown and grown since I moved from the Parrot to the Shakespeare. A few other customers turn and raise their glasses to me. Matthew grins.

'And how is Mr Visconti?' he asks.

'Oh, he's very happy,' I say. 'He's quite changed his tune since I first auditioned for him. He was right, though. I had a chance to hone my act at the Parrot, and in front of a pretty lively crowd' – I grin – 'and now it's better than ever.' I pause. 'Can I ask you if you were shocked when you saw it?'

He thinks for a moment. 'Yes, I was, to be candid. I was expecting something a little different' – he grins – 'given that you'd been on at the Parrot, but I was still surprised. The act's so clever, but great entertainment at the same time. I think you are a very talented woman.'

I can't help but smile until my face aches. 'I need to keep thinking ahead, though. Harry's a pearl but he's a businessman and he wouldn't hesitate to let me go if the act doesn't continue to be popular. I'd love to go to America, one day.'

'Oh?' Matthew looks a little crestfallen.

'It's just an old dream really. As a child, when I couldn't sleep, I'd imagine myself on this huge ship, crossing oceans, stretching out my arms to new worlds, and singing and dancing when I got there.'

'It sounds delightful. Can I come?'

I giggle. 'You can. What will you do?'

'Oh, maybe I will become an international music hall sensation. I will sing and dance with a pen, pot of ink and some files. The world will have seen nothing like it.'

'You're not wrong there, sir,' I say, laughing.

'I would miss you very much, though,' he says, looking at me in that way that makes me want to confess my whole heart to him. He should have been a priest.

'And I you,' I cannot resist responding. 'But I will not go because I would never leave ma and Nel.'

I really mean this. And it's felt so good being able to support them both for a bit. I've encouraged Nel not to try too hard for now to find another gent. Since Mortimer, she's stayed at home, looking after ma, doing what makes her happiest. And there's even the possibility of a suitor on the horizon, a great-nephew of Herr Konig.

'From what you have told me of them,' says Matthew, 'and your mother especially, I cannot imagine her trying to stop you, or making you feel awful if you went.'

'She is pure goodness. And she would encourage me to go if she knew how much I wanted it. But I will not. I've led such a selfish life and now I have to look after her and Nelly.'

Matthew looks doubtful.

'It is true. I'm not trying to appear saintly or as some kind of martyr. It's what I must do.'

'In that case, do you think Mr Visconti might consider my act for the Shakespeare? Perhaps we could form a duo?'

We finish our pastis and I have a coughing fit from the fowl cigar.

'You might travel in other ways someday,' says Matthew. 'And there are lots of places in the world that I would love to set eyes upon.'

He gives me that look again and I smile.

'You've barely covered Soho and Covent Garden, yet,' I say.

'That is true. I have a lot of catching up to do.'

'You could maybe begin by meeting ma and Nel next time you're here.'

His face lights up. 'Really? I would be honoured.'

'You can talk to ma about the countryside. She gets more and more sentimental about it every day, and sometimes comes back from the flower market with tears in her eyes.'

'Actually, you know, I do have a small cottage in Herefordshire; it was part of my mother's portion. Your mother would love it.' He pauses. 'I am sorry; I am getting carried away and sounding like a rather desperate suitor.'

'Do feel at liberty to offer up as many cottages as you like.'

We kiss each other quickly on the lips, and there's a loud cheer from the next table.

'Let's take our time,' I say. 'We barely know each other, really, but I'm hopeful.'

And I am. I've let my guard down a lot with Matthew, and my heart flutters before I see him, and at the thought of him when he's away. And the fact that he doesn't seem put off by me cavorting and cursing on a stage, half-naked, whilst being ogled by other men, is testament to a stout-enough heart.

Of course, I haven't told him that I've murdered someone. I think you can be too candid. He might understand, but what if he doesn't? And how many people would? He might never be able to see me in the same way again, or he might even start imagining that he'd be my next victim. No, that's one thing I'll always keep to myself.

CHAPTER 43

Harris Mortimer

THE WITCH IS coming slowly towards me, laughing. Her teeth are as black as her torn black gown, and the tufts of hair on her chin. Her skin is the colour of her long grey hair, which is knotted, and entwined with violets. Her eyes flash red and yellow, the yellow of the long twisting talons that go before her, ready to rip my skin and draw my blood.

I wake up in a cold sweat, and turn to the right to vomit over the side of my bed. I cannot go back to sleep; the weird sister will be waiting for me. She waits for me every night now; it is best if I do not sleep at all. I push myself up to get out of bed but stumble over into the patch of vomit on the floor. My right leg is paralysed and will not take my weight. I cry. I finally push myself up using the side of the bed and my sturdy walking cane, which is always near me. I drink some soda water left on the bedside table by Mrs Hopkinson and drag myself into the sitting room.

My mind is so muddled now that I struggle to string fully formed thoughts together. I am aware that I must find Miss Rosetti, somehow. That is the one thing my mind is able to cling to. I do not believe Nancy Carter and her friend. I do not know why they lie. They may be vulgar good-time girls, but I am sure that their hearts are sincere in some way. It is too much for me to understand as yet.

I light some candles, my hands shaking. I prefer candlelight to gas light these days. It casts an antiquarian glow over my surroundings and softens my spirit. I am standing in the middle of the room. I hobble over to the corner devoted to my professional life, where Cedric Jones is so vividly present in works of science, journalism and popular entertainment. There is much analysis of Jones based on the so-called sciences of physiognomy and phrenology, so that his character, course of life and eventual criminal insanity can all be read from his facial features and the shape of his head and body. One writer claims to have found a hereditary connection through a branch of his family, which is a notorious criminal gang residing in the East End of London, characterised by its low slang speech, unintelligible to the uninitiated. It is believed that other branches of the gang are now terrorising the United States and the Antipodes. I prefer the humorous approach of *Punch* magazine, which has for many years been fighting this pseudo-science, or 'bumpology', with the sword of satire.

There is a street ballad, for which I paid two pennies, devoted to Sarah, Sally and Clara. The words seem rather inane and pedestrian on the page, with their talk of the wretched women grown old, and so cold at the hands of the mad, cruel Jones. But my heart nearly broke when I heard the haunting tones of the ragged ballad singer on the Strand the other day. There are some other verses and poems, which were offered to me from under the counter in a bookshop in Covent Garden, which I will not dwell upon.

There is a large advertising poster for Mad Bessie, the latest show about Cedric Jones. I took down the poster from the wall near the Covent Garden opera house on one of my early-hours perambulations and brought it home. The popularity of Miss Nancy Carter, as well as of Jones, has spurned a host of copycat acts. I have not seen this one. I do not feel entirely comfortable with this fashion for women dressing up and parading around as men for the popular entertainment. What example is it setting for delicate female minds? This picture does divert me, however, with Mad Bessie sat atop a giant poison bottle.

The Cedric Jones ceramic figure and the jack-in-the-box remain on top of my bureau. Without this evil man, my Titania would never have thrown herself into my arms.

In my darling's corner, I have again built up a collection of gowns and other dress items. It is not much. I do regret disposing of my previous collection. I often stroke the gowns to give me comfort. One is in a burnished orange colour, which glows like a sunset, and which will become her so very well, I think. One is in emerald green, the colour of Nancy Carter's gown. The warm velvet, which is both soft and rough, and the smooth coolness of the silk calms my nerves. Their array of jewel-like colours lifts my heart, if only for a moment. I must buy her some real jewels, now I think about it. Why have I not thought of this before? They will be nothing gaudy or tasteless, mind; they will be expensive but simple and pure, and will enhance her beauty, not cheapen it. There is a pair of dainty boots in cream leather, latticed with ribbon and a bow. There is a green silk bonnet trimmed with white flowers and ribbons and a cream fur tippet. I have quite the eye for these things. There is a white parasol to keep the sun from her milky complexion, and a large blue umbrella to keep the rain away; I would not want my darling to catch cold.

I have made so many sketches of my love and placed them everywhere. They are very real to me for I do believe that I am a talented artist. I do have mixed feelings about artists, though, with their tendency towards immorality, which I cannot condone. Perhaps I am a trifle conventional, after all; I pride myself on my moral rectitude. But I must buy some watercolours so that I can really bring my love alive. The pencil sketches are very good, but they can never capture the full light, shade and glow of her skin or the beauty of her eyes and hair.

A Steinway piano is tucked into the corner, for she will

want to sing when she comes. I have been quite extravagant, I am afraid, but I cannot help myself, for it seems to me that there is nothing that can be too good for her. Sadly, my musical talents are no match for my skills with a pencil and brush, but I can tap out a tune, and perhaps she can teach me. How charming that will be. There is a vase of flowers on top of the piano; I have instructed Mrs Hopkinson to change them every three days, so that they are always fresh and ready for her arrival.

Should I go out for my usual nocturnal wander? I generally hobble through the streets of Soho in the middle of the night. It helps to cool my fevered body and mind. I often sing Nancy Carter's song as I go, a wag sometimes shouting the words back at me, 'Oh, there's nothing like a woman when she's dead'. I do not return home until I am wearied out, when I hail a cab to bring me back. The streets at night are not always a pleasant place; I have been robbed of my watch and pocketbook, attacked, for no apparent reason, several times, and am the prey of many unfortunate women.

I had better not, for my leg is worse than usual just now, almost paralysed. Instead, I pour myself a glass of brandy and manage to sit down in my comfortable chair without any mishap. My eyelids begin to flicker along with the candlelight.

'Mr Mortimer, sir?'

I open my eyes. My mind is foggy, my body stiff.

'Mrs Hopkinson. Good morning.'

'It is three o'clock in the afternoon, sir. Have you slept here all night?'

'I believe I must have done.'

'Oh, Mr Mortimer, I'm so very fretful about you. I am, indeed. Have you seen that doctor of yours lately?'

'I am not sure. Perhaps an appointment is due.'

'You must go, sir, you must. My heart's breaking, it truly is.'

I look at Mrs Hopkinson's wrinkled face, tears dropping from her blue eyes.

'Matilda,' I say.

'Yes, dear, that's my name.' More tears drop and she pats me on the shoulder. 'Right, sir, vittles is the first thing and I won't take no for an answer. You look half dead, more ghost than man, if that ain't too dreadful a thing to say. We need to bring you back to life.'

The dear woman bustles round me, trying to make me more comfortable, putting a cushion behind my head and straightening me up. She stares at the right side of my face and looks tearful again. She makes me tea, then toast with butter and boiled eggs on a tray. I struggle to swallow, but it does me good. I must keep up my strength to find Miss Rosetti.

'Will you take a little visit to the barber, soon, sir? I've always admired what a handsome, proper gentleman you are with your neat hair and beard; you don't want to be like one of these wild, over-hairy types you see everywhere nowadays.'

I smile. 'You are right, Mrs Hopkinson.'

She continues to tidy and clean around me. To my great shame, I notice my discarded sheath on the Persian rug. Mrs Hopkinson picks it up quietly and does not look at me. I am afraid that lately I have had recourse to Cremorne once again. I have managed, mostly, to avoid self-abuse, partly, I must admit, because I feel that the witch is watching me. But the lure of Cremorne has been too much for my aching body and mind; I must have some sort of palliative.

'Will you go back to bed now, sir?' asks Mrs Hopkinson.

'I will rest here awhile,' I say.

'If you're sure. Let me get a blanket for you, at least. It's a warm day but you can easily catch a chill when you sleep.'

She finds a coverlet to put over me and gently presses my feet into my old felt slippers.

'Is your leg bad again, dearie?'

I nod. Mrs Hopkinson has fallen into the rather vulgar, impertinent habit of calling me 'dearie', but I find it comforting.

'You must promise me that you'll see that fine doctor of yours soon. I'll be back tomorrow. I've left some cold pie and fowl in the larder for you until then.' She pauses, staring at me. 'I do feel that it's a rum thing to leave you when you're like this, sir.'

'I will be perfectly well, thanks to your good mini…, minist…' I think I say ministrations, but I am not sure if the sound comes out.

Mrs Hopkinson cries a little more, then bends to kiss me on the head. Again, I do not mind. She makes her waddling departure, sniffling as she goes.

CHAPTER 44

I THINK IT IS Sunday today. I will go to church. Then, perhaps, I will go in search of her.

I wash and dress as well as I can and examine myself in the gilt-edged looking glass above the fireplace. I am really quite gaunt and haggard. My hair is a bit too long, falling just past my shoulders, and a bit too wild, as is my beard, which I had planned to keep so neat and trim. There are some white stains on my waistcoat. Good gracious, what a disgrace I am. Mrs Hopkinson will be horrified. She always ensures that my clothes are beautifully clean and pressed, but I do not have the will to change my current ones. The thought drifts away.

I put on my coat and boots, struggling greatly with my right leg, and look again in the glass. I am missing something. A hat, that is it. I do not know where my topper is. I spot the vase of flowers, exquisite in their freshness, on top of the piano, and smile. I pick out a selection – a pale pink rose and some lilac and white larkspurs – and place them carefully in my hair. Ophelias always have flowers in their hair. My love will feel at home when she sees me.

I leave the house and tap my way through the quiet streets to St Luke's church in the pale light. It will soon be hot, but now it is beautifully cool. God will bless my endeavours today. I have suffered, and I suffer still, but we are all born to suffer in some way. I wonder sometimes if my suffering is God's way of making me truly empathise with the plight of the insane, so that I really am the best person to promote that great work of our society. God's ways are mysterious, but always right, and I must try to accept them, and trust that all is working for the best.

I arrive at the church. All is quiet without and within. It must be quite early. I make my way to the altar, the tap of my stick echoing eerily, to look once again at the painting of Christ's deposition. A bit of peace enters my heart. After a little time, I reach out to take the forward foot of Christ so that I can bathe it. I grasp at the painting with my left hand but cannot get the grip I need.

'Sir, sir. What are you doing?' asks a high-pitched voice behind me.

I hear a shuffling and then somebody tapping me on my shoulder.

'Please desist. You must not damage the painting.'

I turn round to see a short, bowlegged old man wearing knee breaches and a pig-tail wig. He smells strongly of snuff, some of which has spilled over his jacket. It is the organist. He is quite of another era and I like him very much.

'Oh, 'tis you, Mr Mortimer.'

He stares at me, his small head cocked on one side. He notes the side of my face and my cane. 'You are not well, sir. Come, sit down, now.'

'I am just a little fatigued,' I say, but sit down on one of the congregant benches at the organist's direction. 'I was trying to bathe the foot of Christ.'

'Yes, I saw. An act for which He will be grateful. But the painting just represents Him, you see? Although his presence is here with us. So, you must bathe the foot in your imagination, as it were, and God will know the good secret of your heart.'

I nod. It is easier than the effort of forming words. I think I understand.

'Now, Mr Mortimer, let me fetch you some tea, and you can take some quiet time here to soothe yourself before the other worshippers arrive for the service.'

He shuffles off. How kind he is. How kind are these people whom nobody usually notices. I notice them now. God is teaching me. The organist returns with a cup of strong tea on a large saucer, and I clutch it with my shaking hands, taking small slow sips, to avoid burning my mouth or spilling any. The organist goes off to greet some fellow church workers and prepare for the service. I am left in peace. He returns, perhaps half an hour later, smiles at me warmly and takes away the cup.

The quiet is replaced by the sound of people arriving,

talking quietly and seating themselves. I turn to look and smile but either people do not notice me, or they are deliberately avoiding catching my eye. I am alone in my pew. My mind drifts through the service, but my soul lifts when the organ plays. I sway and reach out my arms to touch Him, as did the worshippers at Allingsford asylum chapel.

The service ends. Now we are exchanging blessings and taking our leave. I nod at some of the regulars as I walk slowly down the aisle to the door but receive in return only hurried turns of the head and just one quick pitying smile. Gone is the fawning and simpering. I am an outcast, it seems. Well, I shall put away pride and vanity, and disregard the petty thoughts of the foolish throng.

The reverend, once so civil, looks at me with disdain and bids me a cold farewell. But a few moments later, the organist catches up with me, presses my hand and says, 'God be with you, Mr Mortimer.'

I squeeze his hand as a tear falls down my cheek. 'And with you,' I say, very slowly, and walk on.

I turn onto Chelsea embankment, and wander slowly along it, leaning heavily on my stick as I go. It is a very fine construction, having opened only a few years since. I smile at the courting couples and families enjoying their walks as I pass some of the old-fashioned taverns and coffee houses. Now I stop, and take a seat, looking out at the cold grey shimmer of the Thames. 'Found drowned.' The words seem to speak to me from the water. It is a phrase used to describe the poor female souls who have thrown themselves into the great river in despair, either from poverty or shame, their bodies washed up on shore or dredged up by some bargeman or fisherman. I do not know why I think of this. I suppose they are somewhat akin to the Ophelias of the asylums. I think of Titania in the same terrible predicament, her body lying on the shore, her glorious hair wet, knotted and wrapped around her body, and the waves lapping over her skirts. I cannot help but think that it would make a beautiful picture; I am an artist, after all. Lord, please preserve her.

Now, strangely, I see myself in a similar state. I am also lying on shore, the waves lapping over my trouser legs, my feet bootless, pale and wrinkled. I, too, am looking rather beautiful. I stare at this image of myself for some time; it does not frighten me at all. Perhaps one day there will be a painting of this scene on display somewhere, of me making the ultimate sacrifice, like Christ himself.

Perhaps I doze a little, or rather a lot. I awake to an encroaching dusk and a slight chill. Some very dirty urchins, straight from the pages of *Oliver Twist*, are stood staring and laughing at me. I think one of the little devils is about to steal my cane, but he drops it on seeing me open my eyes. I reach for it, haul myself up, and press a few small coins into their hands. They look at each other and scamper off.

I am not sure where I am going. My mind is misty,

as usual, and I note only the blurred grey environment punctuated with dots of white and yellow from just-lit lamps and candles, so that I feel as if I am in an impressionistic painting. My feet and stick are more acute than my brain, however, and guide me to a familiar, dark corner of the wharf. I hear laughs, grunts and shouts of anger or pleasure. A streetwalker approaches me – grubby, dishevelled, in liquor. It is dark but I can see that she is an older woman, perhaps in her forties, although she may just look older due to the life she has led.

'Looking for some fun, Mr floral gent?' she asks.

I do not think I have my rubber with me. I am meticulous, even in these kinds of situations, about cleanliness and purity. I am laughed at, usually, by the whores on the streets, who do not expect it.

'Not this evening,' I say.

Once my carnal needs are satisfied with street whores, I usually dismiss them very quickly. I pay and go; they are filthy creatures beneath my dignity, after all. But now I find myself looking at this creature as if seeing a real woman for the very first time.

'Are you hungry?' I ask her, examining her cracked powdered face and small brown eyes.

'Always, dear,' she says, laughing, then grabbing at my trousers with her stubby fingers.

'No.' I step away.

She scowls, then shrugs, giving up. 'Perhaps you ain't in the market for a lady, sir?'

'I am at no market, madam. Wait, take this,' I say,

pressing several coins into her rough palms. 'Get some food and shelter; go to church; God will help you.'

She stares at the coins in surprise. 'You have helped me, sir, indeed you have. Are you one of those charity fellows?'

'No,' I say. 'Go now, and get some shelter.'

Perhaps I have become a messenger of the Lord. Perhaps. Anything is possible.

The harlot hurries away and I soon hear her propositioning someone else. I walk on, finally sitting down on a large stone. I feel hot now, a little feverish, and take off my coat. I feel for my hat in order to remove it but realise that I am wearing only a few bedraggled flowers.

'Looking for some fun,' I murmur, 'looking for some fun, sir?'

I hear the sound of heavy footsteps approaching, and look up to see a burly man in bulky workman's clothes, boots and cap.

'I'm looking for some fun, pretty boy,' the man says, in a rough voice with an unfamiliar accent. Perhaps he is from foreign shores.

I stare at him. 'Oh, my good man, no, you have made a mistake. I am just taking my rest.'

'Your rest, eh, my g, g, g, g, good man? My little stutterer. Been a busy boy this evening? Turning down trade? Don't be a silly little b, b, b, b, boy.'

He comes closer and gives a shout of laughter. 'Oh, if it ain't Jesus Christ himself, complete with his pretty little crown of thorns.'

He puts his left arm on my right shoulder, and tilts up my face with his right fist. I wince from the smell of beer and raw onions.

'Sir,' I manage, trembling, 'you are mistaken in whatever you think of me. I simply came out to take a walk and get some fresh air.'

He snorts, then pulls at my beard with his fist.

'Have it your own way, boy; I've got no taste, this evening, for Jesus Christ.'

He laughs, lets go of me, then tramps away into another painting, perhaps featuring a fisherman on the edge of a Turner seascape. I close my eyes.

'Looking for some fun, sir?' I say.

'Titania, Titania, Ophelia, Ophelia.

"Before you tumbled me/You promised me to wed/ So would I 'a' done, by yonder sun/An though hadst not come to my bed."'

I get up, pick up my coat from the ground, and head in the direction of home, singing to myself as I go.

'"Come, my coach! Good night, ladies, good night, sweet ladies, good night, good night."'

CHAPTER 45

Nan Carter

THERE WERE TWO objects for me to exact my revenge upon. And how I despised them, with every nerve and fibre of my being. It was the sort of hate that made life worth living, the sort that you consume greedily, and that could consume you whole.

The real trouble for Penny in the Marchmont household began when the governess, who was in love with the master of the house, noticed him admiring Penny. He couldn't disguise his attraction to her, and his desire. He never took advantage, though. She was very young and vulnerable. He loved his ringleted wife and was quite the gentleman. But the governess noticed his feeling, and was furious. She wasn't jealous of the wife, who wasn't worth the effort, but Penny, now, was another matter. Penelope Carter, with her melting brown eyes, snub nose and rather too womanly figure for a girl of fourteen. And she could read, and speak properly – what was she doing there? The governess set out to make her life a misery, and succeeded.

It still amazes me today, when I consider it, that Pen stuck at her general duties as a servant. She got up at half-past five in the morning, carried water and slop pails up and down uneven stairs, cleared fires of ashes and cinders and prepared new ones with paper, wood and coal. She scrubbed steps and cleaned fireplace surrounds with oily black lead, knives with emery powder and old furniture with beeswax polish. She did all this, and more, and the governess stood over her and told her that she wasn't doing things properly, and to do them again, then told the Master and Mistress that Penny was a lazy little slut, or words to that effect.

One day, in what turned out to be the last week of Pen's service, the governess told her that she had to get inside the dining room chimney, climb up inside as best she could and clean it. And Pen did it, and nearly killed herself, choking up coal dust and fumes and unable to get the dirt out of her eyes, skin and clothes for weeks to come.

A few days later, Pen was in her mistress's crammed drawing room, relieved to be simply dusting the endless knick-knacks, small tables, silver-framed photographs, jardinieres filled with flowers and trailing ferns, and glass boxes and bowls stuffed with fake fishes, flowers and birds. She was so very tired, she later told the cook, and glad to just be there in that gloomy, peaceful place, chatting to her mistress's parrot, which, to Pen's delight, occasionally delivered some very bad swear words indeed.

Her peace was interrupted by the arrival of the chimney sweep, there to do his regular duty. Then she realised that she'd been had by the governess, and all her stuffed-up frustration, rage and misery burst out at last. She cried and stamped her feet, then went in search of the governess, who she found in the palm-filled conservatory. As the skylark hopped about and sang its sweet song, Pen punched and scratched at the governess until she was bleeding, quite getting the better of the much taller, older woman. She only stopped when her mistress appeared in the door. What did I tell you, screamed the governess, and hobbled out of the room crying. But the mistress, who wasn't as stupid as she seemed, approached Pen, patted her on her arm and cheek, unpinned a silver, jewelled broach that she was wearing, and pressed it into Pen's hand.

The cook told me and Connie all this after the event. She was fond of Penny, and tried to help, but everyone is so busy in a place like that, it's hard to keep a watch on everything. Pen had told us only a little of it, and we were so upset that she hadn't confided in us properly. Pen left the house that day, never to return, and went to stay with a young man she'd been stepping out with. Tom Sikes was his name. It was then early August in '74.

The cook had seen the young man a few times, and said he was a greasy, pimpled, unsavoury-looking thing, and she couldn't understand it. He worked as a junior clerk in a bank, but had a taste for the high life. He spent his money, and that they got from pawning the broach, before suggesting to Pen that she might like to help out a bit by making herself obliging to a few gentlemen. Connie saw her once, our baby sister, walking slowly up Piccadilly without bonnet or shawl, and turning her head round and about to smile at passing men. It also looked like Sikes had been making great play with her face.

I can't bear it when I think of that; I just can't bear it.

I sometimes think, but I squash the thought, that Pen only did what Nel and I have also done in our lives. But not like that, never like that. And we did it for ourselves, not to please a vile little beast not fit to polish her boots with his spittle.

Well, our poor Penny pretty much died of wretchedness and disease in December '74. She had just turned fifteen years old. And it really was like something from one of those religious tracts or moralistic tales in novels and magazines, the sort of thing you laugh at a little and don't quite believe really happens.

Oh, Penelope, I still can't understand why you didn't just come running back to us, who loved you so; we would have petted you and comforted you and been so proud of what you tried to do for us.

Anyway, I went after Tom Sikes first, but the evil little bastard was dead, killed in an accident on the street, trampled by a horse. It's not such an uncommon death, to be honest. Oh, how I wish I could have seen it, though, seen his pathetic little body writhing in pain. I would have smiled at him, told him who I was, and encouraged the horse to kick harder. And if only I were rich and could have tracked down that horse, I would have housed it in a palace, fed it on venison and claret, and worshipped it until the day I died. That fantasy kept me going for a good while.

So I then turned my attention to the governess in the Marchmont household. You could say that she wasn't on the scale of evil of Tom Sikes. She didn't take the most precious, shiny thing in the world, degrade it, defile it, stamp all over it and send it out to market. But if she hadn't made Pen's life so miserable, none of it would have happened. Pen wouldn't have flitted the house, and ended up running straight into hell. So she made a pretty good target for my revenge, and so I had another new purpose.

I waited outside the Marchmont house a lot, sometimes spotting Mr Marchmont and his pretty, girlish wife, sometimes the servants, but Sarah only once, who I identified from the cook's description. She had a haughty, sharp look about her. I wanted to shout her name, but no sound came out. What would I do if it did? What would I say to her? What would I do to her? Would I really have killed Tom Sikes if he hadn't been done for already? I don't know. Perhaps it was all fantasy, and I was just a coward, or better than I thought I was, depending on your point of view.

So I watched and watched, then went home to plan.

I lay in my bed, going over and over different ideas, like bleedin' Hamlet, because I wanted the revenge to be perfect and couldn't decide what that perfection was, or even rouse myself to do it if I could.

Then Connie and I took the kindly cook for tea again – it was around May of '75, I think – and she told us that the governess had ended up in Allingsford lunatic asylum in Hampshire. I was shocked. I was also half pleased, feeling that she was being punished somehow. I was also half vexed, thinking that she was now out of my reach.

The cook said that when Penny left, Miss Barker couldn't be as triumphant as she might have expected to be, because the household turned on her, blaming her for Penny feeling like she had to go. Sarah wasn't dismissed, but the master of the house, particularly, couldn't bear to be in her sight. This was too much for Sarah's senses because she loved Mr Marchmont and seemed to think that morally she was his true wife. She had known his family from childhood, had been with him as governess to his children for twelve years, and had nursed him through several illnesses.

After everyone turned cold on her, she started to have some strange episodes, talking and laughing hysterically to herself and repeatedly folding and unfolding all items of linen in the house. Then she started to teach the children - two girls, eight and twelve – about nursing, which seemed harmless enough at first, Florence Nightingale being a national heroine, and a perfectly respectable one for little girls. But soon she was telling them that she was actually the real Florence Nightingale, and began dosing them with all sorts of remedies, making one of them quite ill. So she had to go. But they wanted to help her, after all her years of service, in spite of what had happened. So they eventually decided to get her submitted to an asylum, away from London, and settled on one in Hampshire.

When I first heard this, for some reason, I had an image of Penny and the Marchmont's profane parrot, and wondered if that was how Sarah had picked up her occasional inclination for cursing. Or perhaps it was the other way around.

I didn't tell ma or Nel about any of this. As far as they knew, Penny, unhappy in her position, and too proud to come home to us, had gone off, got into vicious company and evil ways, and things went bad from there. They never expressed a wicked thought or intention towards any one or thing in regard to her death. Looking back, I suppose this did not mean that they were not thinking wicked thoughts. Ma and Nel believe in God, and Providence, and things like that, and that we will all be rewarded for our goodness and punished for our sins in a life to come. I wasn't sure myself, and never thought overmuch about it, but when we went through our dark times, I was furious with them for believing such childish and self-deceiving things. It was all just senseless, unfair and cruel, and that was that.

And then the Ophelia idea entered my head and

would not budge. I had a fixed purpose, a monomania, I suppose, and so it began.

I decided on my method right away: poison. It's a woman's preferred method of murder, they say, not requiring physical strength, and also suiting a female talent for deceit and manipulation. Whatever they say, I thought it would be the easiest method to hide. Either they would think that Sarah had died from natural causes or that she'd committed self-murder. I thought about the chemicals used in the photographic studio, there, waiting for me. It took a while for me to get hold of some of the potassium cyanide, but I was patient, for I had the best purpose of my life, and I got what I needed. Then it was just a case of putting it in Sarah's tea. I befriended her, and she didn't seem to mind me; I looked nice and talked properly, didn't I?

I'll admit, I wobbled quite a bit at first. I'd be about to add a little poison to her tea, and I'd hesitate, and the longer I hesitated, the worse it got. Like bloody Hamlet again. I knew that the hesitation would slowly poison me and finish me off if I wasn't careful. I rallied, reminding myself why I was doing it, and that I hadn't put myself through all this madness for nothing. I also decided to act a part, a cross between Macbeth and Lady Macbeth, if you will. If I'm acting, I can do anything. I hardened, grew strong in my purpose again, and finished the job.

Of course, I wanted Sarah to know why she was suffering, and why she had to die; it wouldn't be a proper revenge otherwise. I did it slowly.

When I was sitting next to her on one of the long benches for dinner or tea, the clatter of cutlery around us, I'd whisper sweet nothings into her ear.

'Do you remember Penelope Carter?' I'd say. 'I'm her sister. You murdered her and I'm going to murder you.' Then I would smile and nod. Or I'd vary it a little, depending on my mood and what I could get away with in the situation. 'I had another sister once, a housemaid called Penny, the most beautiful girl you've ever seen. She died; well, she was murdered, to be honest, by a wicked governess, and do you know, I'm going to murder that governess?' Sarah would jump for a moment, then shake her head, and I would keep nodding and smiling along. She tried to tell a few of the attendants about me, and became very nervous about eating. She always drank her tea, though; good old Sarah. Anyway, who would have believed a mad old woman who thought she was Florence Nightingale, and was claiming that someone was trying to murder her? Especially when that someone was beautiful, gentle, innocent me. I happily helped myself to the food she left; it was the perfect setup.

Am I evil for having done this? No, I don't think I am. We're told that revenge is wrong, but we all know that it's natural. Evil is Tom Sikes. Evil is the way Sarah Barker treated the thing I loved most in the world.

When I was sixteen, I met a man in a tavern who claimed he'd murdered two people. He was a terrible drunkard, he said, because he was going mad about it. He hadn't thought twice about it when he'd done the deeds, but years later, he was haunted by phantoms and devils, and could never rest again. I think about him sometimes. Though I had my wobble during the process, I've had no regrets since about murdering Sarah, not one. Will I feel remorse one day? Will it torture me as I tortured Sarah? Will I go to hell, if there is one? I don't know.

I was a bit surprised, and quite upset, about the deaths of poor Sally and Clara. I immediately suspected Cedric Jones, though, and wondered if I'd beaten him to the killing of Sarah. He must have been wondering about that one right up until the hangman's rope tightened around his reptilian little neck. But I got my prize.

CHAPTER 47

Harris Mortimer

I OPEN MY EYES. My surroundings are dark and grey, apart from a chink of light. I must be dreaming. I close my eyes and re-open them, but the view remains the same. My head is aching dreadfully; in fact, my whole body is aching dreadfully; I feel as if I have been thrown into a prize ring for a few bare-knuckle boxing champions to fight over. My aching head isn't eased by the din of shouts and bangs in the building. My throat is swollen, aching and dry; I can feel grit on my tongue and between my teeth and feel as if I have not long dined on a feast of salt and sand. I am shivering, and pull the rough blanket that is over me up to my chin. Am I in some kind of cell? It looks like it. I put my right hand up to my head and see blood on my fingers. I can feel thorns sticking into my hair. I am suffering; I am wearing my crown of thorns; I must be humble and endure for the greater end that is to come. I hear the rattling of keys, echoing the rattle in my head, and the door of the cell opens.

'Good morning, Mr Harris Mortimer. Or is it Ophelia? Do forgive my little joke, sir; us peelers must have our little jokes or we'd be weeping like babbies all over London, and that wouldn't instil fear into the hearts of the criminal classes, now would it?'

I see a large blue stomach circled in a thick black belt with a snake clasp. A snake; this must mean something, I am sure. They are dangerous tempters but then they are associated with the Tree of Knowledge of Good and Evil. I am in a fight between good and evil. I look up. A tall large man with enormous side whiskers is standing over me holding a mug of something hot in his right black worsted-wool gloved hand.

'Wake up, Mr Mortimer. Constable Watkins, at your service, sir. I'm hoping you're sober now, or as good as sober, and we can send you home. Come now, drink this, a hot coffee from Peggy's stall over the way. Not every villain who winds up in here gets given a hot coffee courtesy of my own fair hands, you know, not that I think you're a villain. I don't get many villains thanking me politely for arresting them and coming along with me to the station as meek as a little lamb. No, I usually get a punch in the gut for my trouble, but, happily, as you can see, my gut can withstand a good deal of trouble.'

I blink up at the man, who has a ruddy face and bright blue eyes, a bit like my housekeeper's. He also looks old, tired and rather battered by life. I smile at him weakly, raise myself up, wincing with pain, and manage to half sit up, leaning against a cold wall. I take the mug in both my hands, which warms my numb fingers a little, making them sting.

'Thank you,' I manage.

'Well, well, Mr Mortimer, I was in a charitable frame of mind last night when I found you. And not before time, I assure you. You were singing away – "good night sweet ladies", I believe one of the lines was – drunker than a lord, with nearly your whole body emerged in the water as if you were enjoying a good soak in a bathtub. If I hadn't dragged you back, you would have been a gonner. I didn't want that. I see enough of it on my shifts, I can tell you, what with villains fighting each other and falling in, or those poor women trying to end it all. And a few of us peelers have gone that way, as well, can you believe?'

I blink at the man as he speaks. He is in full police regalia: blue frock coat with white metal buttons and white and blue stripes on one arm, black stovepipe hat with wreath emblem badge and numbers, hobnailed boots, and one of those leather things round his neck that are to prevent garrotting – I have heard of those. Now he sits down on a stool, sighs, and proceeds in a fit of coughing.

'I am very sorry to hear it, constable,' I manage. 'And are you quite well?'

'Not what you'd call well, no. I'm worn out, about as weary as a man can be after twenty-five years on the beat, with barely a rest along the way and only a selection of broken bones and a set of legs and lungs no longer up to the job to show for it. Still, not long now, and I might be granted a bit of pension if I'm lucky. There are plenty worse jobs out there and I try to count my blessings, such as they are. Now, sir, can you remember what happened last night? Take your time; you seem to be having a little trouble with your speech, as I'm sure you know.'

I consider. 'I think I went out in search of a friend. Ophelia; no, Titania; yes, that is she.'

'Well, son, might I advise you to get this here Ophelia, or whatever her name is, not to go a wandering off at night, and then you can also stay safe and sound in your own bed. You could have been murdered out there, and then where would that there Titania be? And you're very lucky you got me – me who's going soft in his advancing years – not one of the seasoned, bitter old coves, or one of those young ones upstairs, still on their probation, and a bit prone to high jinks, shall we say. They would have made mincemeat of you and thrown you to the pigeons in Trafalgar Square. Are you the theatrical type, sir?'

'Why, yes, I believe that I am a little artistic. How can you tell?' I try to smile but it feels as if my mouth is stretching only on its left side.

'Just a guess, Mr Mortimer, just a guess. And after all these years, I'm not one to judge. I've a little bit of the artist in me myself, you know. I've seen it all and I haven't got the time or inclination to waste on harmless musical types like yourself when there are enough true villains out there to deal with. Anyway, bit of sound advice from one artistic soul to another. Drop the flowers from your hair next time you decide to take a night-time walk, and lay off the spirits beforehand as well. I brought you in on drunk and disorderly, but you weren't that bad really. I did it for your own safety more than anything. You can see me as your guardian angel and count yourself a very lucky cove indeed. Do you think you can get up? You're not what I'd call a picture of health, sir. Perhaps you have a bit of the palsy? Are you under the doctor?'

I take a few more sips of the rather nasty coffee, nod, hand the mug to the constable with shaking hands and try to get up. My cane is missing.

'Here you go,' says the constable, retrieving it from the end of the bed and waving it at me like a wand. The wood on it has burst open in places and there is a string of seaweed wrapped round it. 'It's a bit the worse for wear, like it's owner, but you can give it a good clean up when you get home.'

The constable grins, which lights up his face rather delightfully, giving him the look of a Saint Nicholas, and reveals some thoroughly rotten teeth.

'Now, let's get your boots on while you're still sitting,' Watkins says.

He deftly tends to my feet as if he is my valet, fitting the still-damp boots expertly onto my very cold feet.

'Right, up you come, Mr Mortimer.'

I grip my cane with my right hand, and the constable lifts me onto my feet. I wobble and wince but manage not to topple over.

'Try a few steps on your own, sir.'

I do so, and grin at the constable as if I have just completed a difficult task for a favourite schoolmaster.

'Now, let's get this coat onto you. It's still wet, I'm afraid. The good news is that there are some keys in the right pocket, and I'm hoping they will let you into wherever you live.'

I wriggle into my coat with the help of the constable, feeling as if I might wobble over from its weight.

'And here's your pocketbook,' says the constable, finally, 'dried as nicely as my cracked old boots after a night by the fire; and it's a miracle you weren't robbed, sir, and something up there's clearly smiling down on you.'

He comes closer and tucks the pocketbook into the left pocket of my coat.

'Now, Mr Mortimer, I hate to ask the obvious, but it's always best to be sure. You're here at Westminster station on Walton Street, and you live in Chelsea, I believe, so this is your local patch?'

I nod.

'Can you remember exactly where you live and how to get there?'

I think for a moment, then nod again, shamefaced.

'Good man, good man. And you're now as sober as a parson? Mind, I'm not sure how parsons have got a reputation for sobriety, going by some of the ones I've seen over the years.'

I nod again, and smile.

'We'd better get you out of here then. I'd love to chinwag all day, but I've got another long shift ahead of me including a court appearance to get through before I can put my ancient feet up and have a nip and some baccy.'

Constable Watkins takes my arm and leads me slowly out of the cell, past some kind of kitchen or mess, and through to another room, where I am to sign the register confirming my discharge. I hear a number of shouts and whistles as I go. I feel rather amused, if anything. I really feel that my character is transforming in some way, and for the better. It is done, and we are out onto the street. It is pleasantly warm after the coolness of the cell.

I look at the rough kindly man in front of me and feel the tears begin to flow.

'Now, now, son,' he says, 'you'll be alright. Get yourself some sleep, clean yourself up and stay warm; we don't want you developing a fever. Then you'll be right as rain. You're a gentleman, sir, I can see that. We all go wrong a bit now and again. If only all the coves I've arrested over the past twenty-five years were like you, why, I'd be looking thirty years younger now. I'd have fair curling hair and smooth plump cheeks again and be a courting all those pretty maidservants that us constables are apparently so desperate fond of.'

'I do not know how to thank you,' I manage.

The constable grins his angelic rotten-toothed grin, then hails a hackney cab to take me home.

'Take this gentleman home to Chelsea,' he says to the

driver, 'and don't even think about any kind of dodge. I've noted your cab number, and I'll be sure to find it out.'

The driver raises both eyebrows to meet the top of his bald head, but does not say anything.

The constable helps me gently into the cab, stands back and salutes me. I cry a little more as he turns back into the station.

Constable Watkins said that he was my angel, and, indeed, I believe it. An angel in the unlikeliest of places, saving me, treating me with such gentleness and dignity, and me, on the surface a shamed and humiliated creature. There cannot be many police officers like him. I have heard terrible stories and have always been a little suspicious of a state police force, out to steal our good old, British liberty. I must revise my opinion on this, as I have had to do on so many things of late. Still, the Lord sent him to save me, I am sure.

I arrive home. The scowling driver actually helps me out of the cab, and quotes an unusually moderate fare for the journey.

I turn to my house and notice a few figures standing outside the door.

'There he is.'

It's Mrs Hopkinson. She comes towards me in her slow, heavy way.

'Harris!'

It's Mr Rockingham, who comes up behind Matilda.

'Oh, Mr Mortimer,' says Mrs Hopkinson, kissing me on the cheek. 'I'm so thankful, I could swoon right here. My nerves have been on the stretch something terrible. And look at you, looking like some down-and-out from one of those low lodging houses. And smelling like you've just swam across the ocean from America. And me your housekeeper. I could die of shame.'

She bursts into tears.

'He is safe now,' says Rockingham, smiling at me in that warm, familiar way, though his face looks tired and strained.

They take a position either side of me and help me towards the door. Rockingham fishes out the keys from my right pocket, opens the door, and helps me inside. They both help me up the short flight of stairs to my sitting room and sit me down in my comfortable chair.

'Mrs Hopkinson,' says Rockingham, 'if you would be so good, we need a hot bath and something hot to eat and drink. Then he must rest.'

'Yes, sir.'

Mrs Hopkinson goes back downstairs to the kitchen. I notice Mr Rockingham staring at the corner devoted to my Titania. Perhaps he is admiring my sketches.

'We will stay here tonight,' says Rockingham, turning to me, 'and then tomorrow, dear boy, you are coming home with me.'

I nod. Three angels have saved me today: Constable Watkins, Mrs Hopkinson and Mr Rockingham. I am so relieved. I can rest now, and trust in them.

PART III

HAMPSHIRE, ENGLAND

CHAPTER 47

Harris Mortimer

I AM RUNNING, RUNNING, running. As best as I can with my stick. My heart is exploding in my chest; my head is pounding. I am burning up, the sweat trickling down my face. My limbs are heavy, my progress slow. I can go no further, and come to a halt. The gate is locked. I pull at it anyway, to no avail. I grip the bars and squash the middle of my face into one of the gaps.

'Titania, Titania. Miss Rosetti. My Ophelia. Come back to me, please. Do not abandon me like this. You promised me to wed. How will I live without you? Oh, do not break my heart, my darling, do not break it. Where are you?'

I am sobbing now, and feel a gentle tap on my left shoulder.

'Now, sir, now, what's all this? Don't upset yourself,

Mr Mortimer. Come into the cottage now and take a cup of tea.'

I turn round to see the gatekeeper, who was so affable to me in November last year when I first visited the asylum.

'Do you know where she is?' I ask. 'My darling?'

'I'm not quite sure who you mean, sir.'

'Miss Rosetti. Titania.'

'Ah.' He nods, looks sorrowful and shakes his head. 'She's left here, Mr Mortimer, a good while ago now. She went home, back to London, I believe, but perhaps other places since.'

'Yes, London and other places; I must try them.'

'Come and say hello to my wife first, Mr Mortimer, or she'll be cross with you.'

He takes my arm and leads me into the cottage. It is cosy; there is a kind feeling here. I drink tea and let his wife's smiles and blandishments soothe me. I am drowsy again now; I am often drowsy here; it is pleasant, forgetful. I see the world through a glass darkly, but it is a comforting shadow. One day I may see the whole, if I can bear it.

I must have fallen asleep for now I jolt awake, my mouth dry, my senses bewildered. Mr Rockingham is smiling down at me.

'I am glad you have rested,' says Rockingham. 'Now let me take you back to the house and we can have a little discourse before tea.'

I smile and let Rockingham help me up from the armchair and out of the cottage, the gatekeeper and his wife saying their kindly farewells and waving at me. We walk slowly back up the main drive, me leaning heavily on Rockingham's right arm. He points out the beauty of the flowers as we go. A crop of snapdragons, some roses of a deep, red colour. The latter make me think hazily, but not too painfully, of the colour of one of my Titania's gowns. I nod appreciatively. It is a lovely August day, but I will be glad when the leaves begin to fall. I prefer the winter now. Summer is too stark, too intrusive, too exposing. It does not leave a man in peace, constantly prodding him to thoughts and memories he would rather stay buried.

I think about my first time on this road, that dark November afternoon last year. Was it only nine/ten months ago in my life? I feel as if I have endured centuries on this earth since then. I remember the surly cab driver and his horse, and above all, She, her face at the carriage window. And yet, it is if I am watching another person, in another life, and though I feel a little uneasy, I do not seem to mind the vison so very much.

We arrive at Rockingham's office, another pleasant place. Yes, this is the time of life for small pleasant things. I sit down in one of his comfortable leather chairs and he offers me a small brandy.

'A little will do you no harm,' he reassures me, 'though we must not mix too much with your current medicines.'

I grasp the cold glass, my hands shaking, and take a few sips.

'How are you feeling, dear Harris?' Rockingham looks at me tenderly, his eyes more drooping than ever, his large forehead wrinkled in concern.

I think, ponder the question.

'Oh, quite well, I believe, quite well.'

'And how are your dreams? Has the hag visited recently?'

I think. 'Yes, a few nights ago, I believe. But she is less frightening. She approaches my bed but stops. She raises her hands, then they fall.'

'That is good news, indeed. Soon she will depart forever.'

'Oh,' I say, 'and last night I dreamt of my mother. She appeared at the end of my bed, looking well and neatly dressed. She smiled at me, then disappeared.'

'Oh now, see, that is even better news. You are making wonderful progress, my dear Harris, and will make a complete recovery, I am sure. But we must take our time. I am glad to observe that your partial paralysis has not grown worse. In fact, I think your face has improved slightly. And your speech is a little better.

'You are safe in my hands; I am sure you know that. I have made a personal commitment to you. We are old friends, are we not?'

I nod, my smile now extending a fraction to the right side of my mouth. What a wonderful man Rockingham is.

'As such,' he continues, 'I do feel that I owe you the utmost candour. Now that the terrible business that took place here is over, and we have made a new start here at the Allingsford Public Asylum for the Insane, I can tell you how it all was. Indeed, I must confess that I have been feeling the weight of this knowledge, and it will do me good to unburden myself.'

I nod dreamily, and take another sip of brandy, which numbs my lips pleasantly.

'Mr Cedric Jones, now,' he says.

I squirm a little, something awful touching on the borders of my memory at the sound of that name.

'He was a truly evil man,' continues Rockingham, 'and we have done a great service to society to rid it of him. The opinions he held, and worse, the power he was gaining to turn them into a reality, were truly terrifying.'

Rockingham stares at me, his eyes full of fear. He breathes out and smiles. 'But it is over.'

Now he looks thoughtful, and pauses for several seconds.

'Of course,' he says, 'Mr Jones did not actually commit those crimes for which he was executed.'

Something seems a little odd about this comment, I think, but no matter.

'No, dear Harris. Indeed, you must know that it was I. Or, at least, it was I who sent dear Sally and dear Clara to a better place. I do not know who or what was responsible for Sarah's demise. That one quite confounded me, I can assure you. She was on my list of three, you see. But perhaps it was self-murder, after all. It served my purpose and all to the good. God's hand is behind everything, driving us towards our destiny; He helped me along.'

'All to the good,' I say. I nod, then shake my head. Something is not quite right here, but I cannot grasp things; they slip away from me.

'You see,' says Rockingham, 'Mr Jones's views and future policies and plans, if he had been allowed to execute them, could have rid our world of the fairer sex almost entirely. The fairer sex, our comfort and our helpmeets, our dear mothers, wives, sisters and daughters. What sort of world would that be, dear Harris? What sort of a world? It is unthinkable.'

Rockingham is crying a little. He glances at the photograph of his wife and daughters, smiles at it, kisses the fingers of his right hand and touches the glass with them.

'I had to stop him,' he continues. 'Somebody had to. I could have just disposed of him myself, and that was my first plan. He would have been out of the way, and unable to cause harm. But then, I thought, the problem is bigger than this individual. I needed to fight not just him but his ideas. And then it occurred to me that if he was found guilty of pushing his views to their logical conclusion – which surely he would have done at some future point – that is, by murdering some of our women of a certain age, the world would know of his madness and its results. There would be outrage, and his poisonous opinions would be entirely discredited.

'And only look at the outcry in the *Times*, proclaiming the danger of men like Jones, and how that outcry has spread. All that was begun by you, dear Harris; you should be so proud of yourself. Of course, I did suggest the initial piece to you. I knew that it would serve my purpose beautifully, you see, and also help you in your career. You needed a little direction, a cause, and how superbly you rose to the challenge.

'And, you know, Sally and Clara died in this great cause. For women are self-sacrificing creatures – the good Lord bless them – and I know that they would not blame me; they would see only the greater good. I did think about Mrs Christie at one point; she was the right age and so on. But then she was so useful that she did not quite fit the brief, and I did not think I could manage without her, or easily replace her here in the asylum. Patients are more expendable. I am sure that poor Mrs Christie suspected me of the killings. She began to struggle to look me in the eye, and when I caught her glancing upon me there was a queer look in her eyes that I had not seen before. But I know that she would never say anything to me, or accuse me to the world; she will take the knowledge to her grave. She, too, understands the greater good, you see, and is sacrificing herself to it.'

Rockingham seems to have confessed to killing two women. I think about this, but it does not resonate deeply. I feel at little uneasy, but still relatively calm. He smiles at me.

'You understand, do you not, Harris? Only think of your poor dear mother. Imagine what evil plans Mr Jones might have had for somebody like her?'

I feel a quick pain at my heart, but it passes. Yes, that is true; an evil man is out of the way.

'You are so very like her, you know, so good,' he says. 'Though, alas, you have very likely inherited from her a taint of madness. But, whatsoever may have caused your current illness, we will get you well. For what are we here for, if not to care for the poor afflicted insane members of our communities, and make them better when we can?'

I smile, begin to hum a little, then softly sing the song:

'For there's nothin' like a woman when she's dead.

'Even better than when she's bad, or not right in the 'ead.

'She's so pretty, she's so quiet, so delightfully compliant,

'Oh, there's nothin' like a woman when she's dead.'

A tear rolls down Rockingham's right cheek.

'Come, my dearest Harris. It is time for tea.'

ACKNOWLEDGEMENTS

Editors, Cat Cobain and Claire Baldwin, for their hugely insightful, intuitive and thought-provoking reviews of my script, which made me so excited to finish this book. I can't imagine how I would have achieved the final result without them.

A NOTE ON SOURCES

There is an extensive field of work on lunacy in the nineteenth century. Prominent names include Andrew Scull and Elaine Showalter, one of the first feminist literary critics to analyse depictions of female madness in Victorian culture.

In terms of writing this novel, the most helpful work I found was *Life in the Victorian Asylum* by Mark Stevens (2020), which takes the reader on the patient's journey, from admission to the asylum, through life inside it, and finally to discharge or otherwise. I have drawn extensively upon it for my depiction of the physical aspects of the asylum. It also attempts to show the benevolent motives driving much of the mental health work in the nineteenth century, a fact that might surprise us. Future historians may wonder about the way we manage such things today.

My literary depiction of a nineteenth-century lunatic asylum owes more to the Victorian genre of sensation fiction than the real world of asylums. However, the novel's themes reflect the period's real-life preoccupations, particularly the focus on female lunacy with its emphasis on the primacy of biology and life cycle (from puberty through to menopause). The fantastical idea of the Ophelia-type female lunatic really existed. Clitoridectomies were carried out, but rarely.

ABOUT THE AUTHOR

Author photograph by Tessa Carroll

R S Leonard was born in Cheshire, England, and after a long stint in London, then Hampshire, now resides back in her home county.

She has a PhD in Nineteenth-century Literature and Culture and MAs in Creative Writing and Victorian Studies.

This is her second historical mystery novel. Her first, *The Body, the Diamond and the Child*, is a tale of murder, slavery and the theft of a famous diamond.

By day she works in the charitable sector.

rsleonardbooks.com

Printed in Great Britain
by Amazon

62317060R00231